"Both my Granny and my Grandmother approved of him." Poppy was leaning forward in his chair. "They said we were lucky to have him along."

"That's right," Lotus murmured.

"Zahara says we need him to balance the expedition," Jazz said. "I think she's right."

"If you don't want me along, I'll just go home," Bailey said, though he was glad to hear Poppy and Jazz speak out in his favor.

"No you won't." Lily spoke first, but Iris was just behind. "Not a chance. Zahara has decided that you're coming so you'll come."

"It's a question of balance," Heather said. "You're right—we don't know what he'll do. And that's important."

"You see," Zahara said, her voice steady. "The crew agrees that he is an essential part of the expedition." She turned to look at the norbit. "Bailey, we need you. Will you come with us?"

Bailey looked at the others. Under Myra's gaze, he felt very small, but he spoke up as loudly as he could. "If you all want me to, I will."

"Then you'll come," Zahara said. Her eyes were fierce as she glared at Myra. "As expedition leader, I insist on it."

But Bailey wasn't listening anymore. It seemed to him that he had just passed an important turning point. He had decided, for better or worse, not to go home just yet.

THERE
AND BACK
AGAIN

BY MAX MERRIWELL

PAT MURPHY

TOR®

A TOM DOHERTY ASSOCIATES BOOK
NEW YORK

THERE AND BACK AGAIN

A Tor Book
Published by Tom Doherty Associates, LLC
175 Fifth Avenue
New York, NY 10010

www.tor.com

Tor® is a registered trademark of Tom Doherty Associates, LLC.

ISBN: 0-812-54172-3
Library of Congress Catalog Card Number: 99-38395

First edition: November 1999
First mass market edition: October 2000

Printed in the United States of America

0 9 8 7 6 5 4 3 2 1

1

His courage is perfect! And that, after all,
Is the thing that one needs with a Snark.

—"The Hunting of the Snark,"
Lewis Carroll

BAILEY WAS HEADING HOME IN HIS STEAM-POWERED ROCKET
when he found a message pod. It was only by luck that
he spotted it, disabled and drifting in an eccentric orbit
around a large M-type asteroid. Strange to find a message pod so far from interstellar trade routes. The pod's
radio signal was silent; Bailey could see in the viewscreen
that its antenna had been snapped off.

Just luck that Bailey had taken that route home, that
the pod was in orbit around that particular asteroid, that
Bailey had happened to be in a scavenging mood and
that his detectors had called his attention to the blip that
was the pod. Otherwise, centuries might have passed before anyone found it. The Asteroid Belt was crowded
with tumbling rocks and bits of space debris, and there
was no reason for this one to attract any attention.

Through the viewscreen, Bailey could see that the
pod's metallic surface was decorated with elaborate
glyphs in purple and gold. He recognized the glyphs as
those of the Farr family, the galaxy's largest, richest, and
most famous clone. One side of the pod was badly
dented and scraped; it had collided with a few asteroids
along the way.

Bailey matched the pod's orbit, grasped it with his

ship's external manipulators, and took it home. He was no postal pirate, but rather a good-hearted soul who hated to think of a message gone astray.

When he got back to the Restless Rest, the hollowed-out asteroid that was his home, he sent a radio message on the frequency noted in the glyphs. Someone would come to claim the pod, if the Farrs thought it was valuable enough. Bailey put the pod in his storeroom and forgot about it.

That was the beginning of the adventure, though Bailey didn't know it at the time.

BAILEY'S HOME WAS part of a jumble of tumbling rocks located between the fourth and fifth planets orbiting a yellow dwarf star on the inner edge of the Milky Way galaxy's Orion arm, about two thirds of the way from the galactic center. A quiet little backwater. Sure, Bailey's asteroid was in the same planetary system as the ancestral home of the human race, the planet Earth, but few interstellar travelers had much interest in that. And Bailey's home was far from most of the wormholes that had been mapped and were commonly used for interstellar travel, which made visiting it inconvenient and time-consuming.

Bailey was a norbit, and norbits as a group didn't care much about interstellar travel. In the centuries since people had left the planet Earth, the human race had scattered, traveling many light years from their home system and colonizing planets hundreds of light years away. But few norbits had ventured away from the Solar System.

Norbits liked where they lived, preferring the comfort of the known to the wild adventures that could be found elsewhere in the galaxy. Thousands of years ago, their ancestors had left the planet Earth and settled in the Asteroid Belt. That adventure (which was comfortably in the distant past and did not interfere with their daily business) had been, most of them felt, quite enough.

The norbits extracted water, metals, and minerals from the asteroids around them. They grew their own food in greenhouse rocks, glassed in with silica glass manufactured using solar energy and silicate rock mined locally.

They made their way from one asteroid to the next in rockets that used the simplest possible technology. Basically, a mirror focused sunlight on a water-filled chamber. The water boiled and the high-temperature steam was vented through a rocket thrust chamber. The steam went one way; the rocket went the other.

Simple and effective. The norbits called them solar thermal rockets. Among interstellar travelers, marveling at the quaint customs of these simple people, they were known as tea kettle rockets. But it didn't really matter what you called them—they got norbits from one rock to another for business or social gatherings (of which they had many, being gregarious people who liked to eat and drink and play games and solve puzzles and tell stories and laugh as frequently as possible).

Over the centuries, norbits had evolved to suit their life style. As a group, they tended to be rather short and stout, a body type well-suited to living in low gravity and confined spaces. Bailey, a well-to-do norbit who had the respect of his community, was a few inches shy of five feet tall, with a girth that suggested he was rather fond of meals.

The word "norbit" came from the adventurous days right after people took up residence in the Asteroid Belt and started hollowing out the rocks to make their homes and farms. The colonists on Mars called themselves Martians, reasonably enough, but the belt dwellers didn't have a name for themselves. Legend had it that the word "norbit" had been conceived at a party where much of the output from a recently constructed solar still had been consumed. Some said the name was derived from the phrase "in orbit." Say it fast with a drunken slur, and "in orbit" easily becomes "norbit."

Others claimed a more erudite origin for the term, citing "orb" as an archaic term for Earth. These pundits suggested that a scholarly belt-dweller had tacked an "N" on the front of "orb" to imply the negative—not from Earth anymore. And since "norb" sounded vaguely insulting, someone else had added "it" to the end of the neologism, creating "norbit."

Whatever the origin of the term, it had stuck. Norbits called themselves norbits and other people called them that as well.

Not being bound by the strictures of a spinning planet with the illusion of a rising and setting sun, the norbits defined day as the twenty-four-hour period during which one had at least five meals: breakfast, morning tea, lunch, afternoon tea, and dinner. Oh, yes—and a snack before bedtime, but that hardly counted as a meal. And sometimes a snack before or after a nap, but those didn't count either.

Several years after he found the message pod, Bailey was finishing breakfast, one of his favorite meals of the day. The previous day, while out checking on a few of his automated mining stations, he had visited a thriving orbital farm and had traded a basket of figs from his greenhouse for a dozen quail eggs. So that morning he breakfasted on fig bread and spore cakes and quail eggs and apple juice from the apples in his greenhouse.

Since you've probably never visited a norbit (few people have), let me tell you a little about Bailey's home. The Restless Rest was an M-type asteroid, composed primarily of meteoritic metal, roughly spherical, with a diameter of about two kilometers and a mass of about thirty billion tons. Bailey lived in a cylinder measuring about fifty meters in diameter, drilled through the center of the asteroid. The asteroid spun around the central axis of this cylinder to produce an artificial gravity equal to about one fifth that of Earth.

Now maybe you think that a cylinder carved in an asteroid wouldn't be a very comfortable place to live. Well, you'd be wrong. Chances are you're imagining a smooth metal cylinder divided with gleaming walls of metal and glass, all slick and cold and polished to a high shine. That's not what it was like at all.

True, the Restless Rest was a cylinder carved in a rock and lined with metal melted from that same rock, but there was nothing slick and cold about Bailey's home. Partitions slicing across the cylinder divided it into sections. Some of those sections had only two walls—the partitions that divided the cylinder—and a single curving floor which followed the cylinder's circumference. In these sections, you could stand on the floor and look up at the floor on the far side of the cylinder fifty meters over your head. That's a nice thing if you want a large airy space—a workshop where you can repair a robot arm, construct a solar panel—or even paint a picture, weave a tapestry, program a computer, or write a story.

Other sections were layered with lofts connected by winding stairways. As you walked up the stairways toward the center of the cylinder, you grew lighter and lighter as the artificial gravity decreased. In those sections were bedrooms and parlors and places to settle down with a book and places to settle down with a snack and places to settle down with a friend for a long chat on a comfortable couch and pantries and kitchens and game rooms. The parlors and bedrooms were decorated with paintings and weavings and sculptures and photographs, made by Bailey's mother (who had liked to paint) and his father (who had liked to weave) and by his many relations who were artistically inclined. The Restless

Rest was the home of a norbit, which meant that it was a comfortable and cozy sort of place.

On that particular day, years after he had tucked that message pod into the storeroom and forgotten all about it, Bailey was eating breakfast in the solarium. Located at the end of the cylinder oriented toward the sun, this section had windows that admitted sunlight, filtering it to remove ultraviolet radiation.

The solarium was Bailey's favorite room, a fine place to have a bite to eat and look out at the universe from a comfortable chair. Through the windows, he could see the sun—a bright spot in a black sky. Positioned at the center of the asteroid's axis of rotation, the sun appeared to remain stationary as the distant stars and nearby asteroids wheeled around it in a spectacular light show.

Above Bailey's head, a glass divider ran lengthwise down this section of the cylinder, separating him from the greenhouse, where a riot of leaves pressed against the glass. From where Bailey sat, this divider was a ceiling, high overhead. The air in the solarium was rich with oxygen, piped in from the greenhouse, and it had a wonderful scent of greenery.

That morning, as Bailey savored his breakfast and contemplated what he might do that day, he noticed a note, attached with a magnet to a metal file by the communicator screen. He didn't remember writing the note, but he must have, since it was in his own handwriting. *"Eadem mutata resurgo,"* it said. Beneath that was a spiral. And under the spiral, there were three more words: "Harvest the figs."

How odd. He didn't remember writing the note. The words at the top meant nothing to him. Some foreign language. He'd seen the spiral before—it was the symbol of the College of 'Pataphysics. He had heard of the pataphysicians but he had never met one and he didn't know why he would have drawn their symbol and tacked it to the noteboard. Fortunately, the last line made sense. The figs were ripening fast—he had noticed that the other day—and he really should harvest them.

So he put the note in his pocket, put his breakfast dishes in the washer, which would rinse them clean and use the water for the plants in the greenhouse. He strolled up the curving floor, to where it met the glass that divided the solarium from the greenhouse. He was walking the circumference of the cylinder and down was always the direction in which his feet were pointing. The floor curved to meet the glass divider that ran the length of the cylinder, and as Bailey approached, it ceased being a ceiling and became a wall. He stepped through a door in the wall into the greenhouse.

HE HAD GATHERED three baskets of figs, had made three loaves of fig bread, and was just taking them out of the oven when his hailer chimed, indicating that an approaching ship was calling with an urgent communication. He answered immediately. He wasn't expecting company, but it could have been one of his many relations was stopping by for a cup of tea and a chat.

"Calling Restless Rest," an unfamiliar voice on the hailer said. "Calling Restless Rest. Brita, are you there?" Bailey's great-grandmother, Brita Beldon, had hollowed out and named the asteroid. She had died when Bailey was very young. He remembered her as a frail old woman with an unnerving tendency to bark orders. "Brita, come in. This is Gitana, aboard the *Jabberwock*."

Gitana! I could tell you many stories about Gitana and there are many more that no one but Gitana knows to tell. Some said she was a pirate; some said she was a scavenger; some say she was an adventurer, in search of glory and profit. If you asked her, she would just smile and shrug and say that she was a seeker of truth. And maybe she was. But wherever she went, adventures followed.

Her description was the stuff of legend. She was a tall woman with blonde hair cut short, in the fashion of the old-time spacers who had no time to spare for grooming. Viewed in profile from the right side, she looked like a beautiful woman from Old Earth. Thin face with high cheekbones. Smooth curve of skull beneath that crewcut blonde hair, so short it begged to be stroked. Her right eye was a brilliant blue, a blend of glacial ice and tropical seas. Blonde eyelashes against fair skin. Natural, organic, warm. From the right, she looked honest and warm-hearted, a person to be trusted, a person to be treasured, a person to be cared for. You could fall in love with that profile.

From the left, you got a very different view. The same thin face, the same smooth curve of skull. But her left eye was capped in black. She had, decades before, dedicated that optic nerve to input from her ship's sensors. A crimson light glowed on the optic cap, indicating that the cap was receiving input from the sensors.

Surrounding the cap were blackwork tattoos. A streak of black lightning crossed her eyebrow and ran up onto her scalp, its dark pattern visible through her pale hair. A gentle curve flowed downward beside her nose, then spiraled clockwise on her left cheek, rising high on the cheekbone and circling inward like a coil of rope or a chameleon's curling tail. A pattern of fine lines radiated from the eye cap, as if a spider had been spinning a gossamer web of black against her pale skin. Such facial tattoos had been the fashion some forty years back, inspired by the Maori and the blue men of Morocco, part of a wave of nostalgia for the ways of Old Earth. The fashion had passed, but Gitana had never opted to have the tattoos removed.

From the left, she looked exotic and sinister, touched

with shadow. Powerful. Not necessarily evil, but not necessarily good. Tricky and confusing. Her beautiful face was patterned in darkness.

"Gitana?" he said, pushing a button to activate the view screen. Gitana's face filled the screen, and Bailey smiled at her nervously. According to family legend, his great-grandmother had been traveling with Gitana when she made her fortune. But Bailey's mother had not told him much about that. Great-Grandmother Brita had not been entirely respectable. "My great-grandmother passed away many years ago."

"So soon?"

"She was over two hundred years old when she died," Bailey said. Having no unifying orbital period of their own, the norbits continued to use Old Earth years as a unit of measurement.

Gitana glanced off screen, consulting her instrument panel. "I've been gone longer than I realized," she said. She studied him again. "And you must be at least fifty."

"Fifty-five," Bailey said.

"I see," she said, regarding him steadily. Her gaze was disconcerting—one blue eye and one mechanical sensor fixed on his face. "So you sent the message to the Farrs. You've got a message pod for them. I need that. And I'm looking for someone to share in an adventure I'm arranging."

"That last won't be easy," Bailey said. "Most people around here aren't looking for adventures." Her scrutiny was starting to make him nervous. He tried to sound brisk and businesslike. "But I'm sure I have the message pod. It's in the storeroom." He scratched his head, trying to remember when he had seen it last. "Why don't you come aboard and I'll get that pod for you. And you can join me for lunch."

He figured he would get her the pod and have an entertaining lunch during which she would tell him about adventures. He liked to hear about adventures—things could get very interesting out in the great universe. Her stories would be a big hit at the next party he went to; everyone liked to hear about other people's adventures. After lunch, he would send her on her way. It seemed like a plan.

When Gitana stepped out of the airlock, Bailey began to wonder if it had been a good plan. Gitana unsnapped her helmet and slipped out of her space suit, leaving them on the rack by the airlock. She was an imposing woman. She studied him with unnerving intensity, then smiled an ambiguous smile. "Not looking for adventures?" she said. "And why not?"

Flustered, Bailey didn't know what to say. "Well, not just now, anyway," he managed at last. "I'm very busy harvesting the figs. But do come in."

She followed Bailey into the solarium. "Your great-grandmother and I were good friends, you know. I would have recognized you as her great-grandson anywhere. By the way, the others will be meeting me here quite soon."

"Others?" he said, startled.

"From the Farr family," she said. "I advised them that this was a message that would interest them greatly."

"Of course." He nodded, as if a visit from one of the galaxy's most powerful families was an everyday occurrence.

"I trust you will invite them to lunch." She smiled. "I remember how proud Brita was of norbit hospitality."

"Oh, yes. Lunch. Of course, of course. It depends, of course, on when they get here," Bailey began, thinking he might plead urgent business elsewhere, but before he could finish his sentence, the communicator chimed.

"Allow me," Gitana suggested, and before he could move she was chatting on the communicator with two women named Poppy and Jasmine. "Come on in," she said. "We were just going to fetch the message pod."

Bailey watched through the solarium windows as another deep-space craft locked onto the asteroid beside Gitana's scout ship. This one was larger than Gitana's, and decorated with the Farr clone's colors.

"Jasmine Farr and Poppy Farr," Gitana introduced the two women who entered through the airlock. They were the same height. They had the same broad face, the same high cheekbones, the same hazel eyes with a hint of an epicanthal fold. Jasmine ("call me Jazz," she said immediately) was muscular, with a build that made Bailey think painfully of how rarely he used the exercise equipment in his recreation room. Her hair was as short as Gitana's and colored a startling shade of gold. Her nose had been broken years ago, from the look of it, and hadn't been set quite right.

Poppy was a decade or so older than Jazz. She had a well-padded body that suggested a love of good food. Her long hair, tied back in a single braid, was dark brown, shot with streaks of gray.

"Jazz is the chief engineering officer. Poppy is the expedition's cook and general housekeeper," Gitana said.

Bailey wondered vaguely about Gitana's use of the word "expedition," but decided not to ask about where they were headed. It really wasn't his business, after all.

"We were just going to fetch the message pod," Bailey began, but the chime of the communicator interrupted him again. Another deep-space craft and two more members of the Farr clone: Heather and Iris. The same face again, but more variations in hair and dress. Heather's hair was very short and curled in tight knots; Iris' golden hair was in two long braids. Both were about Jazz's age.

"Heather is navigator; Iris is weapons officer," Gitana explained.

"At your service," they greeted Bailey politely. "Hello, sibs!" they called to Poppy and Jazz.

"At yours and your family's," Bailey managed, though the solarium was feeling a trifle crowded and he had started wondering if he had enough fig bread and spore cakes to feed this crowd. "Gitana told me that you're here for the message pod. If you'll follow me. . . ."

Again, the communicator chimed. "Not so fast," Gitana called to Bailey. Poppy and Jazz and Heather and Iris were laughing and talking to each other. "It's not hospitable to rush your guests."

A deep-space cruiser, larger than the other crafts, docked, and three more Farr sibs came through the airlock and into the solarium. Lily and Lotus Farr entered, laughing and shouting greetings. They both looked younger than Jazz. Bailey glanced at them: Lily's hair was brilliant red and cut in a crest; Lotus had tied her dark hair into dozens of tiny braids, decorated with beads.

And finally, Zahara. She looked considerably older than the others. Her head was shaved clean, no trace of hair of any color.

"Lotus is the expedition's anthropologist and expert on the Old Ones. Lily is head of computing, and Zahara, of course, is the Captain."

Having learned, Bailey greeted the three and said nothing of going to the storeroom.

"What are we waiting for?" Zahara asked. "We are all eager to see the message pod."

In some confusion, Bailey led them through the Restless Rest to the storeroom at the far end of the cylinder.

The storeroom housed castoffs of the last three generations of Bailey's family—some packed in carefully labeled boxes and some scattered helter skelter. Broken mining equipment that could be cannibalized for spare parts; solar panels that Bailey's father had somehow never gotten around to installing; a portrait of Bailey, lovingly completed by his mother, that had never seemed to him to be a good likeness; toys abandoned by generations of norbit children. Bits and pieces, odds and ends—all stored on a series of lofts, connected by ladders.

Bailey found the message pod on the third level up, tucked between his first steam rocket (an antique now, but one that he kept for sentimental reasons) and an unattractive sculpture created by one of his cousins. The Farr sibs gathered around the pod while Zahara entered the code to open it. Lily prepared to download the message from the central unit into her belt computer. She would then decode it, since all messages were carefully encrypted to avoid hostile interception.

Bailey stayed back with Gitana, studying the group. "I've never met any of the Farr sibs," he said softly to Gitana. "I thought they would all be the same."

"Same genetic material," Gitana said. "But they try very hard to be different from their sibs. Myra Farr, the original, was a very independent woman. She wanted to continue herself, but not necessarily to duplicate herself. They all feel the same about that. And they love to argue."

"Maybe you should try . . ." Lotus was saying.

"Look," Lily interrupted. "Why don't you all get out of here and let me handle this."

"I don't know," Poppy said. "I think . . ."

"Better that Lily handle it," Zahara said. "She has the most experience. And didn't Gitana say something about lunch?"

So they ended up in Bailey's best parlor, lounging about on pillows and sofas, eating all of his fig bread and drinking his best wine, and waiting for Lily to return with the message. The lights were dim—Gitana had turned them down.

Bailey, in his anxiety, had drunk several glasses of wine. Now he was feeling more excited than nervous, listening in on conversations as his visitors, all of whom seemed to know each other rather well, shared news about where each of them had been and what adventures had transpired.

". . . trading in spices and whiskey and of course we got roaring drunk," Jazz was saying to Iris. "I made a tidy profit, but. . . ."

". . . met up with an expedition of pataphysicians. Nice enough folks, though dreadfully fond of word games. Don't play Scrabble with them, or if you must, don't wager. I almost lost my ship, but then. . . ."

". . . took the wormhole through to the Scorpio-Centaurus Association. Nasty war, out that way."

". . . told me that the sector near Fomalhaut is crawling with Pirates. You'd be wise to route any messages around it."

". . . just a small war really. But still, a sector to avoid. You see, one side is in league with the Resurrectionists, and . . ."

". . . he found an artifact from the Old Ones. Couldn't figure out what it might do, so he traded it to a pataphysician and . . ."

As he listened, Bailey's heart beat faster. He imagined dodging Pirates and diving down wormholes and trading in whiskey and playing word games with pataphysicians.

Lily returned from the storeroom and the group fell silent, turning their attention to her. "Decoded and ready to go," she said, and inserted a disk into Bailey's holographic projector.

The woman who appeared in the center of the group, sitting at ease in a command chair, had a face like Zahara's, like Poppy's, like Lily's. Decorated with tribal tattoos, but essentially the same. She was, as near as Bailey could tell, about Zahara's age.

"That's Violet," Gitana said, identifying her for Bailey.

"Greetings, sibs," said the holographic projection of Violet, gazing at a point between Gitana and Zahara and smiling at no one in particular. "I'm sending this message by way of three pods—two by conventional routes and one by a new route. I hope one of them gets through." Her smile widened. "I have found the ultimate Snark, and I could use some help. Come as fast as you can. This will show you the way."

The face disappeared and the space that Violet had occupied was suddenly filled with brilliant points of light, connected by glowing golden arrows.

"What is it?" Zahara said, her voice taut with excitement.

"It is a holographic enlargement of an alien artifact that I gave to Violet," Gitana said evenly. "Violet believed it's a map showing the wormholes that lead from this sector of the Orion Arm to the very center of the Milky Way galaxy."

As Bailey leaned in to look more closely, he caught the flash of a reflection from a transparent surface—the pattern of lights was contained in a cube of transparent material at least two meters across. The sibs on the far side of the parlor were inside the cube, surrounded by glowing arrows and points.

As Bailey studied the holographic projection, he realized that the cube was not quite complete. One corner of the cube and one edge had been broken away. But that shattered edge did not hold his attention.

At the center of all the lights and arrows was a translucent silver sphere that held a translucent golden cube filled with points of light, a tiny replica of the cube that filled Bailey's parlor. Mesmerized, Bailey stepped into the holographic projection to study that golden cube.

*   *   *

PERHAPS IT'S TIME to tell you a few things. It's a bewildering universe and you need to know a little about it. Hang on—this is going to be a crash course in the history of humanity. No details, just the big picture.

Thousands of years ago, humans left the planet Earth—first establishing orbital colonies, then ranging out to colonies on the Moon, on Mars, and among the asteroids. A few hundred years after people had settled Mars, a consortium of engineers on Mars developed the Hoshi Drive, which propelled ships at near-light speed. With the Hoshi Drive, it became possible for humanity to spread even farther, journeying first to the trinary dwarf system of Alpha Centauri, just 4.3 light years away, and then farther, to Barnard's Star at six light years distance, Sirius, at nine light years, and Procyon at eleven light years. The explorers found planets, some of them habitable, and distant colonies were established.

Though people were traveling distances that were minuscule on a galactic scale, the malleability of time quickly became apparent. Cruising at 99.50% light speed, the travelers experienced just one year while ten years passed back on Earth. Travelers who went to Procyon and back spent two years on-board ship and came back to a world that had aged twenty years. And the messages that they brought from the new colonists were ten years out of date.

As humanity spread to nearby stars, communication became more and more of a problem. No information can travel faster than light. Not a carrier pigeon, not a radio signal, not a human brain. No way. So if you want to send a message back to Earth from your colony on the third planet orbiting Procyon A, it'll take eleven years to get there. And it'll take eleven years for a reply to reach you, putting you a bit out of touch.

Things got even more interesting when Aidlan Farr, an early member of the Farr clone, dove down a wormhole, while on the run from a Resurrectionist ship. Some fifty years later, she showed up at Farr Station, having traveled back from Aldebaran.

What's a wormhole, you ask? Where have you been? A wormhole is a passage through the space-time continuum.

You say that doesn't help much? Well, then try this: take a strip of paper and bring one end to the other, making a loop. Now put a half twist in the loop, so that the top surface of the strip meets the bottom surface of the strip. Voila! You have a Moebius strip—a two-dimensional piece of paper.

A Moebius strip has only one side. Start at any point on the strip and draw a line, following the length of the strip. Without picking up the point of the pencil, you'll go around the loop twice and end up back where you started. The line will go all around the inside of the loop and all around the outside of the loop—even though you never picked up the pencil to change sides. That's because a Moebius strip has only one side.

Now suppose, just suppose, you punch a hole through a Moebius strip. You might think that hole goes from one side of the strip to the other—but the strip only has one side. So where does the hole go from and to?

It goes from one location on the one-sided strip to another location on the one-sided strip. If you were a two-dimensional Flatlander, this hole could provide startling short cut to a distant location (a spot that the Flatlander would ordinarily have to trudge a long way to reach). That short cut goes through the third dimension, something that a Flatlander living on the strip might have a tough time visualizing.

That brings us, at last, to wormholes. A wormhole is a short cut through the fourth dimension that connects one location to another. It's a black hole and a white hole, hooked up with exotic material to keep the passage between them open. It leads from one place to someplace else—and the someplace else can be four light years away or four hundred. The distance between the points doesn't make any difference to your travel time.

But here's the difficulty: as Aidlan discovered, a wormhole takes you from here to there, but it's a one-way trip. For reasons having to do with black holes and gravity and the space-time continuum, you can't dive back down that wormhole and come out back where you started. It just doesn't work that way.

So Aidlan's Surprise, as it came to be named, can take you from near Alpha Centauri to Aldebaran. But to get back, you have to either take the long way through the regular universe, as Aidlan did. Or you could take your chances and try another wormhole. You might end up closer to home or—the universe being a very large place and odds being what they are—you might end up a few hundred or a few thousand or a few million light years farther away. You just didn't know.

A few adventurous souls dove down other wormholes to see where they went. They were never heard from again, and that discouraged other would-be explorers.

The Farr clone took a different approach, one that seemed sensible enough to patient folks willing to take a long view of time. They chucked a radio beacon or two down every worm hole they could find, established a listening post on Farr Station, and began waiting for some results.

Why does this require patience? Remember—information can't travel faster than the speed of light. Suppose the beacon you tossed down a wormhole travels to the vicinity of Beta Centauri, one of the brightest stars in Earth's sky. Beta Centauri is about three hundred light years from Earth. That means you'll be listening for three hundred years before you hear a peep out of that radio beacon.

By galactic standards, Beta Centauri is a relatively close neighbor. Suppose the radio beacon popped out somewhere near the center of the Milky Way galaxy, some thirty thousand light years from Earth. Suppose the worm hole led to the Magellanic Cloud, the closest galaxy to the Milky Way galaxy. That's about 150,000 light years away.

To find out where some of those beacons went, you're going to be listening for a long, long time. Fortunately, Myra Farr and her sibs didn't mind taking the long view. That's where it helped to be a clone. Though each member of the Farr clone knew that her particular body wouldn't be around for the results, she knew that a version of her would. Over the next few hundred years, the Farrs listened and charted the wormholes that led to nearby locations. They sent explorers out through those wormholes and established colonies hundreds of light years away. Those colonies tossed radio beacons down more wormholes and listened for the returning signals.

Eventually, a radio beacon tossed down a wormhole by a Farr colony located some two hundred light years from home popped out just a few light years from Farr Station. Farr Station read the glyphs on the beacon and sent a messenger ship to the colony, establishing a way back for those colonists.

Just one more thing, before we move on. Wormholes were, as near as anyone could figure, artificial constructs, created by an alien civilization that had apparently visited our galaxy a long long time ago. Explorers had found other strange artifacts left behind by these aliens. The fragments of the vanished civilization were known as Snarks and the folks who sought them were called Snark hunters, after an ancient bit of verse from Old Earth. But the most useful artifacts that the Old Ones had left behind were their wormholes, shortcuts across the galaxy.

All this takes us to where we are now: the universe is riddled with wormholes that let you travel from one place to another with no ensuing travel time. But each wormhole is a one-way street. The Farr clone knows where a hundred or so wormholes go. But all of the other wormholes lead to unknown destinations. Dive down one and you don't know where you'll end up— or how you could get back.

WHEN WE LEFT our company, the sibs were studying the holographic projection in Bailey's parlor, while Gitana sipped her brandy. "I recognize the patterns," Zahara said. "There's Alpha Centauri . . ." She pointed at three dots near one wall of the cube. ". . . and that . . ." She indicated a golden arrow that led to two dots. ". . . is Aidlan's Surprise, which leads from Alpha Centauri to Aldebaran's binary system. But this. And this." She reached into the projection and ran her fingers through the cat's cradle of golden arrows criss-crossing the pattern of stars. "All new routes for us to follow."

"This one . . ." Gitana's finger indicated an arrow. ". . . leads from near the galactic center to a previously unmapped hole less than a light year from here. That must be how the message pod got here. Violet told me she was going to follow this route." Gitana ran her finger over a series of arrows, following a route that led from near Alpha Centauri to the galactic center.

Bailey leaned close, interested despite himself. He had always been fascinated by maps and puzzles and ciphers, and he fancied himself rather good at them.

"Where did Violet come by this?" Jazz asked.

Gitana looked grim. "This is an enlargement and replica of a cube that I gave her. I obtained the original in the hold of a Resurrectionist ship," she said. "It was entrusted to me by one of your sibs. I did not get her name—she did not remember it herself by that time. She had been there for sometime."

All the sibs shuddered, imagining what happened to a person in the hold of a Resurrectionist ship. The name of these space pirates came from an eighteenth century term for the bodysnatchers who exhumed bodies for dissection by surgeons. The space-faring Resurrectionists harvested human brains and nervous systems and used them in the construction of cyborg control systems for space ships, mining stations, automated prospecting probes, and the like. Their philosophy was one of aggressive individualism, and they disliked clones, regarding the sibs as spare parts. In the hold of a Resurrectionist ship, a clone would be kept alive, but just barely, as the Resurrectionists used her body as a source of spare parts to maintain their cyborgs.

"What were you doing there?" Zahara asked Gitana.

"I was finding things out, as usual. A nasty and dangerous business. And having learned what I could, I was leaving as quickly as possible. Even so, I barely escaped, and I could not save your sib nor find out her name nor find out the details of how she had obtained this map. I learned only that she had found it on an exploratory trip."

"But I did what I could. I promised your sib that I would give this map to her family. So I gave it to Violet. She was working in the museum on Farr Station and she was getting restless."

"And Violet went off adventuring on her own," Zahara said, with an edge in her voice. "Just put together an expedition and took off. Not stopping to ask Myra's permission. Disgracing her family."

"And I'd guess you would have done the same in her position," Gitana said. "A family trait, this going off on adventures. She went off and sent back this message pod. I got wind of it and let you know. And so we are here and you are all eager to go off adventuring yourselves. It's a wonder there's ever anyone in Farr Station."

"But what was she looking for?" Zahara asked.

"The source of the map, of course," Gitana said. She reached out and touched the silver sphere that had caught Bailey's attention. "This was her destination. She thought she might find more maps there—and she figured there would be some interest in detailed maps of the other wormholes."

Gitana grinned wolfishly. An improved map of the wormholes would be beyond price, and everyone knew it. Not only would it open up areas of the galaxy, it would provide travelers with routes to take around troubled sectors. The known wormholes functioned a bit like mountain passes along trade routes on Old Earth: a good spot for banditry and interception. Travelers taking the known wormhole routes were likely to encounter Resurrectionists, postal pirates (who intercepted message pods and sold them to their intended recipients or sometimes to higher bidders), and any number of other undesirables.

While the sibs chattered about the value of such a map, Bailey peered at the glowing lines in the hologram. He studied the broken place, wondering what had happened there.

"We could follow her route, but I don't like the look of a few things," Zahara was saying.

"Yeah," said Jazz. "That path takes us near Epsilon Eridani. Not a good place to be just now."

"Here," said Poppy, running her finger along another possible route. "Look at this."

"No good," Lily was saying. "That sector's crawling with Resurrectionists."

Bailey ignored them, studying the pattern of arrows as the sibs continued to argue. It was an interesting puzzle, requiring a different sort of focus. It didn't matter how far you traveled on the golden arrows, since all jumps were the same length, regardless of the distance traveled. What mattered was the distance between the end of one golden arrow and the next one you caught. That was what took the time.

"Over here," he said at last, tapping on an arrow that led to the one wall of the cube and on another arrow that led back. "Through here and here and here. And we're there."

Zahara leaned closer. "Not bad. We're clear until here, where we go through a bad patch, over here. After that, the trouble will begin. But otherwise, not too bad."

Zahara and the others were still studying at the map, but Lily was examining Bailey with narrowed eyes. "What do you mean—we?" she asked.

Bailey hadn't meant anything by it, but Gitana spoke before he could say that. "Zahara asked me to choose the final individual for your team, and I've done so," she said.

Gitana was, among other things, an expert practitioner of *jen chi*, a system of interpersonal dynamics that involved balancing energy and personality to create an ideal working team. Developed more than a hundred years ago by Su Orenda, a businesswoman and mystic from Groombridge 34, the system employed psychological profiling developed on Earth during the twentieth century as well as modified versions of two ancient Chinese astrological systems. Its proponents compared it to *feng shui*, the Chinese discipline designed to establish a harmonious environment. But *jen chi* differed from *feng shui* in one very important respect: practitioners of *jen chi* did not always seeks to create a harmonious group, since harmony was not always the ideal working situation. Rather, they sought the perfect balance of order and chaos, of wild intuition and careful focus.

"For very good reasons, I've chosen Mr. Beldon as

the final member of your party, exactly the fellow you need along for balance on this adventure."

Zahara was looking up now, frowning. Seven pairs of identical eyes regarded Bailey with suspicion. The Farr clone had never been noted for its willingness to accept outsiders. In fact, they tended to be clannish and distrustful of those who were not part of the clone, always concerned that they might be cheated and often driving a hard bargain as a result.

"I suggest," Gitana continued, "you offer him a share in the adventure."

"I don't know," Bailey began. "I think . . ."

"Mr. Beldon has talents that will prove quite valuable—I'm confident of that," Gitana said, interrupting Bailey and speaking to Zahara as she filled her glass and Bailey's with brandy. "I think some of you knew his great-grandmother."

"Yes, yes," said Iris, "but we're talking about this fellow, not his great-grandmother."

"That's right," Gitana said, "but blood will tell, and I'm saying that you need this fellow along."

Bailey was about to protest that he did not really want to go along, when Lily let out a breath with an exasperated sound. "That's all very well for you, Gitana, but we don't have any room for dead weight on this expedition."

"Dead weight?" Bailey said, glaring at Lily and drawing himself up to his full height. He was offended now—these people were in his home, drinking his brandy, and dismissing him as if he were nothing. Lily was half his age and he didn't like her dismissive tone. "I think you should reconsider that statement."

Lily shrugged. "Correct me if I'm wrong, but you have no experience outside this sector. You've probably never been farther than Old Earth."

Bailey did not bother telling her that he had never

even been as far as Old Earth. "What does that have to do with it?" he said. "I found your message pod. I've shown you a route far better than the one your sibs found."

"Have done with it," Gitana said suddenly, just as Bailey was trying to think of another contribution he had made. "You asked me to chose the final member of your expedition and I have. If any of you believe that I have chosen incorrectly, then you may do as you like. Go as you are and remain out of balance. Or go home to Farr Station and give up. Your choice, but you will have no more help from me. I've told you that Bailey Beldon will be a valuable addition to your group and that should be enough."

Gitana glared at the sibs—her blue eye cold and steely, her mechanical sensor glowing red. Bailey decided that it would be best not to raise an objection to this plan just then; Lily leaned back in her chair and said nothing more.

"It's enough," Zahara said. "Consider it done. He'll come along, then. And now, we need more brandy and we need to make our plans."

More brandy and more talk and more brandy and Bailey wasn't sure when talk of Resurrectionists and postal pirates and alien artifacts gave way to dreams of the same, where he was wandering through a long tunnel, following a glowing golden arrow, and wondering why he had ever left his comfortable asteroid behind.

2

They roused him with muffins—they roused him with ice—
They roused him with mustard and cress—
They roused him with jam and judicious advice—
They set him conundrums to guess.

—"The Hunting of the Snark," Lewis Carroll

TO THE END OF HIS DAYS, BAILEY COULD NOT REMEMBER THE
rest of that evening with the sibs. He remembered drinking more wine. He remembered being in the kitchen
with Jazz, the muscular sib, scrambling all his quail eggs
to make a midnight snack for his hungry guests. Jazz
was telling him about her last visit to the Fomalhaut
system, a trip that had involved smuggling and piracy
and a business deal gone wrong.

Her story was one of many told that evening. Elaborate tales of gambling and clever trades, of wealth beyond measure and bad luck that came without warning,
of exotic food and intoxicating drink, of romantic liai-
sons and daring escapes. Bailey remembered Gitana telling of a ritual practiced by Gelasias, a nomadic people
who sailed the stellar winds near Vega. Following the
death of their leader (you could call him a king; they
called him the Stellar One), the Gelasias constructed a
mass of ice, extracting the water from asteroids and
packing it around the dead body. At a time agreed upon
by court astrologers, hundreds of steam rockets were
used to launch the ice mass into orbit around the star.

The king's body became a comet, with an orbit carefully calculated to exactly match the span of the king's life.

Bailey remembered Zahara, standing inside the holographic map and speaking of what the Snark could make possible. In the light of the glowing lines, the smooth skin of her shaven head gleamed like polished gold. "So many places we could travel," she murmured. "If only we knew the way. First, we will journey to the center of the galaxy. Then onward to new galaxies, new stars, new worlds to explore." She spread her hands as if to catch hold of the glowing lines and gather them like a cat's cradle. They slipped through her fingers.

Bailey did not remember going to sleep, but he remembered waking up slowly, thinking that his bedroom was rather chilly. He felt a little lighter than usual, and wondered if he had to adjust the spin on the Restless Rest. He thought vaguely about the mess in his best parlor—the party had left it cluttered with empty bottles and plates. His eyes still closed, he lay in bed thinking of how sad he would be to say good-bye to the Farr sibs and politely excuse himself from the expedition. "Thank you very much for asking, but no, I really couldn't," he would say. That's what any sensible norbit would say, after all. He really couldn't go. He felt a pang of disappointment, as he thought about saying it. But he couldn't go; he had to harvest the figs and take care of the Restless Rest. Besides, they really didn't want him along.

Still drifting toward consciousness, he fumbled for the blankets, but they seemed to have slipped away. His groping hand ran over a soft mattress, bumped into a cold metal surface. He could hear an unfamiliar humming, a soft beeping, the rattle of fingers on a keyboard.

He blinked, rubbed a hand over his face, wiping sleep from his eyes, then blinked again. He was not in his bed; he was not in his bedroom. He was in a cold-sleep cylinder, wearing the clothes he had been wearing the day before.

There were two other sleep cylinders in the room, neither of them occupied. Across the room, Jazz sat at a desk, peering at a screen. Her hands were on the keyboard.

Bailey sat up and the woman looked up. "Good morning, Mr. Beldon," she said cheerfully. "I tried to wake you earlier, but you seemed determined to sleep."

Bailey stared at her, stared around him. He was on a deep-space craft. Navigation sensors beeped softly as one viewscreen displayed the positions of the dozens of tumbling asteroids that surrounded the ship. For a moment, still half asleep, he gazed at the display, puzzled that he did not know exactly where they were. He would have claimed that you could put him down anywhere in the Belt and he could establish his location immediately by looking for a few familiar landmarks. But this pattern of tumbling rocks was strangely unfamiliar.

"I thought you'd best come on my ship," Jazz said cheerily. "Poppy went with Zahara. She and I had gotten sick and tired of each other. She's been on Farr Station while I've been traveling, so she's older and thinks she's much wiser. So I said you should come with me."

"Very kind of you," Bailey managed.

On the other side of the cabin, a bell rang softly. "There now," Jazz said. "Tea is ready. I thought you might like some when you woke."

"Very thoughtful of you," Bailey said, still groggily polite, still trying to make sense of the viewscreen. They were following two ships—Zahara's ship and Heather's ship, he figured. Gitana's ship might be behind them. All right then, he'd have a cup of tea and then explain that he had to be getting back home. Very nice of them to invite him along and all, but he really had no use for an adventure just now. Perhaps some other time.

He got up and followed Jazz to the commissary unit, which was filling insulated squeeze tubes with tea. Very light gravity, just barely enough to keep his feet on the floor. He figured the ship must be accelerating slowly, just enough to provide the sensation of light gravity.

He sat in one of the contoured seats by the viewscreen and eyed the tumbling asteroids. If he could figure out where they were, he could suggest somewhere Jazz might drop him off, perhaps at the asteroid of a friend or relative who could give him a ride home.

Jazz handed him a squeeze tube. "You'll feel better soon. I wake up slowly too. Tea helps."

"Thank you," he mumbled. "Very kind of you." He wasn't really listening. "But you know, I'd best be getting back home. I think . . ." He hesitated. Describing his muddled state as thinking would have been overly generous. "I guess . . ." That was closer. "I wonder if there's been some mistake."

"Mistake?" Jazz raised her eyebrows. "What do you mean?"

"I mean . . . what am I doing here?" He took another sip of tea.

"Simple enough. Gitana vouched for you. Zahara drew up an agreement. You signed it and here you are."

"Agreement?"

"Details on your share of the profits, promise that any surviving members of the expedition will defray your funeral expenses, if that becomes necessary. The usual."

While they were talking, Bailey had leaned back in his chair. The sharp corner of a folded paper in his pocket poked him. He pulled the paper from his pocket and discovered it was an agreement between Zahara Farr and Bailey Beldon. Discussion of expenses and profits and funeral expenses. The usual.

He shook his head, staring at the paper. He'd just

have to explain that he couldn't go on an adventure just now. Surely they'd understand.

"You're probably feeling a little confused," Jazz said. "Wine and cold sleep aren't a great mix, if you aren't used to it. But you'll be fine. We spent about a year in cold sleep and made the jump through the wormhole called Farr Way Home. And now we're almost home. Less than a day's travel from Farr Station."

Bailey shook his head, trying to clear it and make sense of what she was saying. They were almost to Farr Station. He blinked. Farr Station was more than eleven light years from the Asteroid Belt.

Bailey stared at Jazz, then at the viewscreen. As Bailey watched, the view shifted as the ship turned, still following the other ships. An orange dwarf star blazed in the center of the screen. It wasn't Sol.

"Exactly where are we?" Bailey asked faintly.

"Well, that's Epsilon Indi. We're making our way through the Meat Grinder on our way to Farr Station," Jazz said.

ABOUT A MILLION years ago (give or take a hundred thousand years), two planets collided in this system. The collision had smashed both planets into tens of thousands of pieces, leaving a tumbling, churning, jostling crowd of orbiting asteroids. That's the Meat Grinder.

In Earth's Asteroid Belt, the asteroids have had four and a half billion years (give or take a million) to find their places. In the millions of years right after the Solar System formed, they were bashing into each other and splintering into families of asteroids. Mars and Jupiter were tugging on them, rearranging their orbits. But after a billion years or so, they had settled down to relatively stable orbits. The largest asteroid left, after repeated collisions, was less than one thousand kilometers across and most of the rocks were less than a tenth that size.

Compare that to the Meat Grinder. Here, the young planetary fragments were still jostling for position. They were in a tight cluster—in just a million years they hadn't had the time to spread out. Some of the rocks were almost as large as Earth's moon, and most were larger than the largest asteroid in the Belt. Some of them had a strong enough gravitational field to hold other Asteroids in orbit around them—mini-moons orbiting moon-sized planetoids which were, in turn, orbiting the star. Sometimes a planetoid would capture a new rock, adding to its collection of mini-moons; sometimes one planetoid would steal a mini-moon from another. It was a chaotic system, with orbits that could be predicted in the short run, but not in the long run.

Myra Farr and her sibs had chosen to locate Farr Station in the center of this crowd of shoving, bumping, unruly rocks. To reach Farr Station, a pilot had to navigate among the asteroids, a difficult task with dangerous consequences for any lapse in judgment.

Friendly ships tapped into constantly updated transmissions from the main computer at Farr Station, which dedicated half its capacity to calculating asteroids' orbits and determining a safe path through the asteroids. To date, no ship had successfully navigated the Meat Grinder without the assistance of data from Farr Station. The Meat Grinder kept Farr Station safe from pirates, Resurrectionists, and other hostiles.

"THE MEAT GRINDER," Bailey muttered, realizing that he had come too far to turn back. They were almost to Farr Station, eleven light years from the Asteroid Belt. Since they had been traveling at near light speed, only about a year had gone by for them—and he'd spent that in cold sleep. But back home, more than eleven years had passed. Even if he turned around right now and headed straight back, he would get home twenty years after he left.

"Exactly. But we've got nothing to worry about," Jazz said cheerfully. "We're following Heather, and she's an excellent pilot." Jazz had turned toward the viewscreen. "Though I have to say, this is the craziest path I've followed yet. Seems like the wrong direction entirely. I wonder . . ."

They had swung around a planetoid, still following Heather's ship. The viewscreen showed a clear patch, and far ahead a glowing point of white light. Jazz touched the communicator switch, turning up the volume. "Jazz to Heather," she started. "Jazz to Heather, come in."

There was static on the hailing frequency, a hash of white noise that ebbed and flowed. Bailey and Jazz listened to the rhythmic rising and falling of the sound.

"Jazz to Heather," Jazz repeated. "Jazz to Heather. Can you hear me, Heather?" Her voice fit into the rhythm, matching the beat rather than fighting it.

The steady beat of the static grew louder, and Bailey heard other sounds emerging from the background noise. Was that a drum beat, matching time to the ebb and flow of the static? No, not a drum, it was the pounding of his heart in perfect time. Was that a flute—or perhaps a human voice—singing along? No, it was the singing of blood in his ears, the background symphony of his living body. Bailey found himself leaning closer to listen to the communicator.

"Wait," Jazz said, her eyes growing wide. "Trancers." And her voice merged with the static, which grew louder until it filled the cabin. "A Trancer trap."

The words matched the rhythm and the rhythm matched Bailey's heartbeat and the static and the words and the heartbeat combined to make a music so compelling that he felt the urge to close his eyes and dance.

There are songs that get stuck in your head and play over and over and over in an endlessly repeating loop until you want to scream. Certain patterns of rhythm and melody affect the human nervous system and induce trance states that lead to the internal physiological repetition of the rhythm. The songs that get stuck in your head do that. So does the music used in Inuit shamanistic ritual and in Voodoo ceremonies; so do the Gospel tunes sung at Christian revivals and the tunes transmitted by Trancers.

Throughout the inhabited galaxy, Trancers set up stations (which they called "meeting houses" and non-Trancers called "Trancer Traps"). These stations transmitted music and electromagnetic pulses that reinforced the music by acting directly on the nervous system (nerve signals being nothing more than electrical currents, after all). Like the Sirens of Greek legend, the Trancers used music to lure ships in. Captured by the Trancers, the ship's crews became Trancers, brainwashed by the music and unable to break free.

"Trancer trap," Jazz said again. Her words slid into a syncopated beat, blending with the original rhythm. "Trancer trap. Trancer trap. Trancer trap." She was beginning to move in time with the music. Bailey felt the urge to join her, but he wasn't much of a dancer; never had been. So he pushed himself deeper into his seat. One foot tapped along with the rhythm, but other than that, he didn't move.

Oh, it should never have happened. Heather should have noticed the rhythm in the static and switched frequencies before it caught her. Someone on her ship should have noticed what was going on before she turned up the volume and caught the others. Jazz and Heather should have noticed that something was up and suspected Trancers. But they were all heading home; they were on familiar territory and thinking themselves already safe. And of course Gitana should have . . . Wait a beat. Where was Gitana?

Gitana should have been there. "Where's Gitana?" Bailey asked Jazz, but she didn't answer. She was caught by the rhythm now—up and dancing. Though her eyes passed over him, she didn't seem to register his presence. "Trancer trap," she said. "Trancer trap."

As Bailey watched, the bright white light in the viewscreen grew brighter. They were approaching the Trancer station.

The communicator screen had been showing static that pulsed in time with the rhythm. Now the static cleared and a man appeared on the screen. He was the happiest looking man Bailey had ever seen. He was wearing a broad, beatific smile, content with his world and eager to share his joy with those around him. His face was surrounded by a wild halo of curly hair that bounced as he moved in time to the music, which had swelled to fill the cabin, its rhythms growing in complexity.

"Welcome to the meeting house, my friends," he said, spreading his hands as if to gather them in. "Two of your sisters are here." On the screen behind him, Bailey could see two sibs of the Farr clone dancing: a young woman with hair as curly as Heather's and a middle-aged woman with flame red hair. "These two scouts decided to join us. We're so glad you're joining us, too."

"What if we don't want to?" Bailey said without thinking. His words cut through the rhythm.

The man turned and focused his serene gaze on Bailey. "Don't want to?" he asked. "Not possible."

"I don't like to dance."

"Everyone likes to dance." The man's smile grew broader. "Just listen and you'll find out."

But Bailey was telling the honest truth. He really didn't like to dance. He liked singing, but his relatives discouraged him from doing it in public. He couldn't carry a tune. And I'm not saying he couldn't sing opera. He could render "Happy Birthday" unrecognizable.

In the range of human sensibilities, there are those with no musical aptitude and no sense of rhythm, those who always march out of step. It's a small percentage of the human population, maybe less than a tenth of a percent. This lack of musical aptitude is a liability in many social situations, where singing and dancing are called for. But in other situations, it was an advantage.

This was one of those other situations. Those individuals aren't susceptible to Trancer music. Sure, they can hear the pull of the music, but they can easily resist.

"Just listen," the man said. "Just let the beat take you."

"I'd rather not." Bailey slapped the communicator switch to disconnect, but the man still smiled from the screen and the music continued without missing a beat.

"We've overridden your circuits," the man said. "You can't turn off the music."

"We don't have time to stop," Bailey said, feeling uncomfortably out of his depth. "We're heading for Farr Station, and people are expecting us."

"No problem. They'll find you here. Everyone's welcome here."

"But we have places to go." Bailey glanced at Jazz, hoping she might help him out. But the sib was dancing, her eyes closed, oblivious to their conversation. "We're in a hurry."

"There's always time for dancing," the man said.

Just then, Gitana came back. Of course Bailey didn't know that. He was studying the control panel, trying to figure out how he might regain control of the communication system. "Jazz," he said. "Help me out here." But Jazz just kept dancing.

"Just listen to the music," the man was saying. "Just listen. . . ." He leaned closer to the screen, focusing the full force of his smile on Bailey. "You don't need to hurry off."

"You don't understand," Bailey said. "I really didn't mean to be here at all. I wish I'd just left that message pod where I'd found it. Then I'd still be home, sitting down to a nice dinner and. . . ."

"Just listen to the music," the man said, his voice a little impatient now. "Just listen. . . ."

A metallic shriek interrupted him, slicing through the music and making Bailey's ears ring. The man's smile faltered and he glared at Bailey. "Stop that," he said.

There was a tremendous crash, like a tower of scrap metal collapsing suddenly.

"We're being overridden," the man was saying to someone off screen. "We've got to block . . ."

Another metallic shriek, accompanied by a throbbing roar, cut through the music. Bailey glanced at Jazz, who had stopped dancing for a moment. "Jazz," Bailey said. "We've got to get out of here."

The throbbing roar continued, and Bailey could barely hear the Trancer music over the din. Jazz was blinking, bewildered, and Bailey pulled her to the control panel. The strange industrial sounds continued to blare from the communicator. On the screen, Bailey could see the man frantically working his controls.

"Zahara! Heather! Jazz!" Gitana's voice interrupted the noise. Her face glared from the communicator screen. Her blue eye glittered like glacial ice; the sensor on her black eye cap glowed faintly red. She worked the panel in front of her and a sound like the rattling of metal claws on sheet metal echoed through the cabin. "Move! Get out of there!"

Jazz was working the controls frantically.

"I've hailed Farr Station," Gitana was saying. "They know about the Trancers now and they're sending help.

Right now, we've just got to get out. Zahara, are you with us?"

"I'm here." Zahara's voice, a little shaky.

A burst of Trancer music came from the speakers. Gitana swore and hit a switch, overriding the music with a high-pitched trilling sound, like mechanical crickets.

Gitana stared at Bailey from the viewscreen. "Bailey, you provide cover."

"What do you mean?"

"Sing. Your grandmother couldn't hold a tune, and I'd guess you can't either. Sing on this frequency. Everyone else, follow me."

Gitana took off, dodging an asteroid half the size of her ship, swinging around the planetoid that had hidden the Trancer trap, and heading back into the Meat Grinder. Jazz followed, blasting her jets to jerk the ship this way and that. Bailey clung to the console chair and did his best to sing.

He began with a boisterous drinking song about a drunken norbit named Jack who decided to dance on the surface of his asteroid. The gravity was so low that when he took a high leap, he jumped into orbit.

> *"A bottle of whiskey,*
> *A bottle of gin,*
> *Jack took the wrong step.*
> *And went for a*
> *spin. . . ."*

In this situation, Bailey's lack of musical ability was a plus. Every note that rang flat and each hesitation that spoiled the rhythm helped break the Trancer spell.

> *"A norbit in orbit,*
> *No way to get down,*

*Thinking of whiskey
And spinning around."*

Acceleration pushed Bailey hard into the chair as Jazz locked onto Gitana's course. They slid past a tumbling asteroid, barely clearing it, then dove fast to avoid a smaller rock. Gitana cut hard left to dodge another rock, and Jazz followed, blasting her jets just enough to slide past.

Bailey's voice faltered, and the Trancer music broke in. He closed his eyes then, figuring he'd be better off if he didn't know when death was imminent. With his eyes squeezed shut, he sang even louder, switching to a song about two lovers who lived on asteroids with orbits that carried them apart. The song involved yodeling, something that Bailey enjoyed but usually did only in the privacy of his bathroom.

His wailing yodel cut through the distant Trancer music, overpowering it. He tried to pretend that he was safe at home, yodeling happily in the Restless Rest. Though his eyes were closed, he felt every jerk and dive and dodge of the small ship, which made pretending difficult. But despite that, he managed to keep on pretending and keep on yodeling. He stayed with the same song. When he finished it, he just started in again, yodeling with steadfast determination.

He was on his fourth repetition of the yodeling chorus when Jazz said, in a voice touched with pain, "You can stop now, Bailey. Please stop."

He opened his eyes. The viewscreen showed a great silver wheel, spinning majestically in a patch of clear space. Light of the orange star glittered on the spokes as Gitana's ship headed for the docking port at the hub of the wheel. Farr Station, the place where so many tales began.

"We're home," Jazz said.

"Quite an adventure." He smiled, happy to be reaching a place of safety.

Jazz glanced at him. "Oh, but we're just getting started," she said with a grin.

3

He had bought a large map representing the sea,
Without the least vestige of land:
And the crew were much pleased when they found it to be
A map they could all understand.

—"The Hunting of the Snark," Lewis Carroll

MANY TALES OF ADVENTURE BEGIN AT FARR STATION: "WE WERE
setting out from Farr Station when suddenly . . ." And
the listener always knows that an exciting story will follow. Many tales end there as well: "At last we made our
way back to Farr Station where we sold our cargo for a
profit. And then . . ."

And then another adventure would begin. Farr Station, where adventures begin and end and pause for
breath along the way.

JAZZ MANEUVERED THE ship to the docking port, where the
ship's external manipulators locked on to the towing cables. She and Bailey sat back as the ship was pulled into
the docking port and cycled through the air lock. Via
communicator, Jazz talked with the sib at the landing
controls—telling her about their narrow escape from the
Trancers. Bailey paid no attention to that. He was too
busy staring through the viewscreen at the busy loading
dock.

Located at the hub of the wheel that was Farr Station,
the loading dock was an enormous cylinder, large

enough to accommodate half a dozen freighters, along with a few dozen smaller ships. At its center, the cylinder was a zero-g environment. Moving out from the center, toward the rim of the wheel, the station's rotation created artificial gravity of about a tenth that of Earth.

The light gravity allowed for complex choreography in three dimensions, an aerial ballet of robot drones and cargo and workers. To the left of Bailey, a broadly built robot riding on magnetic treads yanked metal drums from the open hold of a freighter. With a casual flick of hydraulic arms, the robot tossed a drum aloft. Bailey watched the drum soar in a graceful arc across the center of the loading dock. A jet-propelled robot came up from beneath the soaring drum, caught it neatly, and carried it toward a freighter on the far side of the loading dock.

One by one, the robot hurled drums toward the center of the cylinder. One by one, a series of robots carried the drums away, deposited them beside a loading robot, then returned to repeat the procedure. Every catch precisely timed, every move by one robot matched by a response from another. An elegant dance of heavy machinery where the slightest misstep could spell disaster.

Workers wearing jet packs zipped across the loading dock on urgent errands, but they all steered clear of the air space near the flying drums. All the workers were clad in the Farr colors—deep purple and gold—except for one stout gentleman who was dressed in a forest green jumpsuit with a gold spiral decorating his ample chest. As Bailey watched, this man blasted across the loading dock on a trajectory that carried him directly into the path of a soaring drum.

Bailey froze, his eyes fixed on the man in danger. "Oh, no!" he said. "That man will be hit." But even as Bailey spoke, the man executed a neat back flip. The drum cleared him by a narrow margin. Bailey let out his breath.

"Oh, that's a pataphysician," Jazz said. As if that explained everything.

Bailey watched the pataphysician zip out of sight while the docking cables towed their ship to a landing pad. Jazz flipped a switch to turn on the electromagnets that would hold the ship to the deck. The ship settled into place. "Let's go," Jazz said, clearly excited to be home.

Bailey followed her through the airlock, stepping out into the pandemonium of the loading dock. The place echoed with roaring jet packs, clattering robots, and the thumping and banging and clanging and crashing of loading and unloading. Massive machinery (not heavy, since gravity was light, but still possessing mass and momentum) is noisy stuff. The hot air stank of oil.

Gitana was huddled by a terminal with the pataphysician. Bailey studied the man's face. Older than Bailey by a few years, the pataphysician's dark hair had gone gray at the temples. He looked like a scholar, perhaps a professor of some particularly esoteric branch of philosophy or linguistics. A small beard and thin mustache gave him a slightly impish look. He was smiling calmly, clearly not at all perturbed by his near collision with the drum.

Zahara was striding from the airlock of her ship, followed by the other sibs. Poppy and Iris were waving at a couple of workers, who waved back. Bailey stared around him in confusion.

"Come on," Jazz shouted over the din, grabbing his hand and pulling him toward a trapdoor in the deck. He followed the group down a ladder into a corridor. The trap door slammed closed above them and it was suddenly quiet.

"That's better," said Gitana. "Everyone here?" She glanced around. Everyone was. "Good. Troops are on their way to the Trancer Trap to free your sibs. If you don't have family aboard, report to guest quarters. Dinner—or perhaps breakfast for some . . ." (This with a glance at Bailey.) ". . . will be at the guest dining hall in an hour. We'll rendezvous there. This is Gyro Renacus, a Satrap of the College of 'Pataphysics and a good friend of mine. He'll be joining us for dinner." She turned away, her hand on Gyro's arm.

JAZZ SHOWED BAILEY to guest quarters. He had a small room of his own off a central lounge that was shared by several members of the expedition. In the shower, he found himself humming a tune and thinking about how well they had done so far. Certainly, they had come through danger and he had done well. And now they were safe and comfortable.

Jazz had ordered him a clean jumpsuit from the Station store. The only one they had in his size was in the Farr colors, and he felt a little bit silly wearing royal purple and gold. Even so, it was better than the clothes he had been wearing for the past two days (or more than a year, if you counted the time he had spent in cold sleep). However you counted time, Bailey was happy to be out of those clothes.

When he emptied the pockets of his trousers, he found the note that he had found just before this adventure had begun. As you may recall, it consisted of the words *"Eadem mutata resurgo,"* a pataphysical spiral, and the words: "Harvest the figs." Bailey shook his head, still puzzled, and tucked the note into the pocket of his new jumpsuit, resolving to ask Gitana's pataphysician friend what the phrase meant. Jazz led the way to the dining commons, where they joined the others in a banquet room.

Bailey sank onto a pillow beside Jazz, relaxing for the first time since he had left the Restless Rest. The Farrs might be adventurers, but Bailey could see that they believed in being comfortable when they could. The sibs lounged on pillows around an enormous, low-slung table.

The walls were covered with richly colored tapestries woven with elaborate geometric designs. The New Russian Church of Islam, the official religion of Farr Station, prohibited representational art in public places.

The light was soft and warm. Though it shone from bulbs in sconces set in the walls, it flickered and shifted like candlelight. Candles were impractical aboard the station, but people had not lost their affection for light that shifted and changed, light a little too dim for perfect vision. The dining room's environmental control computer had been set to mimic that flickering, uncertain light.

The audio system piped in music—a meandering tune played by flutes and bells. The food was superb. Most of the dishes were vegetarian, concocted from plants grown in the station's greenhouse and exotically flavored with imported spices. There was a salad made of edible flowers—nasturtiums and borage and sage. There were seafood dishes—the station's aquaculture plant raised shrimp and clams and crawfish and fish of various species. Bailey stuffed himself on steamed shrimp with fragrant rice crumbs, scallops sauteed in wine, and Heart of the Sea, a spicy shellfish stew.

Between mouthfuls, Bailey repeated his version of what had happened during their encounter with the Trancers several times before all the sibs were satisfied. The Trancer music had left the others with little memory of events.

"I remember the beginning," Jazz said. "I heard a rhythm in the static."

"That's right. Sort of like this." Bailey tapped the rhythm on the table top with his spoon. Dinner had been wonderful, the wine was flowing, and he was feeling quite content. At that moment, going on an adventure seemed like a splendid idea.

"Stop that," Zahara said sharply.

Bailey stopped. It was unusual for him to remember a rhythm and tune so well, even more unusual for him to be able to reproduce it. It was, come to think of it, the same tune he'd been humming in the shower. Now that the danger was past, he rather enjoyed thinking about the Trancer music. But since the others were understandably wary, he refrained from repeating the rhythm.

"Good thing Gitana came back when she did," Bailey said.

"Good thing you distracted the Trancers while I jammed their transmission." In the shifting light and shadows, Gitana looked benevolent, her blackwork tattoos blending with the shadows. "I'm glad that you inherited your grandmother's ability to carry a tune." Gitana smiled. "Brita was unquestionably tone deaf."

"I've never heard singing quite like yours," Iris said. She had combed out her long blonde hair and it floated around her shoulders like a cloud.

"I'd like to talk to you about those songs," Lotus said. "The tune of the first one had the dirgelike quality of Martian funeral wails combined with the atonal rhythms of Gacruzian war music."

"You certainly have an unusual singing voice," Heather agreed.

"I'd say it was exceptional," said Poppy sweetly, patting Bailey on the shoulder in a maternal way. She had had a few glasses of wine.

"Without equal," said Lily, who had been matching Poppy, drink for drink. "Though I hope we won't have occasion to hear it again any time soon."

"To Gitana and Bailey," Jazz said, raising her glass in a toast.

The sibs drank while Bailey ducked his head modestly and helped himself to another sweet dessert cake.

"Well, now," Gitana said, "thank you very much, but we have a long way to go yet. We've got a galaxy to cross before congratulations are in order. Soon we meet with Myra to discuss our route. I am certain I don't need to warn you all to keep our mission secret from all others. You all realize that if word were to get out about what we're after, we'd have every pirate and every Resurrectionist ship in the galaxy on our tail." Gitana glanced around the room and Bailey nodded with the others.

Gitana smiled, satisfied with their understanding. "But now we can celebrate our small victories. I have a bottle of Ergotian whiskey back at my room. If you will join me in the lounge. . . ."

With that, they retired to the lounge for a night cap, leaving robot drones to clean up.

ERGOTIAN WHISKEY [ALSO known as St. Anthony's firewater) is a blend of two mind-altering traditions: the alcoholic and the psychedelic. Ergot is a fungal disease of grasses, especially rye, that gives rise to hallucinogenic alkaloids. The production of a superior blend of Ergotian whiskey involved balancing of infected and clean grains. The resulting brew induced a mellow drunkenness accompanied by colored haloes, insights that were sometimes brilliant and sometimes foolish, and an occasional vision.

In the lounge, Bailey found himself seated on the couch beside Gyro Renacus, the pataphysician who had met them at the loading dock. Gyro was smiling again, an expression that seemed to come naturally to him. He leaned back on the couch, comfortable in his body, in this lounge, in the universe.

"Congratulations on your narrow escape," Gyro said to Bailey, lifting his glass of whiskey.

"Thank you," Bailey said. He lifted his glass and gingerly sipped the whiskey. "You know, I've never met a pataphysician before."

"But I'll bet you've heard a few things about us."

"A few. I've heard you're good at word games."

Gyro nodded gravely. "Some are."

"I've heard people say that 'Pataphysics is the ultimate weapon."

"Some say that, and some say it's the ultimate defense. Both are true. You see, we know that there is nothing to fight about. And that's a very powerful position to be in."

"And I've heard people say that pataphysicians think everything's a kind of a joke."

Gyro shook his head. "Now that's not true at all. In fact, only a pataphysician is capable of complete seriousness. You see, we take everything seriously. Absolutely everything." He sipped his whiskey. "According to the Principle of Universal Equivalence, everything is just as serious as everything else. A battle to the death with Resurrectionists, a game of Scrabble, a love affair—all are equally serious."

"But people say . . ."

"People don't always understand," Gyro said gently. "You see people confuse playing with not being serious. We are very serious about our play."

Bailey frowned. "I guess I see. You play—but you take it seriously so that you can win, and. . . ."

"Oh, no. Playing to win—that's not it at all. When you are playing to win, you are in a finite game, a game with boundaries. I was speaking of the infinite game, where one plays simply in order to continue to play."

"So you don't take winning seriously?"

"We take it just as seriously as we take everything else."

Bailey shook his head, still no more enlightened than

before. He was feeling the slightest bit dizzy, and he could not tell if that feeling came from the whiskey or the conversation.

Gyro sipped his whiskey and continued. "In fact, that is the pataphysical privilege—being aware of the infinite game that we are all playing. You see, everyone is a pataphysician. It's just that some of us are aware that we are pataphysicians; we know we are playing the infinite game."

"You see here." He pointed to the words right beside the pataphysical spiral on the chest of his jumpsuit. "College of 'Pataphysics," it read.

"That apostrophe at the beginning of 'Pataphysics is a modest ornament that reminds every pataphysician of the pataphysical privilege. That humble squiggle tells us not to forget that we are playing the infinite game."

Bailey frowned, still baffled.

"Of course, we like finite games, too," Gyro went on. "Playing Scrabble, writing Boolean haiku—all kinds of games."

"Writing haiku doesn't seem like a game," Bailey said.

"You set up strict rules and follow them, while attempting to reach a goal," Gyro said. "What else do you need for a game?"

"I guess it could be a game," Bailey said slowly.

"Of course." Gyro smiled. "You know, you said you had never met a pataphysician. I've never met a norbit before. What was it that inspired you to leave the Asteroid Belt?"

"Well, it was kind of an accident," Bailey said. "A misunderstanding." Thinking about the circumstances of his departure from the belt reminded Bailey of why he had wanted to talk to the pataphysician. "Actually, I wanted to ask you about this." He pulled the mysterious note from his pocket and held it out to Gyro.

Gyro studied the note solemnly. "Did you harvest the figs?"

"Of course," Bailey said with a touch of impatience. "That was the only part of the note I understood."

"Good. It's always best to do the parts you understand. Where did the note come from?"

"That's one of the things that puzzled me. I don't know. I found it when I was eating breakfast a few days ago." Bailey hesitated. "Or a few years ago, depending."

Gyro nodded. "It all depends, of course. Rather a messy scrawl, isn't it?"

"Well, yes. . . ." Bailey shifted uncomfortably. "It looks a lot like my handwriting. But I don't remember writing it."

"How interesting!" Gyro's smile grew broader. "That's lovely."

Bailey did not think it was lovely. "So what does all this mean?" He ran his finger over the words that he couldn't understand.

"*Eadem mutata resurgo*," Gyro said. "It's Latin, an ancient language of Earth. In translation, it means 'Though changed, I arise again the same.' And then, of course, we have the pataphysical spiral. You know the meaning of that, of course?"

Bailey shook his head.

"Every point on our spiral is a turning point," Gyro said.

"What?"

"Every point is a turning point," Gyro repeated. "That's one of the basic tenets of the College of 'Pataphysics. Each point along any path is a turning point. The spiral represents that tenet."

"Your most serene serenissimus," Gitana interrupted, leaning over the back of the couch and staring at the note in Gyro's hand. "What's this?"

Gyro grinned and handed her the note. "Bailey

showed me this note. He found it back at the Restless Rest, just before you arrived."

"I see," Gitana said slowly, first examining the note and then studying Bailey with equal intensity. In the shadowy room, the blackwork tattoos on the left side of her face seemed to pulse and flow.

Bailey shifted in his seat, uncomfortable to be under such scrutiny. Gitana exchanged a glance with Gyro and handed the note back to him.

"It bodes well, I'd say," Gyro said, then gave the note back to Bailey. "I'd save that, if I were you. You may need it later."

"But I don't understand," Bailey grumbled. "I don't know where it came from or what it was doing in the Restless Rest or. . . ."

"Let it be. These things have a way of becoming clear over time," Gyro said. And then he shrugged. "Or not. In the end, it doesn't really matter does it?"

It mattered to Bailey, but it was clear that he would get no more information from Gyro or Gitana. After that cryptic statement, Gyro had turned to Gitana. "Myra is bound to have an interesting perspective on your plans," he observed mildly, and the two of them began chatting about Myra and what she might think of their plans.

Bailey would have liked to stay, but his dizziness had increased. It was not an unpleasant sort of dizziness, just a gentle disorientation. The overhead lights were surrounded with vividly colored haloes. Iris was playing an intricate tune on a stringed instrument that rested in her lap. The notes seemed to echo, blending with the ebb and flow of conversation in the room, creating an intricate rhythmic pattern. Watching her play, Bailey reminded himself that she was the weapons officer—the hands plucking that delicate melody were accustomed to firing lasers and missiles.

He felt as if he were drifting above the others. He had the sense that if he stayed and listened for long enough, he would understand many things that were mysterious to him, including Boolean haiku and the pataphysical privilege and the note in his pocket. But at that moment, sleep seemed more important than understanding. He finished his whiskey and retired to his room where he slept soundly. In his dreams, he battled a forest-green dragon that trailed golden spirals and recited haiku in Gyro's voice.

WHEN HE WOKE, there was a message from Poppy and Lotus, inviting him to dinner in their family's quarters. The meal was a chaotic gathering of sibs of many ages, presided over by a pair of gray-haired matriarchs. Poppy and Lotus called one woman "Granny" and the other one "Grandmother" and listened fondly while the old women argued about how to spice the soup and how long to boil the crawfish.

"Granny is cooking the right-handed food," Poppy explained to Bailey. "And Grandmother is cooking the left-handed food. How many lefties have we got around, just now?" she asked Grandmother.

"Just a few. You and your sister and your friend, of course. Your sisters Daisy and Delphina and your cousin Elodia. They're just back from Vega and they took an odd number of jumps. A repeat trip will set them right."

"Zahara went to some trouble to make sure that our expedition is all one orientation starting out," Poppy told Bailey. "It makes provisioning so much easier."

Bailey frowned at Poppy. She was talking about a side effect of wormhole travel that Bailey had heard about. The person who emerges from a wormhole is a precise mirror image of the person who entered. If you're right-handed when you enter, you emerge a sinister lefty. If you had a dueling scar on your left cheek, it's now on your right. "Wait," he said. "We all went through the wormhole, but I'm still right-handed."

"Are you?" Lotus grinned at him. "Hold up your right hand."

Bailey held up his left hand. Lotus laughed and Poppy patted the norbit on the shoulder. "This is your right," she said. "That's your left."

"I'm right-handed," Granny said, waving a stirring spoon in her right hand.

Bailey stared at his own hands, flexing his fingers and regarding them with suspicion. The hand that he had been certain was his right was now his left. He shook his head. "Why didn't I notice?"

Lotus shrugged. "Everything changed, and you changed along with it," she said. "If you had changed and everything else stayed the same, I guess you'd have noticed sooner."

Poppy laughed. "I was wondering how long it would take you to notice. It always takes new travelers a while. You're a lefty now, and you'll eat left-handed food."

Most organic compounds—such as proteins, sugars, and the like—come in two forms: right-handed and left-handed. On Earth, the right-handed form is most common. It's the form that the enzymes of the human body evolved to digest. Someone who has never traveled through a wormhole can't digest left-handed molecules. Trying to digest a left-handed sugar with a right-handed enzyme is like trying to put your left shoe on your right foot—it just doesn't fit. Left-handed food won't hurt those equipped for right-handed food, but they can't get nourishment from it.

And now you see the difficulty. A traveler who has made one jump through a wormhole must eat left-handed food, composed of molecules that match the traveler's digestive enzymes. Fortunately, the provisions aboard the ship (having made the same jump) are also left-handed. But when the traveler reaches his destination, he must be careful to seek out the appropriate food, a necessity that plagued the cooks on Farr Station and other places where interstellar travelers gathered.

"More salt," Granny said, tasting the soup.

"I don't think so." Grandmother shook her head. "More pepper, I think. It needs more of a bite."

"The soup is a mixture of left- and right-handed stock," Poppy told Bailey. "It will work for both orientations."

Bailey nodded.

"You there," Granny said, gesturing at Bailey. "Come taste this soup. What do you think?"

The soup, thick lentil-vegetable medley, was exotically spiced. Bailey declared it to be perfect as it was—no need for any more fussing—and both matriarchs beamed. Then each credited the other with its success. (They argued genially about that for a time.)

Lotus introduced Bailey to the assorted sibs, some of whom she called sister and some cousin. Poppy and Lotus were sisters. They were also from the same generation of sibs. All the sibs in a given generation had names that were of a type: flowers or gems or colors or names of prophets. All the sibs on the expedition except for Zahara were from a single generation.

Bailey could make no real sense of the family relationships among the sibs. Lotus explained a bit about how the sibs were divided into clans, and those clans into families. She talked of how the sibs formed group marriages of two or three or four, banding together to raise cloned children and natural children as well. Lotus's sisters and one of her cousins had married men from outside the clone; the others were single or had married within the clone—pairing either with members of the same sex or the opposite. The children, of which there were many, were both clones and natural offspring from heterosexual pairings.

Lotus explained that Bailey was going on "an expedition with Zahara," carefully omitting all details. After dinner, Bryan, one of the husbands from outside, drew Bailey aside. "Are you the only non-sib on this trip?" he asked Bailey.

"No, Gitana will be coming along."

"I see. That's good." He gazed past Bailey into the kitchen, where the sibs were preparing dessert and discussing whether cream whipped using a wire whisk had a texture superior to that of cream whipped using a power mixer. "They take some getting used to," he said. "But I'm sure you'll do fine. You certainly charmed the Grannies."

Bailey hadn't intended to charm anyone; his compliments were sincere, and he told Bryan so. Bryan nodded again, smiling. "You'll do fine," he repeated. Bailey was glad that Bryan was sure, because he wasn't so sure himself.

After dessert, they played word games. Bailey's favorite game was "Riddle me haiku." The name of the game came from an ancient nonsense haiku:

> *Riddle me haiku.*
> *Refresh me with conundrums.*
> *Riddle, puzzle, pop!*

The younger members of the clan played a clapping, dancing game that involved reciting that nonsense haiku while the older members composed riddles in haiku form—a line of five syllables, a line of seven syllables, then a line of five syllables that poses a question—and attempted to stump the rest of the party with them. Bailey enjoyed himself immensely.

Over the next few sleep cycles, Bailey wandered about

Farr Station with one sib or another. He learned his way around the public areas of the station and grew accustomed to hearing the call to prayer echoing through the corridors, a signal heeded only by the most devoted. ("All of us on the expedition are members of the Reform Church," Lotus explained. "We don't attend daily prayers. We drink alcohol in moderation.")

Iris, her blonde hair tied neatly in braids, took him to the performance of a zero-g dance troupe. The star performer was a Farr sib who looked to be just a couple of years younger than Iris.

"My daughter," Iris told Bailey.

Bailey frowned. "Your daughter? But she looks like she's almost your age."

Iris shrugged. "I've been traveling. She's been staying put. I broke up with Rosemary, her mother, when she was a child. Haven't seen Rosemary for a while."

After the performance, they went backstage to join the cast party. There, Iris introduced Bailey to Raisa, her daughter, and Rosemary, her daughter's mother. Rosemary was a Farr sib who looked old enough to be Iris's mother.

Raisa was surrounded by friends and well-wishers, but she took a moment to greet Iris. Then Rosemary introduced Iris and Bailey to other members of the troupe, treating them with conscientious courtesy.

"It was a beautiful performance," Iris told Rosemary.

"She has worked very hard," Rosemary said. "In a month, she'll be competing at the dance festival. Perhaps you'll be able to attend?"

Iris shook her head. "Unfortunately not. We're heading out on an extended expedition. . . ."

"Of course." Rosemary's voice was cool. "I assumed that." She glanced at Bailey and smiled a brittle smile. "Interstellar adventurers can spare so little time for their families. It's good that some of us prefer to stay at home."

He nodded sympathetically. "Staying at home sounds like a much better choice to me," he said, with a touch of wistfulness. "I'd be ever so content to go home and stay there."

Rosemary looked startled, then her smile softened, becoming more genuine.

"I know it was a difficult choice," Iris said softly, and Rosemary nodded.

Not long after, when Bailey excused himself to return to guest quarters, Iris and Rosemary were talking easily, reminiscing about old times.

The next day, Jazz took him to a bar and lounge that had viewscreens that showed the ships docking with the station, a comfortable place from which to watch the bustle and movement and a favorite drinking place for visiting traders. They were sipping right-handed wine when Bailey saw Zahara sitting with a group of older sibs. The expedition leader looked grim.

When Bailey pointed her out, Jazz shook her head. "Let's not interrupt. I'd rather not get embroiled in station politics."

Bailey frowned. "What do you mean?"

"It all has to do with prestige and power," Jazz said. "Her family has been out of favor since Violet left on her expedition without asking Myra's permission. Maybe when I'm Zahara's age I'll worry about gaining glory for my family, but right now, I can't be bothered. Tell me: do norbits seek glory?"

"Glory? Not really. I think most norbits would rather have a pleasant dinner than a grand adventure."

"Good. Then let's go get a pleasant dinner."

And they did.

As the days went by, Bailey had a chance to explore other parts of the station. Lily took him along when she went to the Market to trade a few gems she had picked up on her last trip. (She wouldn't say exactly how or where.) While a sharp-eyed gem trader bargained with Lily (her red crest of spiky hair bristling, her teeth gleaming in a predatory smile), Bailey explored corridors scented with spices and exotic perfumes, brought direct from a thousand planets. Farr Station was a center for the trade of spices, perfumes, and botanical drugs. The complexity of these biologically produced compounds could not be easily duplicated—synthetic substitutes lacked the nuances of the original. So these luxuries were still traded from world to world.

Heather took him to the Farr Museum, dedicated to the history of the clone. In one room, a glowing timeline showed how Myra Farr had spent her biological life. She had been born on Mars some two thousand years ago, give or take a century or two. Her family was wealthy, her grandfather having been one of the developers of the Hoshi Drive. Museum displays depicted some of the highlights of Myra's early years.

One display described her role in the liberation of the Martian colonies from Earth rule. Another provided a model of the ship she had piloted to Capella—she had been the first person to reach Capella's third planet, located some forty-one light years from the Solar System.

A set of wall panels summarized how Myra had founded the interstellar branch of the New Russian Church of Islam, a matriarchal religion based on a radical reinterpretation of the Koran by the prophet Katrina. By that time, Myra had established the Farr clone. The endogamous, community-style family characteristic of the new Islam, which did not discourage the marriage of cousins or clones, fit in with her plans for Farr Station.

There were displays depicting more adventures than Bailey had imagined possible. Myra was a bold and adventurous woman who did not shy away from conflict.

Myra had been a robust woman, who had lived to a ripe old age. Calculating exactly how old her biological body had been when it finally gave out was difficult. Myra had spent much of her life criss-crossing the galaxy—sometimes in cold sleep, sometimes at near light speed, sometimes diving down wormholes. Some five hundred years passed on Earth between the time she was born and the time her body died. But that was planet time, not personal time. Long before her biological death, she had given up calculating her age or celebrating her birthdays.

Some one hundred years after her birth (measured by Earth time), Myra cloned herself, creating a generation of sibs. In the following years, there had been many more generations. Each sib was a genetic duplicate of Myra, more or less. There were, of course, some sibs in which one of the X chromosomes had been altered to make a male version. And there had been a few adjustments here and there—a correction to remove an allergy to a certain variety of mildew, an adjustment to correct for a tendency to flat-footedness. But very few changes, really.

The timeline showed when Aidlan Farr dove into the wormhole that came to be known as Aidlan's Surprise and when she returned from Aldebaran. It showed when Myra founded Farr Station and began her long-term investigation of wormholes. And it showed when Myra's biological body finally gave out. At that point, her brain patterns and knowledge base were downloaded into the main computer at Farr Station, allowing her to continue her consciousness without the inconvenience of a body.

Bailey and Heather followed a giggling school group (twenty-five ten-year-old sibs, all named for precious gems) into a room dedicated to the Farrs' efforts to map the wormholes. Bailey stepped into a holographic display of the galaxy, with wormholes marked, just as the teacher began quizzing her charges on the display.

"Crystal! When did we begin mapping the wormholes?"

"Three hundred years ago," Crystal said.

"Ruby! Why did we bother with this project?"

"So we could explore the galaxy," Ruby said, her voice a little hesitant.

"That's true, but that's just part of it. What else? Emerald?"

"It puts us in control of navigational information." Emerald was a smug-faced child. "So we can sell that information and get rich."

Bailey remembered the old saying: "Trust a Farr to know the way; trust a Farr to make you pay." Both were true. From their radio beacons, the Farrs had learned routes that let them traverse the galaxy—and for a price, they had shared those routes with others. The financial arrangements had been complex, but always navigational knowledge had come dear. The Farrs were known to be greedy—both for knowledge and wealth.

"Crudely put, but true. It allowed the clone to assume our current position of wealth and power. Why do we continue it? Sapphire?"

"Because there's always more to learn."

"That's quite right."

The teacher gestured to a display of alien artifacts discovered by the Farrs. "Now why are they called Snarks?" the teacher asked. "Jewel?"

"It comes from an ancient Earth text about hunting a fabulous beast that's very hard to find. The Snark is now extinct on Earth."

"That's quite right. Now let's move on."

They left Bailey and Heather alone in the holographic galaxy.

"There's always more to learn," Heather said softly. "There are so many wormholes that are still uncharted."

A navigator and astronomer, she stared with longing at the holographic stars around them. "The map Violet sent fills in some of the gaps. Maybe we can fill in the rest."

Bailey nodded, still feeling uncomfortable. He was wondering just a bit about the clause in his agreement with Zahara about his share of the profits. It seemed so unlikely to be proposing to share in even a fraction of the wealth of the Farrs. And it seemed unlikely that the Farrs would want to share.

"You don't look happy," Heather said.

Bailey shrugged. "I guess I'm just not sure what I'm doing here," he confessed. "I'm not really an adventurer."

Heather smiled, but she was kind enough not to indicate that she had already observed that. "Gitana says we need you, and she's been right so far. If not for you, we might be dancing with the Trancers right now."

"Gitana would have saved you."

Heather shook her head. "Even Gitana needs some help, now and then. And if she says we need you to balance the group, then we need you. I've studied a bit of *jen chi* myself, and I think she's right."

BAILEY WAS AWAKENED by the sound of Gitana's voice on the intercom. He had been sleeping soundly and dreaming happily of the Restless Rest. "Time to get up," Gitana said briskly. "We're meeting with Myra Farr in an hour, so make yourself presentable."

"Surely you don't need me," Bailey said.

"Oh, yes we do. She asked that you be there."

"But . . ."

"She knew your grandmother."

"But . . ."

"Trust me—we don't want to keep Myra waiting."

"But . . ."

"No time for that. I'll see you in the lounge in ten minutes."

With that, she was gone, and Bailey was sleepily splashing water on his face and scrambling into his jumpsuit. He had just walked into the lounge, the last of the group to arrive, when Gitana said, "Follow me."

He trailed along at the end of the group with Gyro. Gitana and Zahara were in the lead, with the other sibs following in twos: Iris and Heather, Jazz and Lily, Lotus and Poppy.

"I don't know what I'm doing here," Bailey grumbled to Gyro. He had been out drinking with Jazz the night before and his head ached from too much wine and not enough sleep. He was not in a mood to bustle off to see Myra Farr. "It's all quite inconvenient. People back home will be wondering where I'm off to. Without a note, without a word." He shook his head fretfully.

Gyro smiled. "There's an old pataphysical saying: 'An adventure is only an inconvenience, rightly considered.' Adventure is never convenient. And everything is an adventure, if you take the right perspective."

"So everything is inconvenient?" Bailey grumbled.

"Oh, yes. That's exactly it! Life is terribly inconvenient, which makes it quite entertaining." Gyro seemed happy about this, though Bailey could not understand why. "And here we are."

Gitana led them through door marked "Director's Office" to a lavishly furnished lounge. Along the wall, which curved to follow the outer wall of the station, were viewscreens, each of which showed a different view. One showed the tumbling rocks of the Meat Grinder, glittering in the light of the central star. Another showed the activity outside the loading dock, ships waiting for entry to the station. Still another showed a view of the distant stars.

Floating in the center of every view was an elderly

woman in a rocking chair. She looked quite at home there, though asteroids tumbled past her and ships by the loading dock maneuvered nearby, oblivious to her presence. She studied the group as they filed into the room.

Myra's face came from the same basic template as the others—it was the original from which the others had arisen. But Bailey would no longer say that she had the same face as the others. In the time he had spent with the sibs, he had come to see the differences in their faces, rather than the similarities—the laugh lines around Poppy's eyes, the wrinkles on Zahara's forehead that came from frowning, Jazz's broken nose and crooked happy-go-lucky grin. Though the sibs had eyes of precisely the same color, they wore different habitual expressions: Lotus studied the world with an anthropologist's detachment; Lily with the appraising eyes of a trader, ready to bargain; Heather with the distant gaze of an astronomer. Their faces had started out the same, but life had traced different patterns on each.

Savage glee filled the smile with which Myra greeted them. It was the smile of a predator—a wolf scenting a fawn, a killer whale closing in on a fleeing seal. Her eyes burned with fierce passion, stoked by an inner fire. A dueling scar sliced across the soft wrinkles of her face, running from forehead to her temple and narrowly missing her right eye. (Bailey remembered seeing a display in the museum about dueling on Mars in Myra's youth.)

"Well, Zahara, it seems you have brought home quite a treasure." Myra studied Zahara. "It's too bad that your daughter didn't choose to share this information with me sooner, but I'm grateful to have it now."

Zahara ducked her head and Bailey was startled by the expression on her face. Zahara looked both contrite and surly, like a reprimanded child. "Violet was always willful," she murmured.

Bailey frowned. "Violet is Zahara's daughter?" he murmured to Gyro.

The pataphysician nodded. "Zahara went off an exploratory expedition, but Myra wanted Violet to stay at Farr Station. She stayed for a while, aging while her mother traveled. But when the opportunity presented itself, she left on her own adventure," Gyro told Bailey softly.

"As if you wouldn't have done the same thing in her place," Myra was saying to Zahara. Her eyes were relentless.

"Oh come now, Myra," Gitana said, speaking up for the first time and sounding a trifle out of sorts. "Are you saying you would have stayed happily in Farr Station? The whole lot of you are just the same, willing to blast off across the galaxy in search of glory."

"Knowledge," Myra said, matching Gitana's tone. "That's the point. Not glory."

"Glory, knowledge, wealth, power . . ." Gitana waved a hand. "You could never resist any of them. None of you can. And Violet's Snark offers all four at the same time."

"Are you saying that you are above all that?" Myra leaned forward in her chair, her relentless gaze fixed on Gitana.

"I'm saying let's stop blaming Zahara and talk about what we're doing now. Zahara, tell Myra our plan."

"You've seen the map," Zahara began.

The background in all the viewscreens changed to show the stars and wormholes in the holographic map. Myra sat amid a tangle of glowing lines, like a spider in the center of her web. "Yes, I have."

"Well, here's what we plan to do." Zahara described the route they had planned. As she did so, those lines brightened in the holographic display that surrounded Myra, catching her in a web of golden light.

Myra was nodding, "When you reach the center of the galaxy, you'll find Violet—or more likely the descendants of Violet's crew. And then I suppose I am to believe that you'll bring any Snarks you find back home."

"Of course," Zahara said. "I've given you no reason to believe otherwise."

Myra's eyes burned as she studied each member of the expedition in turn. "Do you think you're up to it?" she asked.

"Yes." Zahara met Myra's gaze and did not drop her eyes.

"The crew you've assembled seems acceptable—with one exception." Bailey stiffened as Myra's gaze focused on him. "I wonder what role Mr. Beldon is to play on this journey. He is, after all, not one of us."

Bailey sat for a moment, frozen in his seat. She was staring at him, as if waiting for him to speak. "Well," he stammered after a moment. "I must say, I've wondered that myself. I had no idea I would be meddling in such important affairs when I found that message pod."

"But find it he did," Zahara said softly. "And he reported its recovery as is proper."

"Oh, he's an honest soul, to be sure. But that hardly seems enough of a qualification for this expedition." Myra's eyes were still on Bailey.

"Gitana, our *jen chi* consultant, has advised that I invite Mr. Beldon join the crew," Zahara continued.

Bailey was uncomfortable being discussed as if he were so much baggage, as if he had no choice himself. They would take him on the trip or not, as they chose.

"No need to argue on my behalf," he said stoutly. "I was perfectly happy tending my mining stations and growing figs in the greenhouse. I have no particular interest in the center of the galaxy. I'd be more than happy to go back home."

"That's settled then," Myra said. "I think that . . ."

"No," Zahara interrupted, her voice louder than before. "Bailey has already proven to be a very important member of the expedition. The Trancers would have had us, if not for him." She had straightened in her chair and she was returning Myra's stare. "We need him to balance the expedition."

Myra frowned. "Being tone deaf is not much of a recommendation."

"Both my Granny and my Grandmother approved of him." Poppy was leaning forward in her chair. "They said we were lucky to have him along."

"That's right," Lotus murmured.

"Zahara says we need him to balance the expedition," Jazz said. "I think she's right."

"He's an outsider." Myra was shaking her head. "You don't know what he might do."

"If you don't want me along, I'll just go home," Bailey said again, though he was glad to hear Poppy and Jazz speak out in his favor.

"No you won't." Lily spoke first, but Iris was just behind. "Not a chance. Zahara has decided that you're coming, and so you'll come."

"It's a question of balance," Heather said. "You're right—we don't know what he'll do. And that's important."

"You see," Zahara said, her voice steady. "The crew agrees that he is an essential part of the expedition." She turned to look at the norbit. "Bailey, we need you. Will you come with us?"

Bailey looked at the others. Under Myra's gaze, he felt very small, but he spoke up, as loudly as he could. "If you all want me to, I will."

"Then you'll come," Zahara said. Her eyes were fierce as she gazed at Myra. "As expedition leader, I insist on it."

On the viewscreen, Myra smiled her savage smile. "Perhaps you are up for this after all," she said. "You've passed the first test of leadership. You've disagreed with me." She waved a hand, dismissing the matter. "Take him or not. It doesn't matter to me."

"We'll take him," Zahara said firmly, and Myra's smile broadened.

Bailey thought about the pataphysical spiral and glanced at Gyro, who was smiling. Every point was a turning point indeed.

"Be very careful on the first leg of your journey," Myra was saying to Zahara. "You have an excellent ship, but the Resurrectionists have grown bolder of late."

But Bailey wasn't listening any more. It seemed to him that he had just passed an important turning point. He had decided, for better or worse, not to go home just yet.

THEY SPENT ONE more sleep cycle on Farr Station. Then they bid farewell to Gyro. Bailey was sorry to say good-bye. Though the norbit did not feel that he really understood the pataphysician's views, he found Gyro's imperturbable calm most reassuring.

"I wish you were coming along," Bailey said.

"I have my own path to follow." The pataphysician was about to begin an exploratory mission on behalf of the College of 'Pataphysics. "But I'm confident that we will meet again. Be patient. And remember: *'Patiens quia aeterna; aeterna quia pataphysica.'* "

"What does that mean?"

"Patience because eternal; eternal because pataphysical."

Bailey frowned. "And what does that mean?"

"You can be patient because time itself is an illusion."

"Bailey!" Jazz called to him. "Come on. We have to get aboard."

Gyro clapped Bailey on the shoulder. "Don't worry about it, my friend. We will meet again. You can be sure of that."

Soon they were all aboard, except for Gitana, who followed in her own craft. Through the viewscreen, Bailey watched Farr Station grow smaller, until it was nothing but a speck of light in the distance.

4

He would joke with hyenas, returning their stare
With an impudent wag of the head:
And he once went for a walk, paw-in-paw, with a bear,
"Just to keep up its spirits," he said.

—"The Hunting of the Snark," Lewis Carroll

THE GALAXY IS RIDDLED WITH WORMHOLES, A TANGLED NETWORK
of secret passages, each of which might carry you a few
light years—or a few thousand light years—from your
starting point. The expedition made its way toward
Stone's Throw, thewormhole nearest Farr Station. The
hole was part of a binary system, orbiting and being
orbited by a main sequence red star known as Red
Stone. One of the first holes mapped by the Farrs, the
name Stone's Throw referred to its proximity to the station. The distance it took you—some 140 light years to
an open cluster called the Hyades, was much more than
a stone's throw.

Their ship, the *Odyssey*, was an exploratory vessel,
equipped for long distance travel into unknown territory.
It had comfortable quarters for all, a communal lounge,
and a well-equipped galley (since good food was known
to be one of the best ways to maintain morale on long
journeys). Since they expected to be traveling through a
number of dangerous sectors, the vessel was also well-
armed, equipped with radar detection equipment, missile decoys and jamming devices, and laser cannons.

Shortly after the *Odyssey* left Farr Station, the ship entered interstellar space. Bailey noticed that Zahara seemed exhilarated by their departure from Farr Station. She smiled more and joked with the others over meals. On Farr Station, she had looked beleaguered and set upon, her face set in grim lines, her eyes hard. As the *Odyssey* entered interstellar space, her face softened and she relaxed.

She joked and smiled, but she also insisted on battle drills—both regularly scheduled drills and ones that came without warning in the middle of a sleep period. In a battle drill, each member of the expedition assumed his or her battle station and prepared for the worst. Bailey's station was by the tail port, a rarely used entry into the ship, and he felt a bit useless during the drills, which invariably began with much shouting of orders and ended with a long discussion in which Zahara detailed how their response could have been improved. At these times, she was stern, but fair, noting problems and discussing how they could be avoided.

Two members of the expedition were always on watch, monitoring the ship's radar for possible hostile forces. There was some argument over whether this was necessary. Heather maintained that the ship's automatic warning system was sufficient as long as they were in a sector patrolled by Farr forces. But Zahara insisted and two members of the expedition were on the bridge at all times.

When they weren't on watch or participating in drills, the sibs had other tasks to occupy their time. Heather studied Violet's map, correlating information from that with data the Farrs had gathered. Iris spent her time working on original composition for her qanun, a plucked trapezoidal zither of Arabic origin. Poppy cooked, experimenting with new combinations of exotic spices. Jazz worked out in the recreation room. Sometimes, she convinced Zahara or Lily to play handball. When no one wanted to play, she played solo, returning from these games drenched in sweat. Lotus and Lily played long and complex card games. Occasionally, Bailey convinced them to play Riddle Me Haiku.

Sometimes Bailey studied Violet's map with Heather, sometimes he cooked with Poppy. But he spent most of his time gazing out the viewscreen at the stars.

He was used to travel in the Asteroid Belt, where there was always something to look at. A mining station here, a bit of space debris there, a friend tootling by over yonder. A cozy sort of place, the Asteroid Belt, crowded with tumbling rocks and the people who lived in them.

By comparison, interstellar space seemed terribly lonely, a vast expanse of emptiness. They were only about eleven light years from Earth—no distance at all on the galactic scale. Looking toward the galactic center, he could still pick out reassuringly familiar constellations: Sagittarius, Scorpio. Looking toward Sol, he could still make out Orion and Taurus and Sol itself, a dim star notable only because Bailey knew it was home.

Bailey noticed subtle changes in the stars as the Hoshi Drive kicked in and the *Odyssey* gradually accelerated. The positions of the stars seemed to shift subtly, moving in front of the ship. The colors of the stars ahead shifted toward the blue. Aldebaran, the red giant that marked the eye of the Taurus, became orange, then yellow, and finally green-blue.

Late one sleep cycle, while on midwatch with Lotus, Bailey asked about the changes he had observed. "The stars are changing," he said hesitantly. "Changing color, changing position."

Before Lotus could speak, Zahara answered from the doorway. "Yes, they are," she said. "Isn't it wonderful?" She strode into the room and sat down in the chair beside Bailey's, gazing at the viewscreen. "Sometimes, I can't sleep for thinking about them," she told him. "And I have to come and take a look."

Bailey did not find the changes wonderful. Rather, he found them disturbing, but he did not want to tell Zahara that. "Why are they changing?" Bailey asked.

"The color change is the Doppler blue-shift. As we move toward a light source, we meet the light waves coming toward us. That shifts the light's frequency—higher frequency, bluer light."

Bailey gazed at the stars. "But why are they changing position?"

"As we catch up to the light, its perceived direction changes," Zahara told Bailey. When she saw that he was about to ask another question, she shook her head. "Don't think too much about it. It'll just make your head hurt. Just accept that it tells you we're moving. Moving fast and leaving it all behind. It feels great, doesn't it?"

Bailey did not agree. He liked the home he was leaving behind; Zahara did not seem as fond of Farr Station.

"If you like traveling so much, why do you ever go back to Farr Station?" he asked her.

Her smile faltered; her forehead furrowed in a frown. "I have duties," she said somberly. "To my family, to my clone." Zahara gazed at the viewscreen. "Violet neglected her duties and brought disgrace to us all. But now, I can return my family to a position of honor."

"This trip will bring glory to us all," Lotus said. She had looked up from her work.

Zahara nodded and smiled brilliantly. "We'll go to the center of the Galaxy and find the Snark to end all Snarks," she repeated. "If that doesn't gain Myra's respect, nothing will."

Bailey followed her gaze to the viewscreen, where the constellation Sagittarius blazed in its new, altered form, and wondered if anything would gain Myra's respect.

Later on, after Zahara had returned to her bed, Bailey

asked Lotus about Zahara's sense of family honor. "I don't understand," Bailey said. "She seems so much happier away from all the politics of Farr Station. Yet she's tied to it by this need for family honor. Why can't she just leave?"

Lotus studied his face, frowning a little. "You norbits value individual freedom," she said at last. "Independent thinking, individual desires. In a society like the one at Farr Station, the needs of the individual are secondary to the needs of the group. Zahara returns for the good of the group."

"But it makes her so unhappy," Bailey said.

Lotus shrugged, her expression noncommittal. "It's how we are," she said at last.

AS THEY TRAVELED, Bailey had plenty of time to think about what he would be doing if he were back at the Restless Rest. He wondered how long it had taken his relatives to notice his absence. He hadn't left a note behind, and any friend stopping by would just assume he was out checking on his mining stations. The automated systems would keep things going in his absence—at least for a time. The greenhouse would be a riot of vegetation, growing wild. But no one would notice that for the first year or so. He imagined being back at home, maybe going to harvest a few figs, maybe settling down to breakfast in the solarium. But home, like those distant stars, was so far away.

Over meals and between games, the sibs sat in the lounge, a homey room where the walls were hung with tapestries, and talked about what they would do once they had maps of all the wormholes, about what they could do, where they could go, what adventures they could have. Bailey grew bored with the long discussions of possibilities.

"It's always like this between holes," Jazz told Bailey

in the lounge one day. "Long stretches of tedium, punctuated by terror. Near the holes you get Postal Pirates,
merchants, Trancers, Resurrectionists, all kinds of folks.
You hardly ever bump into anything out here."

"And you aren't likely to find any hostiles in this sector
anyway," Poppy said, winding a strand of dark hair
around her finger. "Not with the Farr patrols out."

Bailey wondered a little about that. After all, the
Trancers had been within the area patrolled by the
Farrs. But he refrained from pointing that out.

"Anyway, we're almost there," Poppy went on.

And that was true. Red Stone, the red star that orbited the wormhole, blazed bright in the viewscreen, but
the star appeared insignificant beside its companion. A
great swirling disk of glowing gases surrounded the dark
sphere of the wormhole, sucked into Stone's Throw by
the hole's gravitational pull. As this accretion disk
swirled, hot gases flowed from the red star into the disk,
forming a crimson stream in the radiant vortex.

The sibs did not pay much attention to the wormhole.
They were, after all, in their own backyard, galactically
speaking. They had all been through this particular hole
dozens of times. But Bailey, whose only trip through a
wormhole had taken place while he was asleep, watched
Stone's Throw with excitement and trepidation.

They were just two days journey from the hole when
Bailey and Heather were on midwatch; everyone else
was asleep. Heather was on the bridge, monitoring the
radar. (Well, truth be told, she was napping and trusting
to the automatic warning system.) Bailey had wandered
over to take a peek through the viewscreen at Stone's
Throw. Against the darkness of the hole, he saw a bright
spot, a distant blip coming closer. For a moment, he
thought it was Gitana's ship, then he realized the approaching vessel was much larger than Gitana's scout

ship. "There's a ship approaching," he called to Heather.

Heather blinked awake and yawned. She peered at the radar screen. "Must be your imagination. Nothing on radar. Maybe a star."

"Definitely a ship," Bailey insisted. "Come and see for yourself."

Heather glanced at the viewscreen, still blinking sleepily. "Looks like a freighter. I'm surprised they haven't hailed us." Heather turned a dial. "This is the *Odyssey* to approaching vessel," she said. "Please identify yourself."

Bailey continued to watch the vessel approach. It lacked the markings he had seen on freighters at Farr Station—no identifying numbers or name.

"Something's happening," Bailey said. The freighter had come closer to the *Odyssey* and released a swarm of something: Message pods? Scout ships? Torpedoes? "What are those things?"

Heather glanced back at the screen. "Attack pods!" she shouted. "Resurrectionists!" She slapped switches on the communications console, activating the battle alarm.

"Emergency. We are under attack," said a stern voice. "Report to your battle stations immediately. Emergency."

Bailey took one more look at the attack pods as he ran for his battle station. Small and black and fast, with magnetic heads and dangling appendages. Heather was already taking evasive action. The ship jerked and lurched as Bailey ran toward the equipment locker, but trying to evade the attack pods was like trying to dodge a swarm of bees. Bailey heard the pods bumping and scraping against the hull as he snatched his equipment from the locker and hurried past the sibs who were crowding into the corridor, half awake, bleary, but already shouting questions, pushing toward the equipment locker.

"It's another goddamned drill, isn't it?"

"Not a drill. Resurrectionists!"

"Where?"

"How'd they get past our radar?"

"Must have a new jamming device."

"Sneaky bastards."

"Move, move, move!"

"Where's Gitana?"

There were terrible sounds on the hull—like dentist drills, like jack hammers, like sheet metal torn by giant hands. Bailey felt the ship jerk as Iris and Jazz began shooting the attack pods with the port and starboard guns. He was still struggling into his emergency gear and hurrying toward his battle station, when the stern voice of the battle computer announced. "Ventilation system has been breached by foreign invader."

His eyes drooped shut before he could get his gas mask on.

CENTURIES BEFORE, CYBERNETICISTS had determined that neural networks were extremely efficient for information storage and processing. They had, way back then, begun analyzing the structure of naturally occurring neural networks (like the human nervous system) and attempting to duplicate these complexities mechanically.

Artificially constructing that complexity was difficult. In many situations, it proved far easier to make use of naturally occurring neural networks. Suppose, for example, you wanted a central processing unit to regulate temperature in a space colony. You could build a neural network that would analyze the input information and constantly adjust the solar energy panels and ventilation system to maintain the desired temperature. Or you could simply extract the nervous system of a medium-sized dog—paring away the excess tissue and taking only the neural tissue. You could modify that neural network to serve as your thermoregulatory system. Making use of the dog's brain was, in fact, by far the more efficient option.

Of course, if you had a more complex neural network, you could process more information, manage a more complex system, achieve greater efficiency. Consider, for example, the human nervous system. . . .

Most experimenters stopped there. They considered the human nervous system, but stopped short of anything more. They did not experiment; they did not speculate farther.

There were, however, some who did go on. Resurrectionists, who valued efficiency above all else, decided that the sibs of a clone were not truly human. They were, after all, duplicates of a single individual, The original individual was human; the duplicates were simply spare parts. Following that reasoning, the nervous system of the sibs could be used by the Resurrectionists without guilt. Needless to say, the sibs did not agree with this assessment.

BAILEY WOKE IN darkness. His head ached and his mouth was dry and tasted of strange chemicals. He was lying on a hard, cold surface that throbbed faintly with the hum of distant engines. With an effort, he struggled to a sitting position. His arms and legs felt stiff and wooden, as if he had been lying in an awkward position for far too long.

He felt something constricting his neck and reached up. A collar encircled his throat. It felt smooth all the way around, no buckle, no way to unfasten it. For a moment, he was silent, listening in the darkness. He could hear people breathing.

"Hello?" he whispered. "Who's here? Jazz? Heather? Poppy?"

For a moment, there was no answer. Then a voice

responded, "I am here." A strange, tinny voice—flat and uninflected with no breath behind it. It sounded as if it came from a speaker, rather than a human throat.

"Who are you?"

"The Master calls me Spare Parts," the voice said. "I had another name once . . . but I've forgotten that." Still no inflection, but Bailey read uncertainty into the voice's hesitation.

Bailey heard someone beside him sigh, heard the rustling of clothing as someone moved slowly, painfully. "Bailey? Is that you?" Jazz's voice. "God, my head aches."

"I'm here."

"Who's that?"

"It's Poppy. My head aches, too."

"Me, too." Bailey recognized Heather's voice. "Where are we?"

"Nowhere good," Jazz said. "I hope . . ."

"We are on a Resurrectionist ship," interrupted the emotionless voice. "There is no hope here."

"There's always hope," Poppy said stoutly.

"No hope," said the voice. "Except death. We can hope for that."

"Who else is here?" Jazz said, her voice determined. "Some people may still be knocked out. Feel around you and let me know who you find."

Bailey found a wall and a warm body who groaned when he bumped into her—Iris, just coming back to consciousness. Jazz found Lily and Lotus and shook them awake. Poppy found Zahara, who woke reluctantly. These last three had managed to get their masks on—and they were armed and ready when the Resurrectionists boarded. The Resurrectionists had overpowered them, but only after a fight. They were bruised and battered and even groggier than the rest.

"We're all here except Gitana," Jazz said.

"She probably escaped," Poppy said optimistically.

"If she has, she's heading out of here as fast as she can go," Lily said bitterly.

"You have no call to say that." Iris' voice had an edge in it.

"Hey, she's not stupid. Anyone with a brain would do the same."

"You wouldn't leave the rest of us behind," Poppy said.

"That's different. She's not a sib."

"We don't have time to argue," Zahara growled. Her voice was weak, lacking her usual brash confidence. "Let's talk about what we can do."

"Not much," Lily said. "Sitting up is about all I can handle."

"We can't see anything and we don't know anything about where we are," Iris complained. "How can we figure out what to do?"

"We can start by agreeing to keep our destination secret," Zahara said grimly. "At least we can do that."

"Maybe Spare Parts can tell us more about where we are," Bailey suggested.

"There is nothing to do," said the flat voice. "You will stay here and they will extract you. I know. I was one of you once."

"No," Bailey protested. "It doesn't have to happen that way. The voice sounded so hopeless. He was frightened, but he wanted to reassure the voice. "Maybe we can help you. If we escape, we can take you with us."

"Too late for me. There is so little of me left."

"It can't be too late," Bailey said. He had heard many adventure stories, told by norbits after dinner in a warm and comfortable asteroid. He knew how this was supposed to work. He and the sibs would save themselves and rescue this victim from the Resurrectionists. That was the way it worked in the stories, except when the story was a tragedy and everyone died. He had never liked tragedies. He shook his head. Surely their story couldn't be a tragedy.

Bailey heard the faint click of a switch and the Spare Parts said, "He's coming."

"Who is?"

"The Master."

The room was filled with white light, so dazzling after the darkness that it left Bailey blinking at the room around him. White walls, shiny steel tables and shelves. Bailey and the sibs were confined in a large cage at one end of the room, separated from the door by a sturdy steel partition.

Beyond the partition, the room appeared to be a combination of a medical facility and an electronics shop. The light reflected from a steel operating table. A nearby tray held laser scalpels, forceps, and other gleaming metal instruments. On the walls were monitors that Bailey could not identify. The workbench beside the table was crowded with metal-working tools, soldering guns, and a tangle of wires. On the workbench was a stack of collars, like the one around Bailey's neck, like the ones around the necks of all the sibs.

The door slid open and a man strolled in. He was in no rush. He was a tall, paunchy man, and he seemed completely at ease with himself and his surroundings. He was a man who was comfortable with his world.

Bailey's first thought on considering the man was that he did not look evil. His face was round and jovial, and he was smiling broadly. His teeth flashed silver when he smiled, the natural enamel having been replaced with steel long ago. But that was a practical choice; Bailey had met others who had opted for dental replacements.

The man had four eyes set in a neat line across his face—he had replaced his limited natural eyes with a more versatile set of sensors. The central two eyes still provided binocular vision using light in the visible spectrum, but they could be adjusted for telescopic viewing or closeup work. The other two housed sensors for infrared and ultraviolet. But there was nothing inherently evil about augmenting your sensory input.

The man wore what appeared at first glance to be a cap woven of silver mesh. Closer examination revealed that the silver mesh connected to electrodes that protruded from the man's skull. Bailey had heard that such electrodes were common among Resurrectionists, providing a direct link between the brain and external communications systems. In this case, the electrodes supplied information about the ship's status. The mesh cap connected to a harness that fitted around the man's torso.

As Bailey watched, the man took a small cylinder from a table. The light glinted on a glass lens on one end of the cylinder. The man slid the cylinder into a socket on his harness and stood still for a moment, as if deep in thought. Then he turned to face Bailey and the sibs.

"You've been talking amongst yourselves," he said cheerfully. "And Spare Parts has been telling you what's in store for you."

He patted a glass tank that was beside him. Bailey noticed the tank's contents for the first time. A human brain and other neural tissue, studded with wires and electrodes, floated in the tank. The wires connected to electronic gear on the workbench.

"I told them the truth," Spare Parts' voice said. The voice came from a speaker on the workbench. Bailey felt dizzy and sick.

"That's good." The man continued to smile. "It will help them understand their situation."

"How do you know what we've been saying?" Bailey stammered.

The man tapped the socket where he'd put the cylinder. "I always leave an eye and an ear in admissions.

Just downloaded the recording. Always useful to know what's been going on while I've been out."

"Are you the Captain of this ship?" Zahara asked. She had struggled to her feet. One hand gripped the bars of the partition for support. Though she was weak, she glared at the man defiantly. "I demand to know why you have detained us. We . . ."

The man pointed his index finger at Zahara and pumped his thumb as if it were the hammer of a gun. Zahara made a small, choking sound and clutched the collar at her throat, identical to the one the Bailey had felt around his own neck.

"The Captain? Of course not. The Captain is far too busy to deal with the extraction of a group of spare parts. I'm the Master Technician. You can just call me the Master. And you might as well relax and save your breath. Things will go so much more smoothly if you accept your situation. For one thing, it's no good tugging at your collar. It's an invention of my own. It neutralizes all neural signals to your voicebox at my command. Saves a lot of argument."

Still smiling, the Master surveyed the sibs. "An assortment of spare parts—and an anomaly." He glanced at Bailey again. "Are you the sib of a clone," he asked.

"No," Bailey said, shaking his head.

The Master smiled. "Of course, you wouldn't tell me even if you were, now would you? I'll just have to determine the truth of the matter for myself. So tell me: Where are you from and how did you come to be traveling with a shipload of Farrs?"

"I'm from the Asteroid Belt," Bailey stammered. "From Earth system."

"Earth system?" The Master nodded. "There are clones there. What brings you out here?"

Bailey hesitated, not sure what to say. He couldn't tell the truth. "We're going to meet some friends and relatives." That was true, as far as it went. And when he went traveling in the Belt, that was his main reason for traveling.

"How interesting. So tell me: what route are you following?"

Bailey didn't want to give away any information, but it was obvious that they were headed to Stone's Throw. "Heading for Stone's Throw. After that . . ." He shrugged helplessly. "I'm not a navigator."

"I see." The Master turned to Zahara. "Perhaps you'd like to expand on that." He pointed at her again.

"We are on our way to rendezvous with members of my family. You have no right to . . ."

He shut off her voicebox with another flick of his finger, shaking his head like a disappointed parent. "Now, now. Remember what I said about accepting your situation." He glanced at the other sibs. "Perhaps I should explain. You are all very lucky. We're returning home and you'll all come with us. Whatever your mysterious destination may be, you won't be going there."

The Resurrectionist ship had been exploring a nearby system with an eye toward a future colony. They regarded the fact that this system was in a sector of space controlled by the Farrs as irrelevant. The clone was, after all, just a collection of spare parts. The fourth planet from a G-sequence star appeared to be a likely candidate for terraforming, so the Resurrectionists had come to examine it.

Though the expedition was primarily a scientific one, the ship was a military vessel, equipped with conventional and some experimental armaments. Along the way, they'd been scavenging, picking up ships and material that might be of use. Now, on their way home, the Resurrectionist captain was delighted to capture any Farr ship that happened by.

"You will soon be free of your petty needs and desires," the Master was saying. "Your biological material will be more useful than it has ever been. And after I extract you, you'll be happy to tell me all that you know."

The sibs were staring at him, angry but afraid to speak.

Bailey spoke again, afraid but unable to remain quiet. "Why are you doing this to us?"

The Master frowned at Bailey. "I'm not doing anything to you. Not yet. But these spare parts . . ."

"We aren't spare parts," Jazz said.

The Resurrectionist shrugged. "You sibs are all the same biological template. You must see how redundant it is to repeat the same pattern endlessly, always the same."

"They aren't the same," Bailey said.

"Close enough. Now you—you're a different story. The Captain will want to question you about where you were going and what you were up to. You may or may not be a clone, but you are traveling in very bad company, and that's suspect. The Captain will decide what we do with you." He smiled genially at Bailey.

It may seem strange, but the Master, like most Resurrectionists, didn't think of himself as cruel or wicked or bad-hearted. He thought of himself as rational and efficient and scientific and practical. When his biological body gave out, he would download his consciousness and donate his neural tissue to the ship. Resurrectionist philosophy held that the human body was simply a complex machine: the whole was no more than the sum of the parts. It dismissed questions of spirit and soul as meaningless. You can't dissect a body and find the soul. Therefore the soul doesn't exist.

"We aren't replacement parts," Jazz repeated, and the other sibs joined in with a clamor of protests and threats. For a moment, the room rang with shouts. Then the

Master pointed at the sibs one by one, and each fell silent.

"If you have nothing more to say, we'll begin the extraction process," the Master said cheerfully.

"They can say nothing." The voice of the brain in the tank was flat, emotionless.

"I know that Spare Parts. Just a little joke." The Master eyed the group behind the partition. "Now, where shall we begin?"

A soft tone sounded and the Master looked toward the door. The door slid open and another man rolled a cart into the room. Gitana's body was slumped on the cart. Bailey could see only the right side of her face: fair, pale, delicate looking. She looked so helpless.

"Another one?" the Master said.

"A second ship," the other man said. "The fighters brought it in."

"Lovely. Let's put her on the table."

The two men lifted Gitana's limp body to the steel operating table. The Master fastened a strap to her wrist. On one of the monitors, a green line registered Gitana's pulse. Slow, very slow. The Master frowned at the display and turned away, reaching for the collars on the workbench.

Bailey was watching the monitor as the men continued to talk.

"How much of a dose of gas did this one get?"

"No more than the others."

"Well, based on her pulse rate, she'll be out for a few more hours."

As Bailey watched, Gitana's pulse rate climbed. Gitana, you see, was a practitioner of the arcane practice known as somnimoribundus, the art of feigning a deathlike sleep, sinking deep into a meditative state while remaining aware of one's surroundings.

Bailey did not know what was going on, but he knew

that he had to distract the Master from Gitana's climbing pulse rate. Since none of the others could speak, it was up to him. "Master," he called. "I have a question."

The Master turned from his instruments, holding a collar in his hand. "You make pets of them," the other man said.

"Nothing wrong with treating a prisoner well," the Master said as he smiled at Bailey. "No questions just now." He pointed at Bailey and the norbit could not speak.

As the Master leaned toward Bailey, Gitana's blue eye opened and the sensor by her left eye gleamed red. Without hesitation, she snatched a laser scalpel from the tray beside her and swept it cleanly across the throat of the man who had wheeled her in. Continuing her movement, she slashed it across the Master's back, then brought it back up across his neck.

"How do I get you out?" Gitana asked, her voice steady. She did not look at the fallen men, still twitching as they died, at the blood that had spattered the walls, at the puddle of blood that was pooling around the table. She looked only at the door. "How do I open that?"

"They can't speak," Spare Parts said, in a voice as steady as Gitana's. "The collars prevent it. The lock is electronic, activated at the Master's command."

Gitana swung her long legs down from the table and stepped clear of the pool of blood, still carrying the laser scalpel, her gaze on Spare Parts. "I have an EMP grenade that will fry all the circuitry in this room. It will disable the lock and the collars, wipe out my left eye, and . . ." She hesitated. ". . . take down the systems that maintain you."

"Yes," said Spare Parts. For the first time, Bailey thought he heard emotion in the voice. She was eager. "Please. Do it now."

"As soon as I set it off, every sensor in this room will

be incapacitated and the Resurrectionists will send security. With luck, they won't come quickly. Can everyone run?" She watched as the sibs nodded. "Good." She pulled something from her belt. "Once we leave this room, stay with me."

Bailey was not watching her. He was staring at the Master, wondering at the quantity of blood that puddled on the floor, the metallic stench of it. In adventure tales, people died neatly—or perhaps no one mentioned the mess.

There was a sudden flash of brilliant blue-white light, a loud crackle, and the reek of ozone. The lights went out and the room was dark, except for a glowing light in Gitana's hand.

The explosion, Bailey learned later, was the EMP or electromagnetic pulse grenade. Through a sudden, massive electrical discharge, the EMP grenade created an expanding electromagnetic field that fried all circuitry inside a circle five meters in diameter.

"Let's move!" Gitana shouted, and the sibs were crowding through the door, following her light.

"Come on, Bailey." Jazz's voice, Jazz's hand grabbing his. "Come on." He followed.

Later, Bailey could never give a clear account of what happened. The corridor was brilliantly lit and the walls were polished steel. He remembered coming to a turn in the corridor and seeing a wild-eyed group running toward them—their own terrified reflections. He remembered glancing back and seeing a trail of bloody footprints down the length of the first corridor. He remembered Jazz gripping his hand, pulling him down the corridor, keeping him with the group.

He knew only that he had to follow Gitana and the sibs. Gitana knew the way, ducking down one corridor and then another. Whenever they heard Resurrectionists behind them, Gitana would lob a grenade over Bailey's head. There would be a flash of light, then Gitana would rush away again. The grenade would fry any electronic connections in the Resurrectionists' implants, disabling them more often than not.

"This way! This way!" Gitana cried. And the sibs followed, for once too groggy and disoriented to argue.

Once, they came around a corner and surprised a man in the corridor. Gitana was low on EMP grenades, but Jazz and Lily had stun guns, snatched from fallen Resurrectionists. The others fought with fists and feet. The group overpowered the Resurrectionist. As they hurried past his fallen body, Bailey snatched the stun gun from the Resurrectionist's hand and tucked it in his belt, glad to be armed at last.

Down this way and over that way and up a ladder and down a twisting corridor that opened into a dark cavernous room that reeked of exhaust fumes and oil. The ship's loading dock. "Over here!" Gitana cried. "This way." Ahead, Bailey could see what looked like a junkyard—ships of all makes tumbled this way and that. Gitana was leading the group into a passage between the wrecks. "Quickly now!"

But it wasn't as easy as that. They were running for an opening between two wrecks when Bailey glanced up to see a man's face glaring down from the control seat of a loading crane. "Look out," he yelped, as the crane's arm came swinging toward them. Gitana jumped to the side, throwing her last grenade up into the workings of the crane.

Bailey heard the whir of wheels, and more Resurrectionists came from the darkness, slipping up behind them. There was fighting and shouting. Bailey reached for his stun gun, but someone's arm slammed into his head, sending him staggering to fall onto the hard deck. In the brief moments before he lost consciousness, he crawled away from the trampling feet and flailing arms. That was all he knew for a long time.

5

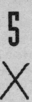

He would answer to "Hi!" or to any loud cry,
Such as "Fry me!" or "Fritter my wig!"
To "What-you-may-call-um!" or "What-was-his-name!"
But especially "Thing-um-a-jig!"

—"The Hunting of the Snark," Lewis Carroll

WHEN BAILEY CAME TO, HE WONDERED FOR A MOMENT IF HE HAD only dreamed of escaping. He was lying on a cold metal surface that throbbed with the distant hum of engines. No one was shouting—no sibs, no Gitana, no Resurrectionists. He couldn't hear anyone breathing. He was alone, lying on a deck slippery with oil.

The air reeked of ozone and smoke. His head ached—from the knockout gas and from the blow that had rendered him unconscious. He found the stun gun still tucked in his belt, and that made him feel a little better. But when he tried to sit up, he bumped his head again—something was above him. He reached up and felt the smooth underbelly of a scout ship. Somehow, in the commotion and confusion, groggy and nearly unconscious, he had crawled beneath a ship for safety.

Carefully, quietly, he crawled out. Along the way, his hand touched something cold—a piece of metal. He grabbed it, hoping that it was an EMP grenade or something else useful, and took it with him as he wiggled out from under the ship.

In the distance, far across the cavernous loading dock,

past the looming hulls of ruined ships, he could see lights creating puddles of brightness on the deck, movement as the great exit lock opened and shut. Something was going on, but it was all very far away.

Bailey sat up carefully, feeling every bruise and pulled muscle as he did so. For a time, he rested in the darkness, thinking about what he'd be doing if only he were at home. Eating breakfast in the solarium, perhaps. The air would be sweet with oxygen and the scent of greenery, rather than nasty with the reek of oil and ozone.

Thinking about home just made him more unhappy. He was hungry and weary and sore. He could use a bite to eat or a sip of something nice to drink, but he wasn't likely to get either of those here. The others were gone, and he wondered what had happened to them. If the Resurrectionists had caught them again, why had he been left behind? And if his friends had escaped, why hadn't they taken him along?

He felt very alone and very lonely. If his friends had escaped, then he should do the same. If his friends had been recaptured, he should go save them. He thought about that and shuddered, thinking of where they might be now. In pieces, most likely, like Spare Parts.

To take his mind off those gruesome thoughts, he fumbled with the thing that he'd found beneath the ship. In the dim light, he tried to figure out what is was by feel. A flexible metal belt that formed a circle with a half twist, just large enough to go around his wrist. A Moebius strip, he thought. When he was a child, Great-Grandmother Brita, in a rare mellow mood, had shown him how to make a Moebius strip from paper, had demonstrated that it only had one side. Perhaps this was a child's toy.

As Bailey continued to play with the metal belt, he realized it was actually two metal bands with their flat sides together, forming a single circle. He couldn't separate the two bands, but there was a bit of metal sticking out from the space between them. He could slide the metal tab one way or another along the loop, but when he released the tab, it always returned to its original position.

He was fiddling with the metal belt when he heard voices and saw a flickering light heading his way. Without hesitation, Bailey sank to the floor and slid back under the scout craft. From this vantage point, he could see only the feet of the approaching Resurrectionists. Two pairs of feet; two Resurrectionists, he thought.

"If you ask me, the Captain's circuits are scrambled," one of them was grumbling. "She's dreaming if she thinks someone's hiding over here. Those spare parts got away clean."

So the others had gotten away. Even in his terror, Bailey was glad to know that.

"Well, you know the Captain," the other Resurrectionist was saying. "The sensors show a warm body in this sector, so we've got to check it out." He was bored, just doing his job.

"Every sensor in the loading dock got a blast of the EMP," the first Resurrectionist continued. "Along with half the crew. And we've got our hands full getting fighters out to chase those spare parts. Besides, you know as well as I do that we're always picking up ghosts in the loading dock. Nothing new there."

The two Resurrectionists had paused about ten feet from the scout craft. Bailey's heart was pounding so hard that he was sure they would hear it. He was nervously fidgeting with the metal band that he still clutched in his hands.

"Yeah, well—I'm getting a reading," the first Resurrectionist said. "A warm body—and some motion."

Bailey pushed the metal tab, a nervous twitch of the hands, and he froze where he was, his hands motionless on the metal band. As he listened and watched, the Resurrectionist's voice rose in pitch, ascending to an inaudible squeaking. The Resurrectionists rushed away from Bailey's hiding place in an unnatural hurry.

It seemed very strange. It made no sense. If they had detected his warmth and movement, they should have hurried toward him. But for some reason, he'd been lucky. For as long as he could stand it, Bailey remained where he was without moving. He didn't hear the Resurrectionists, saw no glimmer of their light returning. The metal band grew cold in his hands.

At last, his muscles aching from the cold and lack of movement, he let go of the metal band, stuffed it in his pocket, and squirmed out from under the ship once again.

He sat by the ship for a moment, feeling a bit sorry for himself. Why had his companions left him behind? Surely the sibs had noticed he wasn't with them. He was certain that Zahara and the others would not be coming back for him. They might have come back for one of their sibs, but not for him.

He was in a nasty spot, to be sure. But Bailey was a norbit, and norbits are a resourceful bunch. Life in the Asteroid Belt demands a certain cleverness. To get by, you have to learn to make do with what you have and what you can make of it. You have to improvise.

Rather than moaning about his fate, Bailey thought about what he could do. He didn't have any weapons, but then he hadn't really used any weapons when they encountered the Trancers, and that turned out all right. Maybe he could manage to get aboard one of the ships that the Resurrectionists were sending after the sibs. Then he'd have to overpower anyone who was aboard and take control of the ship.

Bailey shook his head. That sounded unlikely, but he supposed it was worth a try. So he got to his feet and dusted himself off, and started moving through the junked ships in the direction of the exit lock.

Bailey did not know it, but he was not alone on the loading dock. Wandering among the abandoned ships was another creature who had escaped from the Resurrectionists' lab. A creature, I call her, because she was no longer human. She had been modified by the Resurrectionists, and her humanity had been misplaced along the way.

Bailey was making his way through the junkyard of ships when he heard something rustling in the darkness. He had been clambering past a scout craft that had been shattered—cracked open like an egg. The scout was tipped up on its side, smashed between a freighter and a cruiser. Just then, Bailey heard a voice right beside him.

"What . . . what . . . what is this?" The stuttering voice was inflectionless—cold and dead. Beneath the words, Bailey could hear the rattle of machinery. "What is this?"

In the dim light, Bailey could make out a shadow form, moving toward him. "Who are you?" he asked.

"Who . . . who . . . who am I?" An icy voice. Emotionless, indifferent, and so cold it made Bailey shudder. It stuttered like a broken machine. "The M-m-master called me Rattler. I . . . I . . . I had another name once. But that is gone. Rattler. That is my name now. Rattler. Who . . . who . . . who are you?"

"I'm Bailey Beldon. I've come from the Asteroid Belt with Gitana and the Farr sibs, and I'm trying to get out of here before they find me and take me back to the Master's laboratory."

For longer than she could remember, Rattler had been hiding from the Master. She had lived in the darkness of the loading dock, lurking among the ships, hiding, sneaking, forever fearful, forever hateful. Imagine her as a worm, a caterpillar, a life form that lives low to the ground, hiding in the shadows, shunning the light.

She had been human once, long long ago. The Master Technician had worked on Rattler during a period when spare parts were plentiful. In an experimental mood, the Master had dismantled Rattler's original body and given her a mobile body of an original design. Rattler had a skull, a brain, and a spinal cord extending from the medulla oblongata of the brain through the vertebrae of the spinal column. She had the requisite guts—a beating heart, lungs that brought in the oxygen, digestive tract and so on. But the Master had discarded the rest of the body. No need for arms or legs; no need for eyes or ears or human hands.

Rattler's spinal column stretched the length of a metal frame, supported just a few inches off the deck by magnetized wheels, protected by the burnished steel carapace that housed her organs. She had half a dozen eyes, photosensitive cells that provided images in infrared and ultraviolet as well as the visible spectrum, set on stalks that swiveled, like the turret eyes of a chameleon. Rattler's audio sensors were far more sensitive than human ears, detecting frequencies outside our range. Metal arms equipped with mechanical claws extended from the front and sides and back of the frame, so that Rattler could reach in any direction.

There's no telling how Rattler had escaped from the Master's lab, but somehow she had and somehow she had found her way into the loading dock, where she fed on rations she found in captured ships, oiled her mechanical parts with lubricants stolen from the maintenance stations.

Some of her mechanical parts had broken down. Her wheels creaked. Her speech mechanism stuck and stammered. Her arms twitched and trembled when she reached out. But she survived, living on scraps, hiding in the darkness.

She was more than half mad. She hated Resurrectionists, of course. But she had developed a hatred of their victims as well. The humans that the Resurrectionists captured were made of flesh, nothing more than meat—so soft and weak and vulnerable. Not like Rattler's metal carapace and mechanical claws. She was stronger than meat, faster than meat, better than meat in every way.

Though she did not envy the weakness of the meat, Rattler knew that the soft-bodied humans had something she lacked. She did not know what that something was, but she felt its lack as an emptiness and an aching. She knew only that something was missing, that the Master had stolen something during her reconstruction.

"Do . . . do . . . do you have what I need?" Rattler stared at Bailey in the dim light, her infrared detectors registering the warmth of him, the life of him. Perhaps this meat man had what the Master had taken from her. "I . . . I . . . I must take you apart to find out. J-j-just as the Master took me apart."

She had caught a Resurrectionist alone on the loading dock once, and had taken the man apart in search of that elusive missing part. Though Rattler had enjoyed parts of the process, her search had been unproductive. But she was willing to try again.

Rattler's eyes gleamed in the dim light; all six were turned toward Bailey. She rolled toward Bailey, her wheels rumbling on the deck.

Bailey backed away. His foot slipped in a puddle—lubricant leaking from the shattered scout craft—and he fell backward against the scout craft's console. He flung out a hand to catch himself and, by a stroke of luck (of which he had a more than adequate supply) his hand struck a switch. The scout's emergency light came on, a golden glow shining from a cracked fixture on the console.

The Rattler, in that dim light, looked like something that had been broken and badly mended. Corroded metal parts joined to organic tissue that glistened with mucus. She stank of rot and diesel fuel. Rattler rolled away from the light, just as Bailey snatched the stun gun from his belt and pointed it at Rattler.

"What . . . what . . . what . . . ?" wheezed Rattler.

Bailey interrupted, not waiting for her to finish her question. "It's a gun that will fry your circuits and stop you in your tracks."

"That . . . that . . . that is not necessary. Not necessary at all."

"You said you were going to take me apart," Bailey said. "I don't want to be taken apart."

Rattler stayed at the edge of the circle of light, her eyes on Bailey's stun gun. She paused, considering his statement. It had been so long since she had spoken with another person. How strange to think that this meat man had wants and desires. "You don't want to be taken apart. What . . . what . . . what do you want, then?"

"I want to leave here. I want to escape."

"Escape?" The word touched old memories in Rattler. She remembered fleeing the Master's lab, motivated by a desire to escape. She had come this far and no farther. "I . . . I escaped from the Master."

"Then you know why I need to escape."

Yes, Rattler understood and Rattler sympathized, but she also envied Bailey. This meat man had escaped the Master intact, with his body untouched. He had his arms and he had his legs and he had the piece that Rattler had lost; Rattler was sure of that. That wasn't fair. She studied Bailey with her six eyes, searching her dark and twisted brain for some way she might keep this Bailey Beldon here in the loading dock, might search him for the piece that would fill the ache that bothered her so persistently.

"G-g-games." The Rattler's voice crackled like a burst of static on a broken speaker. "D-d-do you like to play games?"

Keeping the gun trained on the Rattler, Bailey nodded, willing to agree to just about anything that would make Rattler stop threatening to take him apart.

"What . . . what . . . what kind of game?"

Bailey hesitated. "Haiku," he muttered, thinking of the sibs and the games they had played on Farr Station.

"That . . . that is not a game," the Rattler protested.

"Yes, it is." Bailey grew bolder. "I ask you a riddle, a question, in haiku. You have to answer. If you answer, then you ask me one. If you can't answer, then you help me get out of here, get away from the Master."

"If you can't answer, I will take you apart." Rattler made a sound like a junkyard clattering down a flight of stairs. It might have been laughter. She knew that she would take Bailey apart no matter what happened. "We will play. You ask first."

Agitated, frightened, Bailey had a hard time thinking, so he fell back on a riddle from his childhood, set into haiku form:

> *Most precious crystal.*
> *Weeps tears, disappears. Blast off!*
> *Speed me on my way.*

The idea of escape was on his mind. Bailey thought this was very easy, the sort of riddle a norbit child would guess in a minute. But it wasn't easy for Rattler, who buzzed in frustration.

Rattler thought of gemstones that might be used to power a rocket and speed someone away. Diamonds might be burned for heat, she supposed, but why would they weep tears? And she had never heard of a rocket powered by diamonds. What other crystal was precious? What else did the meat man value? What crystal might melt and weep tears?

Then she remembered times she had wandered in the junkyard, searching for a ship that still had water in its tanks. Frozen water was ice, a very precious crystal if you had no water. And somewhere in the distant past she had heard of the norbits' tea kettle rockets.

"Ice melts to water. Evaporates to steam. B-b-blast off in those silly tea kettle rockets."

"All right," Bailey admitted. "Your turn. Remember: it has to be in haiku form. Five syllables, seven syllables, five syllables."

Rattler thought for a moment, staring at the darkness around them. Then she said:

> *Darkness eternal—*
> *Eternal for you, that is.*
> *There is no way out!*

The last line, spoken in Rattler's cold, dispassionate voice, had a spiteful air of triumph that sent a shiver up Bailey's spine and made it difficult for him to think of anything other than how he could get out. Darkness—it was all around him. But the darkness in the loading dock wasn't eternal. There could be light here. Unless he died here in the dark—Bailey didn't like that thought, and he pushed it aside.

He thought about what made things dark. Black paint was dark because it absorbed light. What else absorbed light? What absorbed light and never let it out?

"A black hole," Bailey said. "Light goes in and can't get out. You go in and can't get out. No way out!" Relieved by his success, he came up with a riddle he thought would puzzle this strange mechanical creature.

Four together and
One opposed. Lemurs lack them.
Can you grasp it now?

While Rattler thought about that one, her claws flexed and rattled like castanets. She had not always been mechanical. Once she had a flesh-and-blood body with human hands.

"F-f-four f-f-fingers. And an opposable thumb," Rattler said quickly. "Hands!" She grinned at Bailey, showing an array of glittering steel teeth. "My turn." She was growing impatient now, eager for the contest to be over and certain she would win.

Such bloody music,
A pounding drum—beat by beat.
Death will stop it—yes!

The last word made Bailey shiver. He could think only of funeral processions and dirges, of Trancer tunes that could lead people to death, of war music. He was frightened and tired and he did not know why this cold and heartless creature wanted to take him apart. Cold and heartless.

"Heart," he said. "Pounding in life, still in death. That's it."

His own heart was still pounding with fear. He couldn't think of another riddle, couldn't compose another haiku.

"Ask," Rattler said. "Ask another." She was tired of waiting. "Hurry. It is t-t-time to t-t-take you apart."

Bailey shivered. Rattler's eagerness chilled him as much as the cold air of the loading dock. He couldn't think. "Just a minute," he said. "I need a minute."

"No . . . no . . . no time." Rattler rolled closer, entering the circle of light, her eyes gleaming at Bailey. "Ask."

Groping for a thought, Bailey put his hand in his pocket and touched the metal belt. "What's this?" he wondered aloud.

"Not a haiku," Rattler protested.

Bailey stopped, momentarily confused. He couldn't think of a riddle, but he could make a haiku of his question.

> *If only I knew*
> *What this is in my pocket*
> *I'd be so happy.*

"What . . . what . . . what is in your pocket?" the Rattler grumbled. "That's not a riddle."

"It's a question," Bailey said, gripping the stun gun harder. "It's a haiku."

The Rattler glared at him, rattling her claws. She tried to remember having pockets and tried to remember what she had kept in her pockets when she had them.

"You have to answer," Bailey said, keeping his gun on Rattler. "You have to answer or help me get out."

"N-n-not a fair question."

Bailey shrugged, feeling guilty and uncomfortable. Rattler was right. The question wasn't fair. But he couldn't think of another riddle, so he stuck with the question. "You have to answer."

"Three g-g-guesses." The Rattler drew on her memories of games she had played before she lived alone in the Resurrectionist ship. "You have to give me three guesses."

"All right. Three guesses."

"Your h-h-hands."

Bailey had just taken his hand from his pocket. "No, not hands."

The Rattler growled to herself, a sound like gears

grinding. She thought about things that she carried with her. "Oil can."

"No, not that. One more guess."

More grumbling, more rumbling, and Bailey held the gun steady, sure that he would have to use it. Rattler rolled back and forth on the floor, coming closer and backing away, a nervous and unnerving movement. "N-n-nothing at all."

"That's not it." Bailey tried to sound confident. "All right then. You have to help me find a way out." They had made a deal, but Bailey had little hope that the creature would honor their agreement. He half-expected Rattler to attack him.

"H-h-help you." Bailey imagined there was anger in Rattler's voice. Bailey kept the gun pointed at Rattler as she backed away into the darkness. "I'll h-h-help.

Then Bailey was alone. He heard Rattler's wheels rolling off into the darkness and breathed a sigh of relief, thinking that she was leaving him—not helping, but not attacking either. That was fine with Bailey.

But that wasn't what Rattler was doing. Rattler hadn't survived in the Resurrectionist's loading dock by her wits alone. Hidden in a dark corner, she had a secret, a twisted metal band just large enough to slip over a wrist. Some explorer had found it in the cluttered remnants of an alien space ship, an artifact of the Old Ones. And that explorer had given it to his daughter and his daughter had lost it in a card game and the one who won it had traded it for his heart's desire, and so it had made its way from one hand to another.

What had the Old Ones used this twisted band for? Rattler didn't know. No one knew. Its original use was lost, forgotten. But even now, it was a powerful tool.

That was what Rattler was looking for, the Moebius band that kept her safe. She had worn it not so long ago, when she had ventured into the main body of the ship, searching for food and drink. Surely she had put it back into its hiding place after that. On that trip she had stolen a bottle of Ergotian brandy from the Captain's quarters. The brandy had eased the pain that was always with her, the aches she felt in limbs she no longer had. But the liquor had also addled her memory. She could not remember all of what she had done when she returned to the safety of the loading dock. Could she have dropped her Moebius band? Could it have slipped away from her? Could the meat man have found it?

While Rattler was looking for the Moebius band, Bailey decided that she would not come back. He had climbed down from the scout ship and started to make his way toward the exit lock. He was just past the hull of the freighter when he heard the hum of Rattler's wheels on the deck. The freighter's stern cargo hatch was open a crack, just large enough to let Bailey through. He ducked into the hold, out of sight.

"It is l-l-lost," Rattler said. "M-m-my t-t-wisty b-b-band. It is l-l-lost." Her voice was empty, bleak. At that moment, it reminded Bailey of Spare Parts. "There is no hope," Spare Parts had said, in the same flat, inflectionless tone.

Bailey pushed his hand into his pocket, sliding the Moebius band over his wrist. This was what Rattler wanted, the loss of which had taken the last of her hope.

He hesitated, realizing for the first time that this creature might once have been a sib, like Spare Parts, like Jazz, like Poppy. He clutched the band, wondering why its loss affected her so. He knew that something strange had happened when the Resurrectionists had approached. He'd been playing with the tab on the band, shifting it a tiny bit. Then the Resurrectionists' voices had shifted pitch and they'd hurried away.

"D-d-did the meat man f-f-find it?" The Rattler's eyes were swiveling this way and that, searching for Bailey

among the abandoned ships. "D-d-did he?" Then her
eyes swiveled to focus on the activity at the exit lock.
"He w-w-wanted to escape. He will go to the gate. I
must g-g-go there too."

As Bailey watched, Rattler rolled back and forth,
heading toward the gate and then backing away, forward
then back, talking to herself all the while.

"I . . . I . . . I can't go straight. That would be d-d-
dangerous. I have to go around the back where they
won't catch me."

Rattler set out, not heading directly for the area of
activity, but heading away, following a twisting path
through a maze of ships and junk. Bailey poked his head
out of his hiding place to keep an eye on her, wanting
to follow but worried that she would spot him. As he
fidgeted with the Moebius band, he pushed the tab.

The rumblings of the ship's engines deepened until he
could no longer hear the sound, feeling it as a vibration
deep in his bones. Rattler's voice (she was still talking to
herself as she rolled) dropped to a lower pitch, then even
lower. Then Rattler stopped. Well, she didn't quite stop.
She slowed down to the point where she might as well
have stopped.

Bailey waited, watching. When Rattler did not move,
he pushed the tab back to its original position. The rumble of the ship's engines became audible again; Rattler
continued her soliloquy, rolling toward the exit lock and
searching the abandoned ships as she passed them. Bailey watched as Rattler poked her head into the hold of
a freighter, searching for Bailey, then continued on her
way.

Bailey pushed the tab and again the world slowed
down around him. Slowly, carefully, he approached Rattler, holding the stun gun ready and stopping about ten
meters away. From that distance, he could see that Rattler was still moving—her forward claws were closing,

her eye stalks were swiveling. But the movement was so slow that Bailey could barely detect it.

Bailey circled in front of Rattler, then went behind her and hid in the freighter hold that Rattler had just checked. Once Bailey was safely hidden, he slid the tab back to its original position. Rattler's claws clicked shut and her eyes swiveled wildly, searching desperately for Bailey.

Bailey clutched the band more tightly. The band did something strange to time, shifting his pace relative to the pace of time around him. When the Resurrectionists had been looking for him, he had slid the tab in one direction. Then the world around him had sped up. The infrared radiation emitted by his warm body, electromagnetic waves of a specific frequency, had slowed to the frequency of radio waves, which did not register on the Resurrectionists' sensors. Now, when he slid the tab in the other direction, the world slowed down, making his movements so fast that Rattler could not detect him.

How strange. How interesting. But Bailey did not stop to consider the philosophical implications of this novel device. He found its practical value of greater interest. This artifact of the Old Ones offered him a forlorn hope of escape.

He waited in hiding, watching as Rattler made her way toward the exit lock. Then he pushed the tab, caught up with Rattler, and hid again. Over and over again, close on the Rattler's trail. Fortunately the dock provided many hiding places. Bailey always took care to hide in areas that Rattler had already searched.

As the Rattler drew closer to the exit lock, she slowed down, choosing her way with care, staying in the shadows. The light was bright overhead. After so long in the darkness, it made Bailey squint, even when he hid in the shadows. The cavernous space echoed with the roar of engines, the clatter of equipment, the shouts of workers.

Bailey heard the exit lock open with a great echoing boom, and he peered around a freighter hull. The deck ahead was open; there were no hiding places where he could conceal himself. People bustled around a ship that was being readied for departure. It was a fighter, a low flat craft bristling with weapons. The cockpit canopy was open and a group of workers were attaching the craft's nose to the cable that would tow it to the exit lock. The notation on the ship's fuselage—XF25—identified it as an experimental model, but Bailey didn't know that, nor would he have cared if he did. It was a ship, a way out.

A man in a flight suit stood near the ship. He looked to be about Bailey's height, fighter pilots tending to be short. As Bailey watched, the pilot signaled the man in the control booth overhead, then turned and walked to a nearby structure, pushing open a door and disappearing inside.

Bailey pushed the tab. Taking his time—after all, he had all the time he needed—he walked past Rattler, who lingered in the shadows, and made his way among the frozen workers who clustered around the ship. He felt exposed—Rattler could see him; the Resurrectionists could get him. But nothing happened. The world had stopped around him.

He entered the structure and found the pilot at the urinal, caught in the act of buttoning his flight suit. Still holding the tab in place, Bailey zapped the man with the stun gun. Nothing happened. The man stood at the urinal, frozen as before. Bailey took a step back, then returned the tab to its original position. The man fell heavily, cracking his head against the nearby wall with a thump that made Bailey wince.

Stuffing the Moebius band in his pocket, Bailey knelt by the man's head. The pilot was breathing heavily and bleeding from a scrape where his head had hit the wall, but he was alive. Bailey was glad of that—even if the man was a Resurrectionist, it hadn't seemed fair to kill him while he was frozen helplessly in time.

Working as quickly as he could, Bailey undressed the unconscious pilot. Then he pulled the man's flight suit over his own clothes. It fit reasonably well. He lashed the man's hands together with his belt, used the man's shoelaces to tie his ankles together. One sock became a gag.

It was an awkward, difficult, sordid business. In an adventure tale, it all would have been quite easy. In reality, it wasn't. The man kept moaning while Bailey was undressing him and Bailey had to keep one hand ready to grab the Moebius band in case someone came barging in. It wasn't like an adventure tale at all, but Bailey managed to roll the man into a toilet stall and shut the door behind him.

He was just pulling the helmet on when a voice crackled in his ear as the man in the tower spoke to him through the helmet radio. "Zip up and get your ass in gear, Jim. You're running late."

He pulled on the helmet and checked in the mirror. The dark glass of the face plate hid his features, but he kept his hand on the Moebius band in his pocket as he hurried back to the waiting ship. The workers who clustered around the ship didn't give him a second glance as he climbed into the XF25 and settled into the pilot's seat. He was fastening himself into the seat harness while the workers closed and secured the cockpit canopy. He gave a thumbs up signal to the workers as they completed their task, but they ignored him, hurrying off.

Bailey felt a tug as the towing cable engaged and the ship moved slowly forward. A Resurrectionist would have been wired directly into the ship's controls through electrodes in the helmet. Lacking the skull implants that connected to the helmet's electrodes, Bailey was not wired to the ship. He could monitor the ship's status and position with the displays on the console and fly the craft with the manual controls (ordinarily used only when the electronic connections failed). But he figured he could get by. The basic controls were similar to those of ships he had flown before. The weapons panel reminded him of the computer battle simulation games he had played with his nephew. He examined them, frowning, and hoped that he wouldn't have to use them.

The ship moved smoothly toward the exit lock. The exit lock door slammed close behind him. Moments later, the external lock door opened, releasing the ship into space.

Through the viewscreen, he could see three other Resurrectionist fighters, silhouetted against the bright disk surrounding Stone's Throw. A pair of fighters, and a lone fighter, obviously the craft that Bailey's fighter was paired with. Far in the distance, he could see the *Odyssey*.

He hesitated. He didn't know exactly what to do now, but he was glad to be off the Resurrectionist ship. As he examined the controls, he heard a crackle from the console speaker.

"Who are you?" asked a woman's voice from the console of the ship. "You're not Jim."

6

You may seek it with thimbles—and seek it with care;
You may hunt it with forks and hope;
You may threaten its life with a railway-share;
You may charm it with smiles and soap.

—"The Hunting of the Snark," Lewis Carroll

BAILEY STARED AT THE CONSOLE, MOMENTARILY SPEECHLESS. HE did not know what to say.

"Ragged breathing," the woman's voice said softly. "Rapid heartbeat. Moisture indicating nervous sweat. Not wired for connection. You aren't a Resurrectionist, are you?" She did not sound surprised or alarmed. If anything, she sounded amused.

Before Bailey could reply, his helmet radio crackled. "Bravo 1 to Bravo 4: report status."

The woman's voice spoke again, responding to the hail. "Bravo 4, delayed at take off. Playing catch-up."

"Fluffy, get your ass in gear."

"Copy that."

As the ship accelerated, g-forces pushed Bailey hard into the pilot's seat. A crackle indicated that radio communication was closed, then the woman's voice spoke again. Still calm. Still steady, even as they were accelerating ferociously.

"All right," she said. "We're off the air for now, and I've bought you some time. It'll take a few minutes to catch up. So talk already. Who are you and what did you do to Jim?"

"My name is Bailey Beldon. I . . . ah . . . I left Jim tied up in the lavatory. He's fine, really." Bailey tried to keep his voice as even as hers, but failed miserably. "Who are you?"

"He's still alive? Too bad. I hope you thumped him good. You should have killed him. He's a real asshole, a hard-nosed son of a bitch and a lousy pilot besides. No creativity, no imagination, no sense of humor. We didn't get along. I'm sure he's put me in for a memory wipe and reassembly."

"I left him with a sock stuffed in his mouth," Bailey said. "He's not very comfortable—I can tell you that."

She laughed. "That's just great. I like you already. Whose sock was it?"

"His own."

"Perfect."

"And . . . uh . . . who are you?"

"Me? I'm a construct. The Resurrectionists put me together from various spare parts—you know, a little of this, some of that. I'm a conglomerate, an assembly, an experiment. And I'm a damn good pilot."

"Your name's Fluffy?" Bailey asked hesitantly.

"That's what they call me. It's better than XF25."

"Why did Jim want to wipe your memory?"

"He didn't seem to think I was a very successful experiment. He thought I should be happy to follow his half-assed orders. I didn't agree."

The radio crackled. "Prepare for offensive scissors split. Bravo 3, you and Fluffy head right."

"Roger." Another man's voice; Bravo 3, Bailey guessed.

"Roger," Fluffy said.

In the viewscreen, Bailey could see the last fighter in formation, just ahead of them. More radio traffic, but Fluffy cut that off as she continued to accelerate, sticking with Bravo 3 as the fighter veered to the right.

"The squadron leader has no imagination," she said conversationally, as she accelerated, following Bravo 3. "It's a classic maneuver. Bravo 1 and 2 loop behind left and we take the right. Disable the ship and recapture the spare parts."

Bailey clung to the arms of the seat, staring out the viewscreen, terrified. The head-up display indicated 5 g's and he felt that he was being squashed into the pilot's seat by an enormous weight. Breathing had become difficult.

Fluffy, as you may have noticed, had no loyalty to the Resurrectionists who had made her. Perhaps that was because she was part cat.

Fluffy was the neural network that ran the XF25, and her tissue came from a variety of sources. Her central processing unit was the brain of a woman named Sylvia. A sib of a small clone in the Bellatrix system, Sylvia had run off to space when she was eighteen, a reckless young woman with a taste for adventure. She had landed a job on a mining station, eventually bucked for pilot, and finally became captain of an ore transport.

Sylvia was a scrapper. Her nose had been broken in more than one fight (a mining station being no environment for a lady) and it looked like it. She was tough and practical: she could repair a faulty fuel nozzle, operate a jack hammer in full vacuum, and talk a customs agent into overlooking minor discrepancies. But she'd gotten herself captured by the Resurrectionists and she couldn't fight or talk her way out of that.

The Resurrectionists had merged Sylvia's neural tissue with that of Sylvia's sole companion on the ore transport: a lean tomcat that Sylvia called Fluffy (because he wasn't particularly, even as a kitten). A miner on a outlying rig had given the cat to Sylvia when he was a kitten, a tiny, tiger-striped ball of fur with needle-sharp claws. The progeny of generations of space-going cats,

Fluffy was accustomed to zero-g. In weightlessness, he had propelled himself through the ship's corridors by kicking off the walls with his hind legs. When the transport touched down, he slept as much as possible and complained in a yowl about how tiresome gravity could be. His mind was predatory—always hungry, always prowling.

The Resurrectionists were experimenting with the creation of neural nets that could pilot ships independently or obey the orders of a human pilot. Fluffy was a prototype—an unsuccessful one, from the Resurrectionist point of view. The Resurrectionists had, of course, cleared all memories from Sylvia and Fluffy at the time of extraction and recombination. The resulting neural net had undergone an extensive program of reeducation, intended to ensure her loyalty to her creators. But that program had not entirely succeeded.

The entity that called herself Fluffy was crafty and reckless and interested in adventure, an interest that was tempered only lightly by prudence and practicality.

"You must be one of the escapees from the labs, right?" Fluffy asked Bailey. She didn't wait for a response. "So now where do you think you're going?"

Bailey was finding it hard to breath under the pressure of g-forces, but he did his best to answer. "Gotta catch up with the others. We're chasing a Snark to the center of the Galaxy." He realized, just a moment after he said it, that he wasn't supposed to talk about their mission. But he was tired, his head hurt, he could barely breathe, and it just slipped out.

"Mind if I come along? You see, they haven't been happy with my performance. If I stay, they're going to take me apart. I'd rather not stick around for that. And you seem like a fun kind of guy."

"Sure," Bailey panted. This was all moving a little fast for him. Keep in mind that he wasn't at his sharpest, having been knocked out twice in less than twenty four hours.

"Fine then. First, we have to make sure these guys don't blow up your friends. If they do, we're screwed. This ship has minimal life support—a week out and it turns into a floating coffin for you, and I get to spend the rest of my life drifting in space until some scavenger claims me for scrap. No thanks. So our objective is clear—we've got to save your pals and wipe out the squadron."

Radio crackle. "Bravo 1: launch."

In the viewscreen, Bailey saw a streak of white dart away from the lead fighter, tracing a line across the glowing accretion disk and heading for the *Odyssey*. Bailey glanced at the head-up display. In glowing lines and spots, the display showed a god's eye view of the area. The missile was a brilliant white point, streaking toward the dull blue circle that was the *Odyssey*, homing in on the infrared energy produced by the ship.

"We'd better get busy," Fluffy said. "Or we won't have a ride home."

As Bailey watched, the *Odyssey* released a smaller craft that glowed brightly on the XF25's infrared search and track display. "Decoy with a high-intensity heat source," Fluffy said. The missile turned to follow the smaller craft. "That bought them a few seconds."

As Bailey watched, a burst of fire from a laser cannon shot from the *Odyssey*, missing the rapidly turning fighter.

"They're fighting now, but they don't have a chance without us. I'll do the flying, but you'll have to operate the weapons—Jim, that asshole, has them locked on manual. Can you handle that?"

Bailey stared at the controls in a panic. He couldn't just start shooting; he needed time to think. He reached into his pocket, grabbed the Moebius band, slipped it over his wrist, and pushed the tab as far as he could to one side. In the god's eye view, the missile slowed to a crawl. Then he took a deep breath and examined the controls.

It was very fortunate that Bailey's favorite nephew Ferris liked to play battle simulation games. Not long before Gitana's arrival at the Restless Rest, Ferris had visited Bailey, helping his uncle construct a new mining station. Every evening, Bailey and Ferris had waged war on each other via simulator. By the time Bailey's nephew returned to his family, Bailey had become expert at shooting down enemy craft and evading enemy fire.

The basic layout and function of the weapons panel shared many characteristics with the weapons control panel on Ferris's favorite game, the one that he and Bailey had played together for hours. Slowly, deliberately, Bailey reviewed the weapons. The XF25 was armed with missiles, lasers, and a plasma punch, which accelerated a pocket of plasma to near light speed. The resulting plasma projectile could punch a hole through anything.

He ran his hands over the controls, reminding himself of the feel of the game. Taking a deep breath, he glanced at the god's-eye view where the missile had crept ever so slightly closer to the *Odyssey*. Then he thumbed the tab on the Moebius band back to its original position, returning to normal time.

"Yes," he said quickly. "I'll handle the weapons."

"Let's knock out Bravo 3 first. I'd suggest the plasma punch."

"Right."

A sudden swerve, and Bailey was jerked to one side. On the viewscreen, Bravo 3 was coming up fast. As the g-forces on Bailey increased, he thumbed the tab on the band and suddenly the world slowed. The g-forces continued to press him into his seat with the same heavy hand, but they were inching up on Bravo 3 at a leisurely pace. Bailey took his time targeting the other ship, positioning the crosshairs of the plasma punch precisely on a stress point in the ship's construction. Taking his time, he checked his work, adjusting his aim carefully. Just as Bravo 3 filled the entire viewscreen, he fired the plasma punch and, a moment later, pushed the tab on the Moebius band back to its original position.

The XF25 shuddered violently as the cannon fired. Fluffy swerved again, jerking the ship away from the fragments of the enemy ship as they spun away in all directions.

"Good shooting!" Fluffy said. "Very nice."

Bailey didn't respond. He was watching debris flash past in the viewscreen and hanging on during the XF25's evasive maneuvers. Off in the distance, something exploded in a burst of red and yellow, and Bailey jerked in alarm. "What was that?"

"Relax," Fluffy said. "The missile nailed that decoy."

Bailey glanced at the god's eye view, which showed that their current course would bring them head on with Bravo 1 and 2. The two fighters were closing in on the *Odyssey*, and the glowing spot that represented the XF25 moved toward them with maddening slowness. The *Odyssey* was in front of Stone's Throw now, bright white against the darkness of the hole.

"Time to accelerate. Hang on." Again, g-forces squeezed him.

"Bravo 1: launch," the radio crackled. On the head-up display, Bailey saw another missile streaking toward the *Odyssey*.

"Persistent bastard, isn't he?" Fluffy grumbled to Bailey. Then on the radio. "Bravo 4 reporting. Bravo 3 got nailed by a bandit. Bandit at your nine o'clock.

"That'll throw him," Fluffy said cheerfully as the g-forces squeezed Bailey. "He's flying half blind. Radar's unreliable here, with that wormhole warping space and the exotic matter adding noise to the system. He doesn't have a clue what we're up to."

Bailey was watching the missile close on the *Odyssey*. In the viewscreen, the missile was a streak of fire blazing across the dark face of the hole. The *Odyssey* seemed to hang motionless, cool and serene. The god's-eye view showed that the ship was lumbering toward Stone's Throw, moving at a fraction of the speed of the missile. The ship was close, so close, to the hole's event horizon and escape. But the missile was closing the gap fast.

At last, *Odyssey* dropped another decoy and moved sluggishly to one side, leaving the missile in pursuit of the decoy. So slow, so hard to watch. The XF25 was racing toward the other fighters, closing the gap.

"As soon I can get over there, we can take the bastards out. You'll have to have a quick hand with a missiles. You all right with that?"

"You got it," Bailey said, his hand on the Moebius band. In the viewscreen, Bailey could see Bravo 1 and 2, coming up. Just beyond them was *Odyssey*, still lumbering toward Stone's Throw. "Did I say bandit at nine o'clock?" Fluffy was muttering to herself. "I meant bandit right here. Go for it, Bailey!"

Bailey pushed the tab and took a deep breath. Methodically, he targeted Bravo 1 with the missile launcher and fired. Bravo 2 was out of range. He pushed the tab and returned to normal time just as the ship shuddered.

"Gotcha," Fluffy said. "But Bravo 2 knows we're after him. It's time for some fancy flying. Hang on."

Bailey clung to the tab and closed his eyes, not wanting to see the whirling view in the viewscreen, fighting the g's and nausea, wishing he could breath, glad for once that his stomach was empty.

"I'll get him in range and you nail him," Fluffy told Bailey. The ship twisted and looped, following a spiraling path in pursuit of Bravo 2. Bailey hung on, watching for the right moment to push the tab. At last, when Bravo 2 was almost in range, he slowed the world down. Fighting dizziness and the g-forces that were squeezing him into his seat, he adjusted his aim. As he fired the missile, he pushed the tab back to its original position. He had time to blink once at the viewscreen, catching a glimpse of debris as the ship spun wildly, before he blacked out. As his eyes closed, he heard Fluffy's voice murmur, "Gotcha."

"Just about to bingo fuel, Bailey," Fluffy said to Bailey's unconscious body. "We're coasting into Stone's Throw."

Moving at a steady velocity for the first time since Bailey had boarded, the XF25 coasted toward the hole, following the *Odyssey* to the other side.

7

Come, listen, my men, while I tell you again
The five unmistakable marks
By which you may know, wheresoever you go,
The warranted genuine Snarks.

—"The Hunting of the Snark,"
Lewis Carroll

BAILEY WOKE IN HIS BED, WONDERING WHAT HE HAD EATEN THAT
had given him such disagreeable dreams. A disembodied
brain floating in a tank, a nasty creature that asked him
riddles, a battle against Resurrectionist fighters—he
shuddered, remembering them.

Then there had been a dream that was vaguer than
the rest. He stood in a cavernous room illuminated by
golden light. The light shone from a cat's cradle of in-
terconnecting lines that shimmered in the air around
him. He could hear a voice murmuring words that he
couldn't quite understand. Bailey shook his head and
opened his eyes, ready to get up and have breakfast in
the solarium.

But he was a long way from the solarium. He was
back in his berth on the *Odyssey*. He got up slowly, rubbing his eyes, then rolling out of bed and rubbing his
bruises. He wandered out to find the others. From the
corridor outside the lounge, he could hear them talking.

"He never seemed like a fighter pilot sort," Iris was
saying.

"Maybe not, but that was impressive flying." Lily's voice.

"Don't judge by looks." That was Gitana's voice. "Bailey Beldon is a norbit with hidden depths."

"I just wish he'd wake up and tell us how he ended up on that ship," Jazz said.

Bailey stepped into the lounge. "I'm awake," he said. "And hungry."

"Just in time for dinner," Poppy called from the kitchen.

The lounge was filled with the warm scent of spices and good food. Bailey was grateful to sit in a soft chair at the table with the others. They all looked a little worse for the wear—bruised and battered.

"We're so glad you escaped," Poppy said. She brought a bowl of pasta with a spicy peanut sauce to the table and served Bailey first. "The Resurrectionists would have had us for sure if you hadn't shot them down."

"That was some fancy shooting," Iris said with admiration. "I didn't know you were so fast with a plasma punch."

Bailey shrugged modestly. "I've had some practice," he said, thinking of the games he had played with his nephew.

They were all watching him with such attention and respect that he decided that he wouldn't bother to mention the Moebius band. Not just yet, anyway. It seemed to him that the story was better without it. He certainly came across as bolder and more competent.

"We thought you were lost for good," Zahara told him. "We fought our way through a crowd of Resurrectionists to reach the *Odyssey* and we thought everyone was on board—then we discovered you weren't with us."

"What happened to you?" Jazz asked.

Between bites, Bailey told of waking up under the

scout ship, of crawling out and having a riddle contest with the Rattler. He told about knocking out the pilot and making his escape in the XF25. The only thing he left out was finding the Moebius band.

"Then I made my way to the exit lock and found a fighter that was about to take off. I knocked out the pilot and got aboard. They were in such a hurry to launch, I got away with it."

"It was a good thing for us that you did," Jazz said. "I've never seen such fancy flying."

Bailey shrugged. "That was mostly Fluffy's doing. She's the construct that controls the ship. What a crack-erjack pilot!"

Then Bailey asked Gitana how she had come to rescue them. Over dessert (fruit crumble with ice cream), Gitana told her part of the tale. (She had already told the sibs, but like most of us she never minded telling of her own cleverness twice.) The attack pods had gone for the *Odyssey* first. She knew that if she couldn't outrun the Resurrectionist fighters—and even if she could have, that would have meant leaving her friends in Resurrectionist hands. Fortunately, she had, not long before joining Zahara and the sibs, been visiting a friend on a planet with a slightly noxious atmosphere, which required the use of small filters that fit into one's nostrils to remove the toxins. She had just enough time to find the filters, insert them, then use her skills in somnimoribundus to sink into a deep trance state, slowing her pulse so that the Resurrectionists would assume that she'd been knocked out. Deep in trance, she could remain conscious of the movements and sounds around her.

"Tricky business," she said. "Could easily have gone wrong. Fortunately, the boarding party was in a hurry and didn't bother to search me thoroughly before taking me aboard. So I managed to keep a pocketful of EMP grenades. In a trance that deep, it's tough to be sure that you'll come out of it when you need to, but Bailey's voice brought me out. He had a question to ask and that got my attention." She laughed and Bailey blushed a little, wondering if he had asked too many foolish questions along the way. "You know the rest. Of course I tossed my last EMP grenade among the attack pods before we left, so the Resurrectionists couldn't use them against us. They had to send out the fighters—and that gave you an escape route."

"We had no idea that was you in the fighter," Jazz told Bailey. "We had used a couple of decoys, distracting the missiles with those, but when you came roaring up, we figured we were done for. When you shot down the fighters, we didn't know what to think."

"So we dove into Stone's Throw," Lotus said, "knowing we'd be safe on the other side. The Resurrectionists wouldn't follow us, since that would put them in enemy space with a long, long journey home."

"And what should come popping out of the absolute elsewhere but that fighter of yours," said Lily. "She hailed us and told us that you were aboard. Interesting entity, that Fluffy. She swears like a Bellatrixian miner and certainly has no love for Resurrectionists."

Bailey shook his head in amazement. After weeks of thinking about what it would feel like to make the transition through Stone's Throw, he had slept through it and woken up on the other side. They had all escaped from the Resurrectionists with their nervous systems intact. They had killed the Master Technician, destroyed three Resurrectionist fighters, and stolen another. And now they were having a fine dinner. Despite his bruises and bad dreams, he felt heroic and quite proud of himself.

"Where's Fluffy now?" he asked.

"Following along. She said she'd stick with us. Wanted to know how you were doing."

"Where are we exactly?" Bailey asked. "Where are we going now?"

Gitana answered him. "We're going to visit a friend of mine on Ophir; she may have some useful information for us. You can also replenish your supplies. I'll have to find another ship, since the Resurrectionists kept mine." Gitana leaned back in her chair. "And there, I'll be leaving you and going off on some business of my own."

"Leaving?" Zahara said. Clearly, she was taken by surprise. "Now?"

"That's right," Gitana said easily. "You knew that I wasn't going all the way to the galactic center with you."

"Well, that's what you said before. And of course we don't require your assistance." Zahara sat up straight in her chair, clearly dismayed but trying not to show it. "I just don't see how you could leave such an adventure."

"There are many adventures to be had in this galaxy," Gitana said with a smile. "I agreed to get you started on your way, and I've done that. But I have some pressing business of my own to attend to."

The sibs did their best to talk Gitana into staying with the expedition, but she just laughed and said, "Now, now, Zahara's right. I'm sure you'll do fine without me. This is your adventure, not mine. I'll help you along at Ophir and point you in the right direction before I go."

There was no changing her mind, so after a time they quit trying. They all had a second helping of dessert, Zahara pulled out a bottle of Ergotian whiskey, and they celebrated their victories. Bailey was well-fed and content for the moment. He was on this second glass of whiskey when he realized that he hadn't looked out at the viewscreen yet. He thought he'd like to see what the galaxy looked like, from this perspective.

The viewscreen was filled with brilliant stars. Not just a few bright stars, but hundreds of them, all as bright as the brightest star in the view from his solarium at home. Bailey sank into the seat by the viewscreen, suddenly feeling the effects of the whiskey. He stared at the screen, looking for something, anything, that looked familiar.

Heather looked over his shoulder. "We're in the heart of the group of stars we call Al Kallas. You may know them as the Hyades. It's an open cluster of a few hundred stars, most of them packed into an area just thirty light years across."

Bailey knew the Hyades, the V of stars that made up the head of the constellation of Taurus. But those stars weren't so near, so bright, so abundant. So many stars, and he recognized none of them. He had spent all his life looking at the stars, navigating by the stars, remembering the patterns of the constellations. Now he was lost.

He pictured the constellation of Taurus in his mind. A bright red star named Aldebaran marked the eye of the bull. He focused on a brilliant red star in the center of the viewscreen. "Is that Aldebaran?" he asked Heather.

"No, that's Diona, one of four red giants in the cluster. Aldebaran is back toward Sol some sixty light years. It's not actually part of the Hyades cluster, though it looks that way from Sol."

"I can't see anything I know," Bailey said, shaking his head. He felt dizzy, disoriented.

"Sure you can." Heather was watching him closely now, looking a little worried. "If you look over there, you can see the Pleiades. They're brighter than you're used to, but still in pretty much the same arrangement. Stone's Throw took us about 150 light years closer to them. They're about 150 light years father on."

Bailey peered into the viewscreen. Beyond the nearer,

brighter stars, he could make out the familiar arrangement of the Pleiades, a star group he had learned as a child. "I see them," he said. "But where's Aldebaran?"

"Let me shift direction." Heather worked the controls and the stars swung past. A red star came into view. "There it is—Aldebaran. Now we're looking back toward Sol."

"Where?" asked Bailey, peering at the screen. Seeing Sol would be reassuring, he thought. "Where's Sol?"

"I don't know if we can make it out at this magnification. Here, let me . . ." She fiddled with the controls, zooming in on an area of space near Aldebaran. "There. I think that's it." A faint yellow star, no different from the others.

So small, so faint. "It's very far away," Bailey murmured in dismay.

"That it is," Heather said softly. "We've come a long way. And we have a longer way to go."

Bailey nodded and turned away, feeling very insignificant and not at all heroic.

THEIR JOURNEY TO Ophir, the third planet around a yellow dwarf star called Polyxo, was uneventful. A few weeks after their transition through the wormhole, they docked the ship at the Ophirian space station. Zahara arranged to have the damage inflicted by the attack pods repaired and to have the ship loaded with fuel, food, replacement decoys, and other supplies. They caught a shuttle down to the planet's surface, landing early in the morning in a city called Ha-ha.

Bailey stepped through the port gate, following Gitana and Zahara. Gravity was three-quarters that of Earth—annoying after the half-grav of the ship, but bearable. Bailey glanced up at the pale green sky. He had visited Mars several times, but it still unnerved him to have nothing but open sky over his head. It just didn't seem natural.

He eyed the high, drifting clouds, wisps of white against the green sky, with great suspicion. He didn't know much about clouds but he knew that they were made up of water vapor. He knew that sometimes, on some planets, water called rain fell from the clouds. He didn't like the idea of water falling out of nowhere to land on his head, so he kept an eye on the clouds.

But the air was cool and sweet, a pleasant change from the recycled air of the ship. Polyxo, a yellow G-type star similar to Sol, was just rising.

The sibs were scattering: Lily to the market to trade in gems; Iris to the music halls, Heather to the university where other astronomers could be found; Jazz and Poppy to the section of the city known as Flower Town, where pleasures of all kinds were easily available. Gitana, Zahara, and Lotus were going to visit Gitana's friend, and Gitana suggested that Bailey join them. "You may learn a few things," she said. "And that's always good."

Ha-ha was a city of canals and bridges, on a planet that was almost as wet as Earth. Ophir's primary export was a drug popularly (and affectionately) known as jack—short for "jack-off." Jack was derived from a natural toxin produced by a marine micro-organism native to Ophir. In humans, jack produced a state of relaxed euphoria that many compared to an intensified version of the mental state immediately following orgasm, which is how the drug had earned its name. Though efforts had been made to artificially duplicate the drug, the natural product remained far superior to any imitations. Exports of jack had made Ophir prosperous.

Gitana, Zahara, Lotus, and Bailey traveled by water taxi, catching one of the many small, solar powered, motor boats that plied the canals and lakes of the city. Bailey sat in the stern of the boat watching the driver, a cheerful young man dressed in the knee-length kilt and loose shirt that were standard wear for both men and women in Ha-ha.

Bailey didn't like the way the boat rocked beneath him. It seemed all too precarious. The abundant liquid water made him nervous. In the Belt, water was frozen into chunks of ice, which could be melted to power a rocket or fill a bathtub. On Mars, water was scarce. He had never seen more than a bathtubful of liquid water in one place. He clung to the side of the boat and wished it would stop rocking.

The city was just waking up. They passed a floating marketplace where vendors were setting out their wares on boats and barges. A flower seller called out as they passed, holding up a garland of crimson blossoms. On another barge, men were hauling cages from the water. Through the bars, Bailey could see waving claws and tentacles—some aquatic species native to Ophir.

Gitana said something to their driver, and he pulled alongside a barge on which three women were toiling over a charcoal fire, roasting a tentacle as thick around as Bailey's wrist. Gitana bought three plates of grilled tentacle and Bailey managed to let go of the side of the boat for long enough to eat some. The sweet flesh re-minded him of the crawfish he raised in the aquaculture system of the Restless Rest. Wood smoke and hot sauce added an exotic flavor.

They made their way through a maze of narrow ca-nals past ancient stone buildings covered with tangled vines. Here and there, between the vines, Bailey caught glimpses of bright mosaic tiles set in intricate patterns. Where two canals intersected, a stone statue of an elephant-headed man rose from the vegetation. In his four arms, he clutched a large glass magnifying lens, a mirror that flashed in the light of the rising sun, a bright metal sword, and a crimson flower, obviously placed in his hand fresh that morning.

"That's Ganesh, the remover of obstacles," Lotus told Bailey, nodding in the statue's direction. "A deity of old Earth, adopted by the Ophirians."

"We're in the heart of the old town now," the driver told Gitana.

They took the canal to the right of the statue and pulled up alongside a dock, a solid slab of burnished metal set on stone piers. The bank beside the dock was thick with vegetation, an impenetrable wall of greenery into which a metal gate was set. Beside the gate was another statue, this one an intricate construction of metal. It had the multihorned head and armored body of a Gacruzian ice dragon, but it stood upright on the thick legs of a pachypod from one of the heavy gravity worlds orbiting Vega.

As Bailey climbed from the boat, the statue turned its head to face him and smiled to display a terrifying array of teeth. The color of its teeth—metallic copper, silver, gold, and bronze—matched the horns that ringed its head. It was not a statue at all, but a robot greeter constructed in the toy shops of Flam, one of the three worlds orbiting Fomalhaut. The Flamians were noted from their innovative robotics; their creations were patterned after the life forms of a thousand worlds.

"Gitana . . ." Bailey stammered.

"Greetings," Gitana said, stepping up beside him. "We are here to speak with the Curator."

The greeter inclined its fearsome head toward Gitana and spoke in a Flamish accent. "My apologies, honored one. Curator Murphy is not admitting any visitors today. Strict orders. Perhaps another day."

Gitana returned the greeter's smile. "Tell me: when was the last time the Curator accepted a visitor?"

"Let me see." The greeter gazed into the distance as

if in thought. "That would be two years ago."

"Two years here," Gitana commented to Zahara. "That would be twenty standard years." She turned back to the greeter. "Tell the Curator that Gitana is here with something to show her. She'll want to see us."

"Please wait a moment, honored one." The greeter held its head high, listening to radio signals from within the compound. Then it smiled more widely, showing even more of its impressive teeth. "The Curator will see you. Welcome."

They followed the greeter through the gate and along the twisting paths of a garden. "Please stay on the path," the greeter advised them.

As they strolled, Bailey stared at the exotic vegetation around them. Most norbits liked to garden, and Bailey was no exception. He loved to putter among growing plants and often traded cuttings and seeds with other norbits. Several steps off the path, a vine with orange-and-black flowers twined around an arbor. Bailey paused to admire the blossoms, thinking about how wonderful such a vine would look in his greenhouse.

"Tiger vine," Gitana commented, glancing back at him. "Stay clear." At that moment, the vine twisted toward him, as if suddenly caught by a gust of wind blowing with hurricane force. Bailey caught a glimpse of sharp thorns on the coiling stem as it lashed in his direction. At its full length, the vine stopped just a few inches from the path.

"It's carnivorous." Gitana put her hand on Bailey's shoulder, steering him away from the twitching stem. "And hungry, I would venture to guess. Some things that look innocent are really quite dangerous." She glanced at the back of the greeter's head. "And some things that look dangerous are quite innocent."

After that, Bailey stayed on the center of the path, walking close behind the others.

The greeter escorted them to a long, low building constructed of gray stone. Walking down three steps and through a stone arch, they entered a large room that reminded Bailey, at first glance, of his own storeroom. Junk was stacked everywhere: a curving sheet of metal that looked like the hull of a spacecraft leaned against a stone pedestal carved with ornate floral designs. Other fragments of spacecraft, some of them etched with intricate glyphs, hung from the rafters, swaying slightly in the breeze from the open door. There were crates labeled with the names of distant star systems, broken bits of industrial equipment (Bailey could tell it was industrial equipment, though he could not identify its purpose), a worktable littered with odd bits of metal.

"Wait here, honored ones," the greeter said. In one corner of the room, a brightly colored carpet covered the stone floor and a couch and chairs were arranged to form a sort of living room. The greeter gestured toward the chairs. "Make yourselves comfortable. The Curator will be with you soon."

"Is this a workshop?" Bailey asked, looking at the worktable.

"It's where the Curator does her experiments and keeps her collection," Gitana said. "Part of it, at any rate. Hard to say exactly how many artifacts of the Old Ones the Curator has."

"I still wonder about showing this person the map," Zahara said to Gitana, continuing the argument that they had begun on the ship. "How do I know that I can trust her?"

"If the Curator chooses to help you, there's no telling what information she might offer," Gitana said. "You would be foolish to miss this chance because you won't trust someone who isn't your sib."

Bailey turned away, having heard this discussion at

least three times already. He wandered over to the work-table.

In the center of the bench was a flat metal bar that rested on a half-sphere of the same metal. The flat side of the sphere was attached to the bar; the rounded side of the sphere was down, serving as an unstable base. Kind of like a fried egg, with the rounded yolk down. The whole assemblage was rocking back and forth on the sphere.

Thinking that the vibration of his footsteps had disturbed the device and started it rocking, Bailey reached out and steadied the metal bar, stopping the motion. He let go and began to study some of the other things on the table: a sheet of shiny material etched with strange hieroglyphics; a broken band that looked very much like the Moebius band in his pocket.

He was leaning closer to the band to examine it when he noticed that the metal assemblage was rocking again. He was sure he hadn't bumped the bench, but he reached out and stopped its rocking again.

He turned back to the band, but before he could turn his full attention to it, he noticed that the metal assemblage was rocking again. Frowning, he reached out to steady it.

"Don't waste your time," a quiet voice behind him said. "It'll just start up again."

Bailey turned to face an ancient woman not much taller than he was, dressed in a gray robe. On the label of her robe was a round pin that had a golden pataphysical spiral inlaid on a background of blue-green.

"I'm sorry," Bailey stammered. "I thought I'd bumped it."

She shrugged. "It's been rocking for fifty thousand standard years, as near as I can figure. Perpetual motion. Not at a level that's good for anything much, but mystifying, just the same." She touched the edge of the rocking plate gently, a gesture of affection. "We have no idea what the aliens used it for. It could be a child's toy or an essential component of a space craft. We just don't know." She smiled brilliantly. "Though I've been studying the trash that the Old Ones left behind for many years, I still find them unfathomable."

Bailey pointed to the broken band. "I was just wondering what that is."

"That I obtained from a trader who got it from a pirate who stole it from a Resurrectionist. It was the fool of a Resurrectionist who cut it—trying to figure out how it worked, he was. Those Resurrectionists are always far too eager to take things apart."

"What was it before he broke it?"

"According to the trader, it influenced time, creating a pocket of slow time or a pocket of fast time, depending on how you adjusted it."

Bailey was nodding, grateful for the confirmation of his own observations.

"And why are you so interested in this particular piece?" the Curator asked, smiling.

"No particular reason," Bailey said. He was reluctant to show this avid collector his Moebius band, for fear she might decide it was a valuable acquisition. "I just wondered. That's all."

But the Curator was no longer listening. She was staring past him at Lotus, who was on the other side of the room. She held a golden sphere cupped in her two hands and she was staring into its reflective surface.

"Is that one of your friends?" the Curator asked.

"Yes, that's Lotus." Bailey was grateful to change the subject. He raised his voice, calling to the sib. "Lotus!"

"Oh, she can't hear you. She's caught by the sphere."

Bailey followed the Curator across the room to where Lotus stood. As Bailey watched, the Curator cupped her hands over the golden 'sphere, blocking Lotus' view of the surface.

The sib blinked and looked up. "What . . . ?" she stammered. "Where . . . ?" The Curator took the sphere from Lotus' hands, turning away to hide it from Bailey's view.

"Stay here just a moment," she said. She walked away into a shadowy area of the room.

"Are you all right?" Bailey asked Lotus.

"I'm fine. Never better. I just . . ." Lotus looked around the room, blinking. "I thought I was having an interesting conversation with . . . someone. I don't know who."

"You don't know who you were talking to or what you were talking about, but you would have stood there and dreamed this fascinating conversation until you collapsed from hunger and fatigue," the Curator said, returning from the shadows empty-handed. "My apologies. I shouldn't have left that out. Some artifacts of the Old Ones are very seductive. But I have so few visitors."

"What was that?" Bailey asked.

"Ah, no one knows. Maybe it's a mouse trap, designed to mesmerize the mice. Or maybe it's the alien equivalent of handcuffs, a way to keep prisoners from straying. Or maybe it's an educational child's toy. There's always that option." The Curator shrugged, still smiling. "But I'm sure my friend Gitana is eager to see me."

Bailey and Lotus followed her to the chairs where Gitana and Zahara were sitting.

"Gitana! So good to see you again. Would you like a cup of tea?"

A robot entered, bearing a tea tray on its back. Another Flamish creation, this one was shaped like a Gacruzian carpet worm—about the size of a coffee table with hundreds of thin legs made of translucent crystal.

The Curator poured tea, a spicy blend that had the scent of orange and mint. Bailey sipped his tea while the Curator studied them over the rim of her cup. At last, she spoke to Gitana. "It has been too long since you came to visit. Where have you been? What have you been up to? And where in the galaxy are you off to now?"

Gitana waved a hand. "Too many places to say. Most recently, my friends and I were captured by Resurrectionists in the Farr sector."

"Resurrectionists in the Farr sector? They grow too bold. You must tell me about your escape—but first, introduce me to your friends."

"These are my colleagues, Zahara Farr, Lotus Farr, and Bailey Beldon, a norbit of good family."

The Curator nodded, smiling at Bailey. "Related to Brita, no doubt. A pleasure to meet you. Now you said you had something to show me."

Gitana took the portable holographic projector from her belt and activated it. Suddenly, they sat among the glowing golden lines of the map.

"Beautiful." The Curator smiled.

"You aren't surprised. You've seen something like this before?"

The Curator nodded. "Indeed. But this is only a facsimile. Where is the original?"

"In the hands of my daughter," Zahara said. "At the center of the galaxy. We will follow this map to find her."

"Ah, you've decided it's a map." The Curator leaned back in her chair, smiling. "A bold assumption."

"Many of the golden lines match up with the wormholes we know," Zahara said. "We have no reason to assume the others will not match as well."

The Curator nodded. Bailey remembered what she

had said about the unfathomable minds of the aliens and wondered what she was thinking.

"This is where we are going." Zahara stood and pointed toward the silver sphere at the center of the pattern of lines. "It offers great promise."

"So it does," the Curator murmured. "But great promises are not always fulfilled." She sipped her tea.

"In this case, we have reason to believe that the promises will be fulfilled. Violet reached that destination and sent back a message suggesting we follow," Gitana said. "So Zahara and her colleagues are going to visit the place of the Old Ones. And you know more of the Old Ones than anyone in the galaxy. That's why we came here."

The Curator smiled. "You are flattering me, Gitana. That's usually a sign that you want something." Her voice was teasing.

Bailey watched Gitana's face to see how she would react. "Only your knowledge, dear Curator." Gitana's voice was equally light.

"Well, I believe I can offer you more than that." The Curator got up and walked to the crates. "Help me out here," she asked, and then she directed Zahara and Gitana and Bailey to move this crate off of that one, push this one over that way, shove that one over here. Finally, the Curator said, "That's good," and squeezed through the opening they had created to reach a crate that had been behind the others. She lifted off the top of the crate, rummaged around inside, and pulled out something, which she carried back to the table.

Bailey collapsed in a chair, sweaty and tired, and took a look at the object that the Curator had retrieved. It was a crystal, in which there were glowing spots and golden lines, like the lines in Violet's map. The edge of the crystal was uneven, as if it had broken off a larger piece.

"It looks like it will complete the map," Zahara said, her eyes gleaming with eagerness.

"Perhaps," the Curator agreed. "Adjust the size of the hologram and see if you can match up the edge."

Gitana and Zahara adjusted the controls on the holographic projector to shrink the cube. The lines of the hologram lined up perfectly with the ones of the fragment. A perfect match. The cube was complete.

It was nice, Bailey thought, but not really all that important. They had already traced the route they would follow to the galactic center using the wormholes that were visible on the hologram. The addition of the broken piece didn't really add much information.

"That's good," Gitana said, studying the Curator. "But there's more to it than what we see, isn't there?"

The Curator's smile broadened. "Of course. There is always more. The universe is a place of great abundance." She leaned closer to the crystal. "I had owned this for more than a year before I thought to examine it under ultraviolet light. Such a simple thing. But look at how it changes things." She touched a control in the arm of her chair and the room lights dimmed. In the heart of the crystal fragment, an intricate pattern of pale blue hieroglyphics glowed. Here's what they looked like:

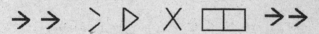

Gitana and Zahara leaned forward at once, staring at the newly visible symbols.

"I believe that the Old Ones could see in ultraviolet, as well as in the spectrum of light that is visible to us," the Curator said.

"What do they say?" Zahara asked eagerly. "Can you read them?"

"It's a series of numbers," Lotus said. She had been

very quiet since the Curator had taken the sphere from her hands. But she was paying attention now, studying the hieroglyphics intensely.

"Quite right," said the Curator. "As Lotus no doubt knows, scholars have managed to decipher the number glyphs. The Old Ones didn't count in base ten as we do. Their system was in base twelve."

"Which may indicate that they had twelve fingers," Lotus added.

"What numbers are these?" Bailey asked. He was very fond of magic squares and puzzles involving numbers.

The Curator smiled at him, as if he had asked a question she particularly enjoyed. Pulling a pad of paper and a pen from the pocket of her robe, she wrote for a moment, then tore off the page and handed it to him. "Here," she said. "The numerals zero to eleven."

This is what she had written on the piece of paper.

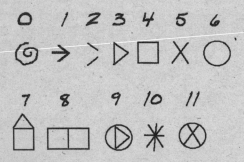

BAILEY LEANED FORWARD and stared at the hieroglyphics. "So these numbers are one, one, two, three, five, eight, and thirteen," he said slowly.

"That's right." The Curator nodded, leaning back in her chair.

Bailey squinted at the numbers, trying to make sense of the numbers. Perhaps they were a sequence of some sort, where each number related in some way to the one before.

Just seven numbers in a row: 1, 1, 2, 3, 5, 8, 13. He could add the first two numbers together to get the third number: one plus one equals two. He could add the second and third number together to get the fourth number: one plus two equals three. He could add the third and fourth number together to get the fifth number, and so it continued. "I see a pattern," he told the Curator and described what he had noticed.

She nodded, smiling. "I noticed that, too."

"That's interesting, but what does it have to do with our destination," Zahara asked. "Can you tell me that?"

The Curator smiled. "I've told you all I know."

"May we make a hologram of this fragment?" Zahara asked.

"I am willing to make a deal," the Curator said, leaning forward in her chair. "If you will agree to stop by at the end of your adventure and tell me what happened, I'll let you take this fragment along with you. I have a feeling it may come in handy."

Zahara nodded. "If I survive, I will gladly return."

"Now tell me about your encounter with the Resurrectionists."

Gitana and Zahara sat with the Curator and told of their recent adventures. After a bit, Bailey excused himself and, with the Curator's permission, spent a few hours examining mysterious alien artifacts. A metal cube that rested, suspended in the air, in a null-gravity field of its own making. A black sphere that bounced inside a glass case, ricocheting off the sides. According to the Curator, the ball had been bouncing for the past fifty years and showed no sign of losing energy. A disk carved from a ruby-red crystal that sang ethereal music.

When they left, the Curator smiled at him. "Good luck with the hieroglyphics, Mr. Beldon," she said. "I'll be interested to learn if you figure anything out about them."

Bailey nodded. His head was filled with wonders, but he was no wiser than before.

THAT EVENING, THEY had dinner with the other sibs in a restaurant that floated on the waters of Lake Ha-ha, the largest lake in the city. The sun was setting. A thin crescent moon was low in the green sky, following the sun down. On the opposite horizon, a full moon was rising. The light of the moon illuminated the clouds from behind, outlining them in golden light.

It was a beautiful sight, but the clouds made Bailey nervous. How odd to have water vapor drifting about overhead. Fortunately, the clouds were far away.

Zahara had ordered a feast of seafood delicacies (right-handed, of course) to celebrate the acquisition of the crystal fragment. She was pleased with the outcome of the meeting with the Curator. She openly admitted that she did not know how the crystal fragment would help them, but she seemed confident that it was important and that the value of the numbers would become evident at the proper time.

The other sibs were weary but happy after their day in Ophir. Iris had learned three new tunes for the qanun; Heather had met with her fellow astronomers. Jazz and Poppy were ravenously hungry after their afternoon in Flower Town. When asked how their day had been, they just laughed.

Lily was happy with her gem trades. Around her neck, she wore a brilliant red stone, into which the image of a scorpion had been carved. "It's for luck," she told Bailey when he asked about it. "We'll need it, in that sector."

"Don't be so gloomy," Poppy said.

"Just being realistic. It's a bad luck sector. Everybody

knows that. Ships disappear when they travel through the Scorpio-Centaurus Association."

"That's not bad luck," Jazz said. "That's the war. There's always a war between the Kakkab Bir and the Lupinos. And neither side seems to accept that some of us are innocent bystanders."

"What are they fighting about?" Bailey asked.

Lily shrugged. "Who knows? But they're always fighting."

"The usual," Lotus told him. "Territory. Religion. Trade rights."

"Right now, they're squabbling over control of the trade routes," Heather said. "Traditionally, the Kakkab Bir controlled access to five of the major wormholes in the sector. But during a period of political turmoil on their home planet, the Bir forces withdrew temporarily, and the Lupino forces moved in. Now there's an ongoing dispute. Of course, they also have different opinions on religion. The Kakkab Bir regard the Lupinos as subhuman scum, having enslaved them a couple of hundred years back. The Lupinos regard the Kakkab Bir as oppressors, a point of view I don't consider unreasonable."

"Enslaved them?" Bailey was startled. "Well then, I'd say that the Lupinos have right on their side."

"Well, you might want to think twice about that. Those Lupino ships are cyborgs, and rumor has it that the Lupinos trade their captives to Resurrectionists."

Bailey frowned. Neither side seemed particularly appealing.

"And on top of that, there's the Great Rift cloud," Lily said.

"Steer clear of that," Gitana called from her end of the table. "I'd say that's the source of the bad luck in that sector."

Bailey knew the Great Rift, a patch of darkness that crossed the Milky Way. And he knew that it was a cloud of interstellar dust. But he didn't know why it would be bad luck.

"Don't worry about it now," Poppy said. "We'll be there soon enough. Have another helping of these lovely tentacles."

But he couldn't help worrying, especially when Gitana said she'd be staying behind on Ophir. "I have to have this replaced," she said, pointing to her left eye. "I need to find myself a ship. And I have matters of my own to take care of."

That put a damper on the celebration. Later, at the shuttleport, Gitana said good-bye.

She patted Bailey on the back when she said good-bye. "Good luck. Take care of these sibs for me, will you?" She studied the rest of them. "Remember, you're heading for the Far Reaches now, leaving civilized space behind. Anything could happen. Be wise, be careful, and avoid the Great Rift Cloud. Stay clear of that no matter what."

"Thanks for the advice," Zahara grumbled. "Very comforting, I'm sure. If you're not coming along, then we'd better be off without any more talk. Good-bye!"

8

We have sailed many weeks, we have sailed many days
(Seven days to the week I allow),
But a Snark, on the which we might lovingly gaze,
We have never beheld until now.

—"The Hunting of the Snark," Lewis Carroll

JUST TWO SLEEP CYCLES LATER, THEY LEFT THE OPHIRIAN SPACE station and headed for Jump-Off, the wormhole that would take them to the Scorpio-Centaurus Association. Bailey watched Ophir dwindle in the viewscreen, dismayed to be going on without Gitana, to be entering a bad luck sector, to be leaving civilized space behind.

Despite Bailey's misgivings, the journey to Jump-Off was uneventful, the Hyades cluster being a reasonably civilized place. They passed through a number of minor territories, but Zahara had paid tolls to all the appropriate governments at Ophir station and they passed without trouble through the sector.

Fluffy traveled with them, though she was under no obligation to do so. In the Hyades sector, cyborgs were recognized as conscious entities with the right to make independent choices. Fluffy could have stayed behind, hiring out as a mercenary craft. But she had asked Zahara's permission to join the expedition and Zahara, conscious of the dangers ahead and aware of the value of a good fighter, had signed her up. So Fluffy and the XF25 came along, sometimes flying alongside the *Odyssey*, sometimes carried as cargo.

Bailey was glad of that. He liked the reckless construct, and knew that he never would have escaped the Resurrectionists without her. She, in turn, considered him to be responsible for creating a situation that allowed her to escape. Their mutual respect served as a solid base for a friendship. Sometimes, Bailey flew with Fluffy in the XF25, just to keep her company. He taught her to play Riddle Me Haiku and she showed him a few high-speed flying tricks.

Though their journey to Jump-Off went smoothly, Bailey believed that Zahara and the others were worried about the prospects ahead. They quarreled even more than usual over poker hands. But they wouldn't admit to their concerns.

"Gitana isn't the only one who's traveled in the Far Reaches," Lily said crossly when Bailey mentioned that he missed Gitana.

"We'll do fine," Heather agreed, but there was an edge in her voice when she said it.

Bailey had a great deal of time to spare—and he spent most of it studying the alien numbers from the crystal fragment. They were interesting shapes. He particularly liked the spiral that served as a place holder, a zero, an empty place. He also liked the arrow that served as a one; it gave such a strong sense of forward movement to any list of numbers. He amused himself by learning to add and subtract, multiply and divide in base twelve, using the alien glyphs.

When he wasn't occupied with the alien numbers, he was looking out the viewscreen, watching the approach of Jump-Off. As the ship accelerated to near light speed, the colors and apparent positions of the stars shifted. Jump-Off was a black sphere in the distance. As black holes go, Jump-Off was on the small side, equivalent in mass to fifty stars the size of Sol, about forty miles in diameter. Since it had no companion star to provide a constant supply of glowing gases, Jump-Off's accretion disk was smaller and paler than the one that surrounded Stone's Throw.

This time, Bailey was awake for their passage through the wormhole, staying on the bridge with Heather and Zahara as they guided the *Odyssey* into the mouth of the hole. On Heather's navigation screen, the heart of the hole glowed deep violet. Around it, a pattern of colors shifted and changed.

"Exotic matter," Heather said, when Bailey asked her what the colors showed. "It's exotic matter that holds the wormhole open, exotic matter that lets us enter without being torn apart by tidal forces. We want to follow this path." On the screen, she ran her fingers over a sweep of colors that ranged from green to blue to violet. "You see, the exotic matter counters the gravitational effects of the hole. We'll be torn to pieces if we end up over here." She waved a hand over sections of the screen that glowed red and orange and yellow.

Bailey decided not to ask any other questions. He didn't want to know all the things that could go wrong and he thought it might be best to avoid distracting the navigator at this crucial time. So he watched in silence as the stars surrounding the black sphere blazed brighter. Such beautiful colors—emerald and sapphire and brilliant blue-white—all of them dazzling against the blackness of space.

"Gravitational lensing," Heather said, glancing at the viewscreen. "The pull of the hole's gravity affects the light."

As Bailey watched, his heart pounding, his breath shallow and fast, the stars shifted to form radiant bands, streaks of colored light that seemed to flow from the hole.

"Almost there," Heather said. "Sliding on in."

The bands of light multiplied, forming a kaleidoscopic

pattern of shifting light. The viewscreen was filled with shimmering color that swirled with the movement of the ship, a vortex of light, drawing them into the dark circle in the center. Bailey started to speak, to force words past the lump in his throat, but before he could, they entered the mouth of the hole.

In that moment, they were somewhere outside of ordinary space and time. They were nowhere at all. In his pocket, Bailey felt the Moebius band vibrating, humming as if suddenly switched on.

He could not speak; he could not move. He was frozen and the world was frozen around him. In that moment, which could have been a microsecond or could have been a hundred years, he saw a pattern laid on top of the swirling colors, a network of lines that glowed brighter than any of the colors on the screen. In that moment, he heard a voice saying something he couldn't understand, something very important.

Then the moment was past. A flash of white light filled the screen. When it faded, the viewscreen looked out on ordinary space once again. The *Odyssey* was rushing forward, carried by the momentum of its entry into the wormhole. In Bailey's pocket, the Moebius band lay still, and Bailey wondered if he had imagined its vibration.

"You have entered a Lupino sector." The voice on the communicator grated on the ear—harsh, unfriendly. "Identify yourselves. You must compensate the parliament of Lupe for passage through this sector."

While Heather and Zahara negotiated with the Lupino forces, Bailey blinked at the viewscreen. He had no time to dwell on the images of the jump; their present situation seemed to demand his full attention.

Just ahead, a Lupino battle cruiser lay in wait for all travelers entering the sector through Jump-Off. Behind the cruiser and to the right, the viewscreen was filled with unfamiliar stars. But the left half of the viewscreen was what caught Bailey's attention. There, the stars were obscured by haze, like streetlights viewed through a dense fog. Nearby stars were dimmed; more distant stars were barely visible through the cloud. Beyond those stars, there was darkness. The Great Rift Cloud.

Bailey gazed uneasily at the darkness where the Cloud blotted out the stars. He had never seen anything like it before. In the Asteroid Belt, the view of the stars was never obscured by clouds or fog or other atmospheric phenomenon. In Bailey's experience, stars shone bright and clear, fading only with distance. It was disconcerting not to be able to see the stars clearly. The haze of the Cloud made the universe seem vague and unreliable, as if existence itself were more precarious here in the Far Reaches.

While Bailey was preoccupied with these gloomy thoughts, Zahara concluded the negotiations for safe passage through space controlled by Lupino forces and the *Odyssey* continued on its way. They were headed for the black hole designated as 569Scorpio. Never mapped, it was unimportant to galactic trade and so had never been named. They traveled with the Great Rift Cloud beside them, following its edge toward their destination.

Even after Heather explained that the Cloud was simply an accumulation of interstellar dust, its presence made Bailey uneasy. The dust obscured the stars by absorbing light, but radio waves and infrared radiation could penetrate it. Bailey convinced Heather to scan the Cloud in those wavelengths.

"Why?" she asked. "What are you looking for?"

"Oh, just take a look," he asked.

A quick scan revealed a variety of objects located not far from the edge of the Cloud: asteroids and planetoids floating in interstellar space. "That's strange," Heather said. "Generally, you find such objects orbiting stars, not floating free. I wonder if they coalesced out of the dust. That would be a good topic for someone to study sometime. But I don't have time right now."

No one had time just then. The ship was on constant alert as they traveled through hostile space. The sibs spent their time hovering near their battle stations or monitoring instruments for hostiles. Zahara sent Fluffy on scouting missions, and sometimes, just to get out of the ship, Bailey accompanied her.

They were returning from such an expedition when they found the *Odyssey* in orbit around a Kakkab Bir battle cruiser.

"Trouble," said Fluffy, opening radio contact and taking up a position near the *Odyssey*.

The battle cruiser was a floating fortress, a sphere the size of the Restless Rest. Curling between the weapons turrets and communications antennae that bristled on its surface was a great scorpion painted in black and red, the colors of the Kakkab Bir. As black and cold as deep space; as red and hot as the coals in the heart of a long-burning fire. The scorpion's claws were tipped with gun turrets; the tip of its tail was a missile bay; its heart was a pulsing red light. Beside this ship, the *Odyssey* was a toy that could be destroyed by accident, and Bailey and Fluffy were less than that.

"We are simple traders, passing through your sector," Zahara was explaining politely to the Kakkab Bir. "We would be happy to pay a fee for safe passage."

The voice of someone on the Kakkab Bir ship began rumbling about hostile forces in this area, and Bailey was leaning back, prepared to listen to a lengthy negotiation, when Fluffy said, "Uh oh. Double trouble."

A pair of fighters was heading their way. Bailey was optimistic. "They're just returning to base, right?"

"Nope. Wrong side."

On the viewscreen, Bailey could just make out the

fighters' colors. Silver and blue: Lupino forces. As Bailey watched, the Kakkab Bir battle cruiser launched four fighters.

"The Lupinos will see that they're outnumbered and they'll turn tail," Bailey said. "Don't you think?"

But the radar showed four more blips, following the first two.

"Maybe not," said Fluffy.

Then one of the Lupino fighters fired a missile and all hell broke loose. The missile, jammed by electronic interference, was veering away from the cruiser, but the Lupino fighters were continuing on a course that would bring them into closer range. Kakkab Bir fighters were racing out to engage the enemy.

In the distance, one of the Lupino fighters exploded, hit by a missile from the battle cruiser. Bailey saw a fountain of scarlet shower erupt on the hull of the battle cruiser as a Lupino laser found its mark.

Viewed abstractly, it was a beautiful scene. The exploding fighter shattered symmetrically with the eerie silence of a space battle, where there is no air to carry the sound. The shrapnel radiated outward to form a golden chrysanthemum with a brilliant red heart. A fighter swooped past with another on its tail, their course punctuated by the bright white bursts of incendiary rounds, like flowers on a curling vine.

It was beautiful, but Bailey was in no position to appreciate that beauty. It was beautiful—if you were not in a cockpit, sweating in terror; if you did not know that the next blossom could end your life. Bailey and the sibs had no role here; they were helpless spectators whose only choice was to watch or to leave.

The *Odyssey* had peeled away from the cruiser and headed away from the battle. On one side, they were blocked by the battle cruiser and the Kakkab Bir forces. On the other, by the Lupino forces. The only direction in which they could flee was toward the Great Rift Cloud.

"Stay with us, Bailey," Heather called on the radio. "We'll lose them in the Cloud."

Bailey watched as the *Odyssey* headed for the Cloud, remembering Gitana's parting words: "Be wise, be careful, and avoid the Great Rift Cloud." It seemed to him that they could not manage all three. They were caught between skirmishing fighters and a battle cruiser with laser beams slicing through the interstellar dust around them, guided missiles zipping everywhere just looking for a place to land, suicidal Lupino pilots coming in and fanatical pilots from the Kakkab Bir heading out, and nowhere to turn for safety. Too late to be careful and perhaps the wisest choice was to get out of harm's way. And that meant heading into the Cloud.

The *Odyssey* plunged into the Cloud. "Come on, Fluffy," Bailey said. "After them."

Just then a laser beam lanced past them, a near miss. A Lupino fighter swooped past them, followed closely by a Kakkab Bir fighter. "All right!" There was a note of glee in Fluffy's voice. "This should be fun."

"No! Not them!" cried Bailey, but it was too late for that. He was hanging to his seat while Fluffy flew in pursuit, whipping around the battle cruiser. "I meant go after the *Odyssey*."

Bailey hung on, while Fluffy went after the pair of fighters. They whipped around the battle cruiser, and Bailey was nothing more than cargo, a trembling norbit surrounded by chrysanthemums of fire.

"We've got to get out of here," he told Fluffy. "This isn't our fight. Follow the *Odyssey*." Bailey did his best to sound commanding.

"But we're flying rings around them." The fighter they were pursuing exploded, hit by a missile, and Fluffy expertly dodged the shrapnel.

"Follow the *Odyssey*," Bailey repeated stubbornly.

Reluctantly, Fluffy turned away, heading for the Cloud. None of the fighters followed.

The Cloud, which had seemed so menacing before, welcomed them in. The ship's engines ran quieter as Fluffy slowed, but it seemed to Bailey that the darkness had somehow muffled them. Bailey felt cooler immediately, as if he had stepped from the hot sunshine into a shadow. Looking back, he still make out the bursts of fire behind him—darker now, softened by the haze of interstellar particles that made up the Cloud.

"Can you find the *Odyssey*?" Bailey said.

"Sure, they're not far ahead." Fluffy sounded cheerful. "That was an excellent fight."

Bailey refrained from sharing his opinion regarding the fight. "Let's just catch up," he suggested.

They made their way through the asteroids and planetoids that Heather had observed on her radio scan of the Cloud. Such strange asteroids. They did not have the slick, metallic appearance of the M-type asteroids nor the dusty, stony look of the S-type. In fact, in the beam of the XF25's lights, they looked shaggy and irregular, like rocks overgrown with moss.

Up ahead, Bailey saw twinkling lights, tiny bright sparks of blue and green and white that glittered in the darkness. For a moment, he thought the lights were an optical effect, afterimages of the explosions playing tricks in his eyes, but then he realized that some of the asteroids were covered with sparkling lights.

"That's beautiful," Bailey said. "What could it be?"

"Haven't a clue," Fluffy said.

They passed two small asteroids, each about the size of the XF25, both shimmering with blue and green lights. The small asteroids were orbiting a larger rock—a lumpy, irregular asteroid on which lights shifted and flashed in ever-changing patterns, a glorious display in the darkness.

"You know what?" Fluffy said. "One of those rocks is sending out a distress signal."

As they rounded the larger asteroid and the XF25's lights played over it, Bailey caught a glimpse of a pattern in a clear patch on the surface: a running wolf in the blue and silver. He blinked, realizing in that moment that the asteroid's protuberances had once been weapons turrets and communications antennae, now covered in moss that sparkled and rippled in the darkness.

"Wait," Bailey said. "That's a Lupino battle cruiser."

"You got it." Fluffy circled the cruiser and the XF25's lights shone on one of the smaller asteroids. It had once been, Bailey saw now, a Lupino fighter. The glass surface of the cockpit was clear of moss and Bailey could see the body of the pilot, lying still in the remains of his ship. Bailey shivered, suddenly feeling very cold. In the light, he could see holes in the hull where the metal had been eaten away. The gaps were ringed with ominously twinkling lights.

"We've got to find the *Odyssey*."

Fluffy veered away from the cruiser, following the *Odyssey*'s radio signal.

Bailey stared at the ruined hulks around them, and wished that they had taken Gitana's advice. Though to be careful and wise, he would have recommended staying on Ophir and forgetting all about the center of the galaxy and the alien Snark. And he knew that Zahara would never have accepted that plan.

"Not too far to go," Fluffy said cheerfully.

They passed the wreck of a freighter and another battle cruiser. Just beyond the cruiser, they passed another fighter-sized hulk, this one dark, no twinkling lights. As the XF25 passed nearby, the ship suddenly lurched, as if struck. The viewscreen went dark, as if the camera had been blocked.

"What the hell . . . ?" Fluffy said, spinning in an attempt to dislodge whatever had struck them.

That was one of Bailey's most miserable moments. Suddenly blind, he was caught in a wildly spinning spacecraft in the heart of a black cloud that he'd been warned against, just moments after seeing the fate of another who had made the same mistake.

FROM THE OUTSIDE, the dense cloud of interstellar dust called the Great Rift Cloud looks like nothing special. Viewed from the Earth, it's a long shadow that crosses the brilliant haze of the Milky Way, a dark patch that runs from the constellation Cygnus to Centaurus. Along the way, this dark cloud, which blocks the light of the stars behind it, hides the galactic center from the view of Earth. The Great Rift appears to be negative space, a nothing. But appearances can be deceiving.

Billions of years ago, a massive blue supergiant exploded in a supernova, tearing itself apart and, in the process, ejecting stellar gases rich in iron and oxygen. These gases cooled and coalesced into dust grains. As centuries passed, the dust was enriched with carbon and nitrogen from a planetary nebula created by a dying red giant. Stellar winds from thousands of stars brought in more gases, which formed more grains of dust, more sites for chemical reaction.

As these dust grains drifted in the interstellar void, atoms of carbon and hydrogen and oxygen and nitrogen abandoned their free-floating existence and stuck to the surface of the grains of dust. Over time, bombarded by cosmic rays, these atoms joined to make molecules. Simple chemicals formed first—molecular hydrogen and water and ammonia and methane—all frozen in the chill of space. Ultraviolet radiation from surrounding stars struck these molecules, causing them to break up and recombine in more complex forms—such as carbon monoxide and formaldehyde and ethyl alcohol and cyanide and a variety of organic, carbon-based compounds—the basis of life as we know it.

All the while—a long long while—these dust grains were gathering, clumping together to form an enormous cloud of dust, hundreds of light years across with a total mass equal to that of a hundred thousand suns. And still the molecules combined and recombined, forming more complex carbon compounds, like amino acids and organic ring molecules called polycyclic aromatic hydrocarbons. Some atoms released heat as they combined in exothermic reactions, warming the dust grains. Amino acids joined together to make proteins, and other molecules combined to make carbohydrates. One thing led to another. And life emerged from the dust.

The first signs of life were microbes, similar in some ways to Earth-bound anaerobic organisms that thrive in oxygen-free environments. You might compare them to *Methanococcus jannaschii*, a one-celled organism that feeds on iron and sulfur and belches methane. Or to the bacteria that thrive in terrestrial oil reserves more than a mile underground. Tough life, capable of surviving in a vacuum.

Those first microbes evolved into more complex forms, multicellular creatures that burrowed in the dust grains, feeding on iron particles. And those creatures evolved into larger creatures, culminating in a sort of insect—or more like a spider, really—that thrived in the interstellar cloud. Life in the Great Rift Cloud evolved to feed on the iron-rich dust—but when other, richer food sources came along, these life forms prospered. For creatures that feed on metal, what could be tastier than a spacecraft? A battle cruiser was a bonanza.

The twinkling sparks that Bailey had admired were

colonies of a phosphorescent sort of microbe that emitted light as they digested iron. On that substrate of microbes lived small insect-like creatures that fed on iron and on the iron-eating microbes. And at the top of the food chain were spiders that consumed the insects and the microbes and the iron itself, given an opportunity.

As the XF25 had passed a derelict spacecraft, one of these spiders had leapt onto the XF25, abandoning an exhausted food source for a rich new one. This spider was a monstrous creature, grown fat on a steady diet of processed steel.

The spider was in no way an intelligent creature. Think of it as an animated feeding machine. It had sensors that detected movement and food, grasping legs to bring the food to its mouth, and a voracious appetite.

"WHAT'S GOING ON?" Bailey shouted over the roar of the engines. The XF25 was careening wildly, spinning and looping worse than it had in any of the space battles. "Is someone after us? Are we hit? What are you doing?"

"Something's on the hull." There was a note of panic in Fluffy's voice. "I'm trying to shake it loose."

"Your strategy doesn't seem to be working." Bailey shouted. "But you may shake me to pieces. Slow down!"

The ship stopped looping and spinning.

"I can feel it," Fluffy said, her voice trembling.

"The viewscreen has gone gray," Bailey said, trying to catch his breath now that the ship had stopped lurching and looping. "Something's happened to the main camera. Do you have an auxiliary camera?"

"Yes. There's one that's used to assess damages. Here." The view shifted as Fluffy switched to the auxiliary camera. Set near the rear of the craft, this camera showed the body of the XF25 and the view beyond as the craft coasted at a steady speed.

Bailey stared at the screen in disbelief. A monster had

wrapped itself around the front of the ship. The spider's body was as big as he was. Its legs wrapped around the XF25, hugging the craft close. Its eight eyes glowed green-yellow in the darkness.

"Well," Bailey said, trying to sound brisk and businesslike. "I guess the problem is clear. We have to get that thing off of us. Now what do we have to fight with?"

"Just get it off me," Fluffy pleaded. "You've got to get it off me."

Fluffy was not accustomed to this kind of fight. From her point of view, a fight was something that happens fast: you chase a ship; another fighter chases you; you shoot; they shoot; someone explodes in a chrysanthemum of fire. She liked that kind of fight. She understood that kind of fight.

But this was a different story, and Fluffy did not know how to respond. She couldn't shoot. She couldn't run.

"Please get it off me."

"Give me a minute," Bailey said, his voice low and soothing. "Let me think." He had, as they were cruising through the Hyades cluster, inventoried the equipment in the lockers of the XF25. The fighter had been used to disable ships; the lockers contained equipment for hand-to-hand combat, to be used in subduing the crews of those ships. Stun guns, tangle guns, gas grenades. Bailey doubted that any of those would be effective against this monster.

"I can feel it," Fluffy repeated, her voice trembling. "Something's rasping on the hull, trying to get in."

"Just stay calm," Bailey said. "I'll think of something."

He stared out the viewscreen, studying the monster on the hull. They were passing another derelict ship and he studied that as they coasted by, considering the environment that had given birth to this monster.

Living in a hollowed out asteroid, Bailey had gotten to know a lot about life and microbes. That knowledge was essential to recycling wastes and keeping all the life support systems of the Restless Rest in balance. Specifically, he had to know about aerobic bacteria, the ones that thrive in an oxygen-rich atmosphere, and anaerobic bacteria, the ones that thrive in an oxygen-free atmosphere.

Suppose, for example, he failed to aerate the compost heap in the greenhouse. (Not that he ever would; he was a conscientious gardener.) Without aeration, there wouldn't be enough air to keep the aerobic bacteria alive, and the anaerobic bacteria would take over. The compost would become a stinking mess as the anaerobic bacteria got the oxygen they needed by yanking oxygen atoms off sulfates, leaving hydrogen sulfide, which smells like rotten eggs.

Or suppose the filter in the aquaculture system got clogged. Detritus would build up, there wouldn't be enough oxygen, anaerobic bacteria would take over, and dissolved hydrogen sulfide would poison his system.

Staring out at the monster and the derelict spacecraft, it was clear to Bailey that this form of life, like those anaerobic bacteria, thrived in an oxygen-free environment. And Bailey knew, from his maintenance of the Restless Rest, how to get rid of organisms that thrived in oxygen-free environments. Add oxygen to the compost heap or the clog in the aquarium filter, and the anaerobic organisms die. Oxygen is, you see, poison to those anaerobic bacteria.

It was a big jump from anaerobic bacteria in the compost heap to a monster spider on the hull of a spaceship. But desperation leads to creativity and Bailey made that intuitive leap. A dangerous thing to do, because intuitive leaps can sometimes leave you dangling in space with no visible means of support. But Bailey, as you may have noticed already, was lucky.

"Oxygen," Bailey said to Fluffy. "Maybe we could kill

it with oxygen. Look—don't do anything sudden."

Fluffy just whimpered and kept coasting, muttering every now and then, "Get it off me."

Equipment lockers are the same all over the galaxy. You might think the equipment locker of a Resurrectionist fighter would be orderly, with everything in its place, with only the things that might be useful on board a fighting ship, with everything strapped down and ship shape.

You're quite right. That's the way it should be. But all over the world, all over the galaxy, equipment lockers hold this and that—a tool left behind by a repair crew, a hose from a tank that's no longer there, a piece of this and a bit of that.

Bailey found what he needed. Norbits, as I've said before, know how to improvise. He improvised for a while and then he was standing in the airlock, suited up and ready to walk on the hull and do battle with the monster. An oxygen tank was strapped to his back; a hose led from the tank to the nozzle in his right hand. One end of a tether was clipped to a fastening on his suit and the other end to a tether hitch in the lock.

"All right, Fluffy," he said. "Keep a steady course. Don't do anything sudden. It'll all be fine."

He closed the internal airlock door and pushed the lever to dog it shut. For a minute, he stood in the airlock, listening to the hiss of air being pumped out of the lock. The hiss faded to nothing as the air left the lock.

Bailey was terrified, but resolute. He did not feel like a hero. He felt like a norbit who was just trying to do what was right and who was, in the process, sweating so profusely that the suit's ventilation system was working overtime to keep up.

When the green, all-clear light flashed, he gripped the hand hold beside the outer door and flipped the lever that opened the outer door. Air rushed from the lock, carrying him with it. He swung on the handhold and pulled his magnetic boots to the ship's hull.

He could see the spider clearly now. Its nearest leg was just a meter from his boots. As the last breath of air rushed past, he thought he saw the leg twitch, just a little. Otherwise, the monster did not move. The lower half of its bulbous body was pressed tight against the hull; its glowing eyes were fixed on Bailey.

Still clinging to the hand hold, Bailey unclipped the tether from inside the lock and clipped it to another tether hitch on the hull of the ship. Releasing his grip on the hand hold, he straightened up. He wrapped the tether around his left hand, holding the line taut so it would hold him against the hull. Over his head, another derelict ship, this one twinkling with phosphorescent bacteria, swept majestically past. In the distance, he could still see the battle cruiser with patterns of lights flashing on its hull.

Tightening his grip on the nozzle, he stared at the spider. The creature stared back. Taking a deep breath, he tightened his grip on the nozzle from the oxygen tank. Pointing the nozzle directly at the glowing, green eyes, Bailey thumbed the control that opened the nozzle, sending a jet of oxygen toward the creature.

Recognizing that it was under attack, the spider reared up on its legs and lunged toward Bailey. On the derelict spacecraft where it had lived for many years, this spider had battled others of its kind, fighting for dominance and territory. The veteran of many battles, it had developed reflexes that had served it well in the past: envelop the attacker and devour it.

Before Bailey could step back, the creature had caught him in its front legs. Rearing back, the spider pulled Bailey into a deadly embrace. Bailey felt his magnetized boots rip loose from the hull as the spider wrapped two long legs around him and began to drag him toward the mouth that gaped on the underside of its abdomen. In the beam of his head lamp, Bailey could see the open mouth in the center of the spider's abdomen; light sparkled a rasping tongue that could dig channels in the metallic surface of an asteroid or drill through the metallic armor of a space suit.

The norbit struggled, trying to free himself of the spider's grip, but the creature's legs were strong as steel. Though the spider's claws gripped Bailey's waist, his hands were free. Pointing the oxygen hose at creature's open mouth, Bailey thumbed the nozzle farther open, filling the gaping mouth with oxygen as the spider continued to drag him closer.

And closer still. If he had wanted to, Bailey could have counted the individual barbs on the rasping tongue. Holding the oxygen nozzle firmly in his right hand and continuing to spray oxygen into the creature's mouth, he swung his legs around and planted his feet on either side the monster's mouth, struggling to keep himself out of that gaping maw. The spider pulled and Bailey pushed, his leg muscles trembling with the effort. Stubbornly, he continued pumping oxygen into the spider's mouth, wondering even as he did so whether it would do any good.

When his leg muscles could not push anymore, he slipped to his knees. The spider's legs were crushing him; his right leg was inches from the rasping tongue. Then the spider suddenly went mad, its legs losing their grip on the hull and flailing wildly.

Still in the spider's embrace, Bailey dangled at the end of his tether, jerked along by the XF25. Even in its death throes, the spider did not release its grip. The monster clung to Bailey, a reflex had served it well with other enemies, smaller spiders who had fought and lost. But as the creature strove to pull him in closer, Bailey continued to point the hose into the gaping mouth, filling it with oxygen. At last the poison was affecting the creature's metabolism, and its legs jerked and twitched, throwing Bailey this way and that. Bailey thought his ribs would crack beneath the spider's legs.

The oxygen tank was almost empty when, with a final squeeze that Bailey thought would crush him for sure, the spider released its grip. Its legs went limp. Bailey took a deep breath and kicked at the monster, pushing it away.

Spinning on the end of his tether, Bailey watched the spider drift away. Its legs were curled up; its mouth was closed in death. Beyond it, the lights twinkled on spacecraft that had once belonged to other adventurers.

Every point is a turning point. At that moment, Bailey knew he had turned a corner. Using ingenuity, acting alone, he had overcome a dangerous enemy. His heart was pounding. His hand still gripped the nozzle so hard his fingers ached. The suit stank of his sweat. He was a norbit who had no business on an adventure—he knew that. But he felt leaner, fiercer, bolder than before. He watched the spider drift away and he felt at peace with himself. Just for a moment, he did not wish he were at home in a comfortable chair. Just for a moment, it felt right to be drifting on the end of a tether in the Great Rift Cloud—bold, stalwart, triumphant.

He shut off the oxygen nozzle and hauled himself back to the ship. In the airlock, he spoke to Fluffy. "Now we've got to find the others."

Bailey hailed the *Odyssey* on the radio, but got no response. Scanning the frequencies, Fluffy detected a faint radio signal, a distress call, and they followed that. They passed another derelict spacecraft, giving it a wide berth lest another spider be lurking there, ready to spring.

In the distance, they saw another hulk, this one twinkling with more lights than any of the others they'd seen. "It's them," Fluffy said.

"What?" Bailey was peering ahead, looking for a sign of the *Odyssey*.

"That's them." Fluffy circled the craft. Bailey could see three spiders crouching on its surface, each one of the territorial creatures keeping its distance from the others. Through the layer of flickering lights, Bailey could see the *Odyssey*'s hull. He wondered if they could see the XF25 in the viewscreen.

"I've made contact," Fluffy said. "Their communication antennae have been severed, but we're close enough."

The radio clicked and Bailey heard Heather's weary voice. "Mayday. Mayday. We are in need of immediate assistance. Mayday."

"Heather! It's Bailey."

"Bailey! We thought you and Fluffy were lost."

"We almost were. But we killed the spider and got away."

"How? Zahara and Jazz went onto the hull with lasers and managed to lop off a couple of legs, but that didn't stop the monsters. They've broken off our antennae, stopped up the engines. . . ."

"Bailey?" Zahara's voice broke in. "How did you get away?"

"Oxygen. It's poison to them." He explained the rig he had constructed and they devised a plan. The sibs were gathered around the radio and while they were talking, the sibs began dragging emergency oxygen tanks from the equipment lockers and started attaching hoses and nozzles.

Heather would remain at the helm of the ship; Zahara, Lotus, Lily, Iris, and Jazz would suit up and arm themselves with oxygen tanks. Bailey would join them with his oxygen tank. They would attack the spiders, with two people to each spider: Zahara and Iris, Lotus and Lily, and Jazz and Bailey.

They would kill the spiders, clear the jets, and make their escape from the dark cloud of interstellar dust, taking their chances with the Kakkab Bir and the Lupino fighters. One can reason with human adversaries. One can find common ground. But common ground does not exist between humans and mindless spiders that devour spacecraft.

And so Bailey found himself in the airlock once again. He swung out onto the hull of the XF25. As the fighter swung close by the *Odyssey*, Bailey blasted across the gap with his jet pack, landing on the hull with a clank of magnetized boots just as the sibs emerged from the airlock.

The hull was covered with a beautiful glowing carpet, microbes that emitted light as they digested the metal in the ship's hull. As Bailey stepped toward the spider number one, the largest of the three and the one that he and Jazz had been assigned, the carpet crept up his boots, his legs, twinkling lights swarming over his suit, joyous to find a new source of nourishment. Bailey ignored them, waving to Jazz.

"We whacked one leg off this one," Jazz said via radio. "Didn't seem to slow it down. Didn't seem to do anything."

Bailey approached spider number one from one side, while Jazz crept up from the other. Before beginning the attack, Bailey carefully snapped his tether into a tether hitch on the hull. Then, acting at the same moment, he and all the sibs opened fire on the spiders. When spider number one lunged for Jazz, Bailey attacked from behind. Half the size of the one that had attacked the XF25, this spider moved faster, swatting Jazz to one side as it turned toward Bailey. Then it was lunging for Bailey and Jazz was attacking from behind.

It was a long, difficult battle. Half the time, Bailey didn't know what was going on. He was blasting one spider with oxygen or fighting off another. Later, he could remember the fight only as a series of sharply defined moments, postcards from the spider wars. Jazz stumbling backward and falling beneath the spider and Bailey ducking under the spider's body to blast oxygen into the gaping mouth. A blast of oxygen hitting the hull and the colored lights fleeing, rushing away from the blast. Zahara and Iris chasing spider number two into spider number one's territory, and a battle between the monsters as they ignored their mutual enemies to squabble for territory. Poppy, menaced by two spiders and the group rallying around her, blasting the monsters with oxygen to drive them back.

There were times when Bailey thought they were lost. But even when he felt hopeless, he kept fighting, kept chasing spiders, kept blasting oxygen this way and that, until at last he looked around and the spiders were gone. The sibs were spraying the deck with oxygen to clear it of glowing microbes. Fluffy was circling the ship. The last of the spiders, number three, the smallest, was floating away, legs curled up like a dried up old spider you'd find in a corner of the greenhouse, nothing to be scared of, nothing at all.

They boarded the *Odyssey* through the airlock. Via radio, Zahara asked Fluffy to lead the way out of the cloud. Though the spiders and microbes were gone, they had stripped the hull of communications and navigational gear, leaving the *Odyssey* disabled.

"We can get out of the Cloud," Zahara said.

"Then what?" Heather asked.

Zahara shrugged. "First things first. We'll get out of the Cloud and get Fluffy aboard and refueled. Then maybe Bailey will think of something."

Bailey turned away. He had no bright ideas at all. He

found his quarters just as he had left them and tumbled into bed for what he hoped would be a long and comfortable sleep. Unfortunately, as has proven so often the case, Bailey's hopes for comfort were dashed.

9

We have sailed many months, we have sailed many weeks
(Four weeks to the month you may mark),
But never as yet ('tis your Captain who speaks)
Have we caught the least glimpse of a Snark.

—"The Hunting of the Snark," Lewis Carroll

BAILEY WOKE TO THE CLATTER OF DOCKING GEAR ON THE SHIP'S hull. He blinked sleepily, wondering if it was worth getting up to find out what was happening. He had just decided it was not when he heard a commotion in the corridor outside his room. Zahara's voice, shouting something about a ship in distress. A man's voice, deep and resonant, bellowing something about lack of respect and something about prisoners.

Half asleep, Bailey scrambled for his clothing. He emerged from his room just in time to see the sibs being hustled down a corridor by a group of strangers holding stun guns. Before the group could notice him, Bailey reached into his pocket and pushed the tab on his Moebius band, freezing the scene so that he could study the situation at his leisure.

This was no military force. One man wore a black and red jumpsuit, the colors of the Kakkab Bir; another wore blue and silver, Lupino colors. The others were in jumpsuits of various colors, not a uniform among them.

In the center of the group was an enormous man dressed in a flame-red jumpsuit. His bushy black beard reached almost to his waist; the dark, curly hair had been braided and tied with red ribbons. His hands were waving in the air and his mouth was open, frozen in the act of shouting. The woman who stood beside him was a sib of the Farr clone, from the look of her. She had a crewcut of flaming orange hair, and she was grinning at Zahara. It was not a friendly grin.

Bailey examined the situation wearily. He was still tired, very tired, from battling the spiders. He could, he supposed, steal a stun gun from one of the men, stun them all, somehow drag them off the *Odyssey*. Then he and the sibs would be back where they started, adrift in a broken-down ship.

He studied the face of the big, bearded man and decided that he would wait and see what happened. So just inside an open door he found himself a spot to hide, released the tab, and waited.

WHILE BAILEY WAS asleep, the *Odyssey* had been captured by pirates.

There were many different varieties of pirates in the galaxy. There were pirates who intercepted ships, stealing their cargo and selling their passengers and crew to the Resurrectionists. There were privateers—pirates under contract to a particular government, acting as mercenaries within the space controlled by that government. There were postal pirates, who specialized in intercepting message pods and selling them to the intended recipient—or sometimes to the highest bidder. Some postal pirates began as scavengers, finding disabled message pods (like the one Bailey recovered so long ago) and charging a finder's fee for their recovery. Others regarded any message that entered their space as subject to toll—in fact, some had set up complex protection schemes in which groups like the Farr clone paid protection money in advance for safe passage of their messages.

In addition to subdividing pirates by their practices, one can also categorize them by temperament. There were businesslike pirates who were motivated by profit, sadistic pirates who were motivated by power, and swashbuckling pirates who were motivated by the love of adventure and the urge to explore.

The pirates who had captured the *Odyssey* combined scavenging and postal piracy. Most of their plunder came from ships that had been attacked and disabled by the life forms of the Great Rift Cloud. These pirates did not usually capture ships nor kill their crews: the giant spiders did that. The pirates made brief forays into the Cloud to reclaim cargo from the ruined ships. Any cargo packaged in metallic containers was destroyed by the spiders, but materials packed in wood or plastic or glass survived.

The pirates braved the perils of the Cloud to search for booty: plastic drums of jack from Ophir or spices from Regulus, bottles of whiskey, gems from all over the galaxy, valuables that could survive the vacuum of space and the predations of the spiders.

When pirates recovered a wrecked ship or its cargo, they used oxygen blasters to clear off the spiders and anaerobic life forms, then hauled the spoils to Rogue's Harbor, a planetoid orbiting a red giant not far from the Great Rift Cloud. Rogue's Harbor was a place where the riff-raff of the sector found safe haven, where unscrupulous traders did a profitable business in reclaimed cargo.

Blackbeard, the captain of the pirate ship that had captured the *Odyssey*, was a swashbuckling romantic with a scavenging streak. He had ordered his crew to board the *Odyssey*, thinking that it was just another derelict drifting out of the Great Rift Cloud. When he had discovered the sibs on board, Zahara had shouted at him.

That was the wrong thing to do. Zahara was in no position to shout at anyone. Fluffy, being very low on fuel, had just docked with the *Odyssey*. The *Odyssey* was disabled, unable to fight or escape. Zahara should have been courteous, respectful, perhaps even humble. She should have meekly requested assistance.

Blackbeard was an expansive man, fond of food and drink and lively women. He was an outlaw, a gypsy, a man with no attachments and a great love of travel. He could, under circumstances that appealed to his romantic nature, be very generous. Had Zahara acknowledged his power and approached him politely, he might have assisted the *Odyssey* in making necessary repairs and merely charged an exorbitant fee for that assistance. But Zahara had shouted at him as if he were an underling and a fool, and that didn't sit well.

The Farr sib who stood at Blackbeard's side was Red, his first mate. She was a renegade Farr who had cut her ties with Farr Station and her family. Like many a renegade, she had contempt for those who had chosen the more conventional path.

BLACKBEARD SAT AT the big table in the *Odyssey*'s lounge; Zahara and the sibs stood facing him. Red sprawled in a chair at one side of the room, her booted feet propped up on the table, a stun gun trained on her fellow sibs. While his crew searched the ship, Blackbeard was interviewing his captives. And Bailey was hiding in the galley, out of sight, but not out of earshot.

"So where are you going?" Blackbeard asked Zahara and the sibs.

"We were leaving the Great Rift Cloud," Zahara said, "barely escaping the giant spiders."

"Yes, yes. But where were you going then? There really isn't much of anything in the direction you were headed."

"We were lost," Zahara said. "Our navigation equipment was not functioning."

Blackbeard regarded her through narrowed eyes. "I see. But if your navigational equipment had been functioning, where would you have gone."

Zahara pressed her lips together, refusing to answer.

"We don't get many Farrs passing through this sector." Blackbeard's deep voice was slow and thoughtful. "What do you think they're up to, Red?"

"Well, it looks to me like they're on some sort of exploratory mission for Farr Station. This is a nice ship, one of Myra's personal fleet. Maybe they were on their way to a newly charted wormhole? Maybe something even more important."

"We were lost," Zahara insisted stubbornly. "Those spiders tried to destroy us. The least you could do is offer assistance to a ship in distress, rather than taking us captive."

"The least you could do is be polite," Blackbeard rumbled. "I ask you polite questions and you treat me like a fool. I don't like that."

"You are treating us as enemies," Zahara snapped. "We don't like that."

"Ah, well, with the exception of Red, I have never been fond of you Farrs. But perhaps Myra is fond of you. Perhaps your expedition is important enough to merit a ransom. I'm a patient man and I am willing to wait for a time. I'll pop you into cold sleep, so you won't mind waiting at all. Perhaps Myra will send a ransom. Or perhaps, if I thaw you out after a few decades, you will decide to tell me what you know. We'll see what happens first."

*   *   *

SO THE PIRATES towed the *Odyssey*, with all the sibs and Fluffy aboard, to Rogue's Harbor. The Moebius band and its time-shifting power allowed Bailey to elude the pirates and make his way from the *Odyssey* to Rogue's Harbor, but it was a tedious and difficult process. He would shift time so that he was very fast and the others were very slow, make his way to a new hiding place, then release the tab and let the world catch up with him. When he was not time shifting, he kept his finger on the tab, ready to speed up if he needed to escape.

Rogue's Harbor was an airless planetoid that supported a rat's warren of tunnels and shops and brothels and taverns and hostelries. From a distance, the planetoid appeared to be covered with warts and bumps. Some of the more enterprising pirates had repaired spacecraft that the spiders had not entirely devoured, cementing the hulls onto the surface of the planetoid. The hull of a freighter formed the great dome of the Freebooter's Bar; the opulent living quarters from a Flamish luxury cruiser had become an upscale brothel, with men and women to cater to every need.

The cold sleep cylinders had once been part of a troop transport, a mercenary ship bringing soldiers augment to the Lupino forces. Now, the cold sleep cylinders held Blackbeard's hostages. There, the sibs were put into deep freeze.

An unpleasant situation to be sure, but more restful than the position in which Bailey found himself. Bailey could hide as long as he shifted time, speeding himself up and slowing the world down. When the Moebius band was activated, no one could see him as long as he kept on the move.

Soon after they arrived at the colony, he slipped into Blackbeard's quarters and hid in a closet so that he could listen as the Captain talked to Red.

"It'll take at least a decade to get word to Farr Station.

It'll be a little quicker coming back," Red told the Captain.

"That's true. You know it and I know it and those Farrs know it. But I suspect they're in more of a hurry than I am." The Captain's voice was deep and deliberate. "We'll see how long they can wait. Maybe I'll thaw them out after a year or two and see if one of them will tell us where they were going. I suspect they were headed for one of the uncharted wormholes in this sector."

Like all the folks who plied the spaceways, the Captain coveted knowledge of the wormholes. To his credit, he did not seek this knowledge for profit alone, though such information could earn a goodly sum. No, he had a wanderlust, a craving for new places, new sights, new wonders.

"The Kakkab Bir would pay well to know where an uncharted wormhole goes," Red said thoughtfully.

"That's so. As would the Lupinos." The Captain laughed. "Let's just be patient for a while."

Bailey time-shifted and stepped out of the closet. The Captain was leaning back in his chair, considering the possibilities. Unlike Bailey, he seemed to be in no great hurry.

ON ROGUE'S HARBOR, Bailey led a strange, unreal existence. Concealing himself by time-shifting made for a frantic, nerve-racking existence—hiding in corners, then dashing about, only to hide once again. Always worried about being caught, he could never relax, never snatch more than an hour or so of sleep.

He ate on the run. At first, he snatched most of his food from the galley in the Rogue's Tavern, time shifting when the cook was at work, grabbing food from the plates as the cook stood frozen in the act of preparing dinner, then dashing away to eat in some secluded corner. Since he could not tell if the food he was stealing was right-handed or left-handed, he often stole the wrong type. When that happened, the food filled his stomach, but he ended up hungry and had to steal more.

While hiding in a storage locker near the galley, Bailey heard the cook's assistant, a bone-thin boy with big dark eyes, complaining about the cook. "He's always blaming me for taking food from the plates. And when I tell him I haven't been eating it, he mutters about ghosts."

Feeling guilty about the cook and his assistant, Bailey began filching choice morsels from the plates of pirates in various hostelries: taking a little from each to make a meal. But that made trouble too: with one pirate accusing another of stealing his dinner. After a few duels, Bailey returned to pilfering from the galley. It was not a relaxing way to eat.

He knew that he was the sibs' only hope of escape. He didn't like having them all depending on him. He wished he could get a message to Gitana, but he had no idea where she might be—or whether she could come and rescue them yet again.

Day after day, he wandered through rooms and corridors crowded with statues, people who were frozen in the inconsequential acts of their daily lives.

In the Freebooter's Bar, for instance, a pock-faced rascal in the mess hall sat with handful of fried potato chips halfway to his mouth. A coquettish pretty boy smiled at a client, his mascaraed lashes stopped in mid-flutter. The redheaded bouncer stood with her meaty hand locked onto the collar of a skinny, young tough, hoisting him aloft to throw him out.

The statues moved—but so slowly, so very slowly. The wink of the pretty boy's flirtatious eye took five minutes, from start to finish.

After wandering among the statues, Bailey would find a place to hide: a closet, a cupboard, a shadowy corner beneath a table, behind a curtain. Once hidden, he book, *The Economics of Galactic Piracy*, published by the University of Vega Press. I advise against more popular accounts (such as *The Lives and Times of the Most Notorious Pirates*) which delight in sensational material at the expense of accuracy. But all that's not important right now. What's important right now is Bailey's discovery.

Each day, many message pods were marked with a seal that advised other pirates to let them pass unmolested. Then the pods were loaded onto an space scow, which carried them into open space and released them.

Rogue's Harbor was not a particularly neat place, pirates generally not being inclined to pick up after themselves, but the rooms adjoining the mail room loading dock were untidy even by pirate standards. They were crowded with unclaimed message pods and other detritus of the space ways. Far in the back of one of these rooms, behind a stack of message pods bearing the glyphs of a defunct empire that had once ruled the region near Miaplacius, Bailey found four intact escape pods, salvaged from some spacecraft or other.

He curled up in the upholstered seat of one of the pods and slept soundly, feeling quite safe. The pod was tucked away out of sight in an unused corner, and anyone approaching it would probably bump into a few message pods, making a racket that would wake him. He slept for hours, and woke feeling more refreshed than he had for ages. When he woke up, he had the beginnings of an idea that might save the sibs.

He didn't do anything just then. He turned the idea over in his mind, considering it from all angles and thinking of how it might be improved. Then one day, when checking up on Blackbeard's doings, he happened to catch the pirate captain in the act of signing an invoice for the delivery of a crate of Ergotian whiskey, Blackbeard's favorite liquor. It was the day before the Feast of St. Elmo, the patron saint of sailors. The pirates on Rogue's Harbor had adopted the saint as their own, and used his feast day as an excuse for wild celebration.

From the safety of the Captain's closet, Bailey listened to Blackbeard chat with the delivery man.

"Celebrating St. Elmo's Day?" the delivery man asked.

"It'll be a double celebration. I'm celebrating both St. Elmo's Day and a very profitable sale to the Kakkab Bir."

Apparently the Captain had completed the sale of the XF25 to the Kakkab Bir. Fluffy would be shipped out the next day.

Bailey knew it was time to act. He waited until Blackbeard had signed the delivery invoice. Then he time-shifted and took two bottles of whiskey from beneath the frozen noses of the deliveryman and Blackbeard. From the deliveryman's clipboard, he took the invoice with the Captain's signature. From Blackbeard's desk, he snatched two sheets of stationery. He stopped by a store that sold drugs (both recreational and medicinal) and picked up some sleeping pills. Then he got to work.

Late that evening, a bottle of whiskey appeared on the desk of Celosia, the woman who ran the mail room, with a note from the Captain wishing her a happy St. Elmo's Day and thanking her for her excellent work.

Bailey was hiding among the message pods when Celosia discovered the bottle where he had left it on her desk. A gregarious woman, Celosia called out to the two mail room workers.

"The Captain must have us confused with some people who actually do good work," she said. "But hey, I'm not complaining. We have to get this scow loaded tonight. But I suppose it wouldn't hurt to have a taste of the good stuff before I get to work. Besides, we need St. Elmo's blessing, right?"

he had to make three trips. By the time he returned to the mail room with the third set, he was panting with exertion and beginning to wonder why he was taking so much trouble with these unreasonable people.

By that time, Jazz had figured out how to run the loading equipment, which was automatically loading the message pods stacked in the bin for outgoing mail. Leaving that equipment running, Bailey closed the sibs neatly into the escape pods (with Lily still muttering about idiotic schemes as the cockpit cover closed). With a feeling of some relief, he took off across the colony with Heather.

They had borrowed clothing from the locker of one of the mailroom workers—a pair of nondescript coveralls to hide Heather's jumpsuit—and made their way through the public corridors. It was very early in the morning, by station time, and the only folks who were out and about had been carousing all night.

Not far from the Freebooter's Bar, Bailey and Heather met a group of women who were singing drunkenly and playing drums. A tall redhead—Bailey recognized her as the Freebooter's bouncer—decided that she wanted Heather to join their party. "Hey, honey, where are you going? Ditch that squirt and come along with us. We're going to a party at Blackbeard's." The bouncer draped her arm around Heather's shoulders and turned her to follow the group. "You need to celebrate, and who better to celebrate with than me?"

"I really can't," Heather said. "I really have to go." But the bouncer had a firm grip on her shoulder. Like it or not, she was going to Blackbeard's.

Bailey trailed the group, desperate to get Heather free. He fell into step beside one of the drummers, just as they finished a bawdy ode to Saint Elmo.

"Here," Bailey said. "Try this rhythm." He hummed the rhythm of the Trancer's tune.

"That's catchy," the drummer said, and picked up the rhythm. Bailey hummed along and the other drummers joined in. The song was contagious, and soon Bailey was not the only one humming. The corridor echoed with the rhythm of the Trancer's tune.

They were not far from Blackbeard's quarters when the bouncer raised her arms to dance, releasing her grip on Heather. Bailey grabbed Heather's hand, pulling her back down the corridor, away from Blackbeard's. She danced along behind him, until the rhythm faded in the distance, then she stopped and blinked, confused.

"Come on," he said. "We've got to get to the *Odyssey*."

It seemed to Bailey that it took a very long time to reach the shipyard. He had grown used to time shifting, and operating in normal time seemed very slow. But they made it to the *Odyssey* at last.

The ship was empty, work on her having been finished not long before. Leaving Heather on the bridge, checking the ship's status, Bailey time-shifted and went to advise Fluffy about her role in the plan.

"You say they agreed to this?" Fluffy said. "Sounds like an idiotic scheme to me."

"Too late now," Bailey said, having grown a little impatient with the repeated criticism. "If you'd rather go work for the Kakkab Bir, that's fine. But if you'd like to come with us, I'd better go add your name to the list of departing ships."

Then, dashing through the corridors past pirates who were frozen in time, he returned to the mail room, where Celosia was just stirring as the scow crew arrived. He hid in a locker, leaving the door ajar. Peering through the opening, he returned to normal time for long enough to find out if his plan was working.

"Loaded and ready to go?" the scow captain was saying.

Rubbing her eyes, Celosia stared at the captain and

the humming loading equipment. "Sure," she mumbled. "Looks like it." Wits scrambled by Ergotian whiskey, she was willing to accept whatever good luck came her way. Somehow, the pods were loaded. Her workers must have managed it before they fell asleep. There were no pods stacked by the loading dock and that was good enough for her. "Ready to go."

The scow captain was closing the hatch when Bailey time-shifted and hurried back to the shipyard. He visited the main office and, still operating in high speed, added the XF25 and the *Odyssey* to the list of ships scheduled to depart that morning. He forged Blackbeard's signature to the addition, carefully copying from the invoice. Then he rushed back to the *Odyssey*. "Let's go!" he called to Heather, returning to normal time as he strapped himself into the co-pilot's seat. And they were off.

THE NEXT FEW hours were no fun for Bailey. The take off went well, but Heather kept worrying about the escape pods and wondering if her sibs were all right. Bailey felt anxious and responsible and not at all heroic as they trailed the scow. He felt a little better when Fluffy blasted past them but only a little.

Pirates and traders were coming and going, and Bailey was terrified that someone would hail them, question them, stop them. But no one seemed to care about one small ship making its way out of Rogue's Harbor.

They reached deep space without incident. Fluffy hailed them on the agreed-upon frequency. They rendezvoused with the escape pods and unloaded the sibs, still grumbling but glad to be off of Rogue's Harbor. Two of the pods had proven leaky, and Bailey was glad he had taken the trouble to fetch the space suits.

Zahara made a very nice speech thanking Bailey for his bravery and resourcefulness and Fluffy for her loyalty. The wormhole that they were about to enter was unnamed, she said, and as the captain of the first expedition to pass through it, she claimed the right to choose its name. "569Scorpio will now and forever after be known as Bailey Beldon's Escape," she said, and all the sibs cheered.

"Thank you," Bailey mumbled, but his eyelids were drooping as he spoke. At last, after many congratulations and much cheering, he made his way to his quarters, to his own small bunk, where he slept comfortably for the first time in many days. While the *Odyssey* was making its way through Bailey Beldon's Escape, Bailey Beldon was dreaming of a network of golden lines, a dream that seemed strangely familiar.

WHILE BAILEY WAS dreaming and the sibs were celebrating their escape, Blackbeard was storming about his cabin. He was in a very foul mood. His party had been disrupted by a gang of drunken women singing a Trancer's tune. Even now, that damn rhythm was running through his head. Then he found out that his prisoners had escaped and he began asking questions that only Bailey could have answered.

"But how did they escape?" he bellowed, his voice echoing from the walls. "How could they thaw themselves out and hijack their ship? How could that have happened?"

He turned to Red, who lounged in a chair nearby. The Captain was majestic in his anger—his dark eyes flashed, his beard was as wild as the ocean waves. But Red had seen it all before.

She shrugged. "The *Odyssey* was posted on the list of ship's scheduled for departure, with your signature. No one questioned it."

"When did it leave?"

"Twelve hours back. We didn't find out about it until this morning, when the work crew arrived at the ship yard. It's my guess that they're headed for 569Scorpio," Red said. "With their headstart, you probably can't catch them before they go through."

"Not before they go through," Blackbeard said slowly. "But afterward, perhaps."

"Who knows where that hole goes," Red said thoughtfully.

"I suspect that those Farrs do." The Captain smiled recklessly. "I have that Lupino battle cruiser that we recovered from the Cloud. I was going to sell it to the Kattab Bir, but maybe I won't. Round up the crew and we'll see who's interested in a little adventure."

10

"For, although common Snarks do no manner of harm,
Yet I feel it my duty to say,
Some are Boojums—" The Bellman broke off in alarm,
For the Baker had fainted away.

—"The Hunting of the Snark," Lewis Carroll

WHEN BAILEY WOKE, HE LAY IN HIS BUNK, FEELING RESTED FOR
the first time in a long time. For a time, he stayed in his
bed, loath to stir himself and find out where they were
and what new adventures lay ahead. Yes, he was happy
to be away from Rogue's Harbor, but it seemed to
him—after battling Trancers and Resurrectionists and
spiders and pirates—that one triumph simply led to
greater obstacles. Success simply led to greater challenges. That didn't seem fair, but the conclusion was
inescapable. He was not the same innocent and cheerful
norbit he had once been. He had learned more about
adventures than he cared to know. And he wasn't done
yet.

If this were a real adventure tale and if Bailey were a
real hero, he knew that he'd leap from his bunk, ready
to meet a new set of challenges. But he was stiff and sore
from lugging space suits across Rogue's Harbor and
wrestling with escape pods. So he stretched his tired
muscles and wished that he could have a quiet breakfast
in his solarium, followed a bit of puttering in the greenhouse.

At last, reluctantly, he rolled out of his bunk. From the corridor, he could hear sibs chatting in the lounge, but he did not stop to join them, continuing on to the bridge, where Heather was busy at the computer. He stopped in front of the viewscreen, blinking. The screen was crowded with brilliant red and orange stars—the color of burgundy wine, of blood, of old gold and tarnished bronze.

"Where are we now?" he asked Heather.

"Hang on. I'm just finishing up." She typed a few lines on the keyboard, studied the results on the computer screen, then leaned back in her chair and grinned at Bailey. "We're right where we thought we'd be. I've checked and double-checked our location, using a few dozen of the best-documented pulsars to triangulate and verifying those results with the short period variables, Cepheids and the like. We're right where we expected to be."

"Where's that?"

"Just a few hundred light years from the galactic center. Another jump, and we'll be there." Heather left her chair and came to stand beside him at the viewscreen.

"There are so many stars," Bailey said.

"We're in the heart of a globular cluster. There are more than a hundred thousand stars packed into a sphere just a hundred light years across." Heather's voice was dreamy. "This is an ancient cluster, more than fourteen billion years old. Over the millennia, most of the stars have evolved into orange and red giants. Isn't it beautiful?"

Bailey wasn't sure. Yes, it was beautiful. But he missed the honest white light of the Hyades cluster, the yellow glow of Sol. There was something ominous about the ruddy glow of these stars. They looked like the scattered embers of a dying fire.

"You can't see Sol from here. It's about 26,000 light

years away," Heather said, and Bailey realized that he had not even thought to ask. Sol and the Restless Rest seemed so very far away, almost like a story someone had told him once. As distant as adventure tales had once been from his comfortable life in the Restless Rest. "But I can show you the way to the center of the galaxy." She worked the controls on the viewscreen.

As the view shifted, the stars become more abundant and brilliant; their colors, more varied. Nebula clouds wound between the stars, glowing silver and blue in the darkness. The viewscreen panned across stars that were separated by a hand's breadth, then stars separated by the width of a finger, then stars so bright and closely packed that they merged into a single blaze of glory.

Bailey caught his breath, stunned by the cold beauty of the stars that filled the screen. Against the blackness of space, they gleamed like precious gems. The nebula clouds held them as a filigree of silver holds jewels in a crown. But these jewels were not organized in a tidy arrangement. The silver filigree was twisted and torn, curling around a fortune in rubies and sapphires and emeralds and diamonds that had been spilled in a heap, with barely a gap between them. Like the hoard of a dragon that had raided the treasuries of a thousand kings, like the treasure of a pirate who had ransomed an emperor, a jumble of fabulous jewels, overwhelming in its glory, terrifying in its brilliance and indifference.

Gazing at those beautiful stars, Bailey realized that nothing mattered to them. All the achievements of humankind were insignificant. Love and hate, death and life, honor and dishonor, knowledge or ignorance—what did any of that matter in the face of this austere and heartless splendor?

"That's where we're headed," Heather said, her voice low. "One more jump, and we'll be there."

All this time, Bailey had been traveling without much

thought for his destination. Sure, they were heading for the center of the galaxy, but he had never given much consideration to what that place might be like. If he'd thought about it at all, he had thought it was a place, much like any other. But the glory of the stars gave him second thoughts about that.

"What will we find?" he murmured, half to himself.

"Millions of stars orbiting a black hole with a mass equal to a million suns." Heather was leaning forward, staring at the screen. "That black hole, they say, is the center of it all, the beginning and the end. It stays at rest, motionless, and the galaxy rotates around it. That's the Heart of the Galaxy. A pocket of emptiness."

As Bailey nodded, Heather worked the controls again, shifting the view back to where she had begun. A scattering of red and orange stars glowed warm against the void. Heather smiled sheepishly at Bailey. "I can't leave the viewscreen pointed at the center of the galaxy. It's too much to look at all the time."

Bailey nodded, agreeing wholeheartedly.

FOR A FEW dozen sleep cycles, they traveled toward the wormhole that Heather had playfully dubbed "Zahara's Hope." As they traveled, Heather occupied herself with charting the stars, documenting their whereabouts for other Farrs who would follow their path. The others kept watch, alert for danger, but finding nothing. The trip was uneventful—there were no pirates or Resurrectionists or traders in this unexplored sector. But Bailey found himself restless. The view of the stars in the direction of the galactic center had left him uneasy, unsettled. Sometimes, he played Riddle Me Haiku with Poppy and Lotus; sometimes, he played a hand of poker with the other sibs. But for the most part he gazed at the viewscreen, turning it to view the terrifying splendor of the galactic center and wondering what they would find there.

At last, they reached Zahara's Hope, a small worm-hole orbited by a dim red dwarf. Zahara was at the helm, with Heather as co-pilot. Bailey and all the other sibs were on the bridge, eager to catch their first glimpse of the galactic center.

The stars grew brighter, formed bands of color, multiplied and swirled in a vortex of color as Zahara expertly piloted them into the mouth of the hole. Dizzy, Bailey closed his eyes against the sight. A moment later, he felt the Moebius band humming in his pocket and knew that they had entered the hole. The sounds of the bridge faded.

Against the blackness of his eyelids, he saw a pattern of golden lines, a spider web of interconnections radiating out from a central point. He heard a whisper—a sound that seemed to be traveling along the spokes of the spider web, growing louder as it approached him. Then the voice was upon him, a deep resonant rumbling that seemed to come from inside him, from his heart, from his bones. The voice was speaking a language he didn't understand. But he wanted to understand it; he ached to know its message.

Then they emerged from the hole. The Moebius band stopped its vibration; the golden spider web vanished. He opened his eyes to the center of the galaxy.

"There it is," said Heather, her voice both fearful and triumphant. "The heart of it all."

The center of the galaxy—a study in darkness and light. The dark heart of the galaxy was a black hole with a diameter equal to that of the Earth's orbit. A black sphere—a void, an emptiness, a hole into nothing.

Surrounding that patch of emptiness, that absolute blank, that glaring nothingness, was a glorious wash of brilliant light, the hole's accretion disk. More than a light year across, the disk was not uniformly bright. Bailey could see currents and eddies and swirls in the light, all feeding into the central blackness as the gravitational pull of the hole brought in molecules of interstellar gas and dust. Those molecules were drawn into the hole, moving faster and faster as they approached, and rubbing and bumping against each other as they sped toward the Heart of the Galaxy. Heated by friction, the molecules emitted electromagnetic radiation—first, infrared light; then, closer to the hole, the visible light that Bailey saw; and finally, closest to the hole, ultraviolet light and x-rays.

The black hole and its accretion disk dominated the viewscreen, but two other objects drew Bailey's attention. To one side of the hole, just beyond the accretion disk was a cluster of dazzling blue supergiants. To the other side was a red supergiant with a tail like a comet, created when the wind from the blue giants buffeted the red star.

Staring at the cluster of stars, Bailey remembered the cluster of blue points on the alien map. There lay their destination, the silver sphere, the alien base, the source of the Snark.

At the control panel, Heather flipped a switch and the bridge was filled with the crackle of static. "Radio hash," she said. "That's the voice of the Heart of the Galaxy. Even though it's several light years away, it's a strong radio source."

Bailey frowned, thinking about the great voice, the terrifying rumble he had felt in his bones as they passed through the hole. That, he thought, was the voice of the galaxy's heart. But he said nothing, just listened to the crackle of static as Zahara turned the *Odyssey* toward the distant blue giants. They had almost reached their destination.

ALMOST THERE! BUT even traveling at close to light speed, under the impetus of the Hoshi drive, that "almost" was a journey of more than a month. Plenty of time to study the alien map and wonder what they would do when they got to the alien base; plenty of time to gaze into the dark heart of the black hole and wonder where it might lead. Plenty of time for Bailey to think about what he'd be doing if he were at home on the Restless Rest.

He tried not to think about his home, so far separated from him in time and space. In his time frame, he had been away from the Restless Rest for less than a year. But he knew that while he was traveling at near light speed, many years had passed back home.

He wondered sometimes about how many years had gone by on the Restless Rest since he'd left. One sleep cycle, when he and Heather were standing watch on the bridge, he asked her.

She looked up from her work—she was mapping the stars as they traveled—and studied Bailey's face. "I don't think you want to know," she said softly.

"I do," Bailey insisted. "I think it would make it easier to know exactly. I was thinking about my nephew and wondering how old he was now."

She bit her lip and pushed her hair back impatiently, looking very unhappy. "It just isn't good to think about that sort of thing. Just put it behind you."

"I can't do that. The Asteroid Belt is my home."

Heather shook her head, looking very unhappy. "If you're going to travel in space, you have to get used to leaving people and places behind. You can't form attachments, except to things that last."

"Like what?" Bailey snapped. He was getting worried. "What are you attached to?"

"Like stars," Heather said slowly. "I miss the light of Epsilon Indi. Like places. I miss Farr Station."

"What about people? Don't you miss them?"

"When I leave a person, I know that I'll probably never see them again. I know that." She shook her head quickly. "When I say good-bye, I mean it."

Bailey turned away from her, staring out the viewscreen at the blue giants in the distance.

"The Asteroid Belt that you knew is gone. You're a different person now and it's a different place. You have to accept that."

Bailey continued to stare at the viewscreen, shaking his head in denial. He didn't have to accept anything. He just wanted to know how many years had passed back home. He didn't want to be lectured on what he should and shouldn't do.

The next day, he went to the kitchen where Poppy was making breakfast, and he asked her how many years had passed in the Asteroid Belt. She stopped kneading the dough for cinnamon buns and gazed at him thoughtfully. "You'd be better off asking Heather that question. She could calculate it exactly."

"Heather wouldn't tell me. She just said I should get used to leaving people behind."

Poppy began kneading the dough again, working her way back into the steady rhythm that Bailey had interrupted. "We learn to do that," she said at last. "We learn that when we are very young."

"I never learned that."

"I know."

The galley was warm; the yeasty scent of rising dough filled the air. It should have been a comforting place, but Bailey was not comforted. He felt restless, ill at ease.

"Just tell me," he asked. "How long has it been?"

She looked up from the dough. Her eyes were dark and sorrowful. "Well, it all depends on how fast we've been traveling. Zahara has been in a hurry, so we've been moving fast. We can't get to light speed, but we can get close. At 99.995% light speed, a year of travel is a hundred years back in the Asteroid Belt. At 99.999%, a year of travel is about 250 years back home. I don't know exactly—I decided it was best not to know. But I'd guess it's been at least 150 years. Give or take a few decades. Of course, that's how long much time has passed as of right now. If you calculated in how long it will take you to get back, you have to figure in at least that same amount of time. So it might be about three hundred years if you turned back right now." She frowned. "Of course, if any of your friends are traveling at near light speed, that would change their time line relative to yours."

He shook his head. "They aren't."

He left the galley then. He skipped breakfast and went to his cabin. He could not begin to imagine all the changes that could have taken place over 300 years. He sat alone in his quarters, thinking of all the friends and relations he would never see again. It seemed so wrong, so unreal.

Finally, he decided that he could not worry about all this now. During all the time that he'd been traveling, he had been imagining the Restless Rest as he had left it. That had made him happy. Thinking about how it might have changed in 150 years made him confused and miserable. So he decided that he would go on thinking of the Restless Rest as he had left it. If and when he headed home, he would worry about the passage of time.

When he left his cabin, he found a plate of cinnamon rolls in the corridor outside his door. That night at dinner, Poppy made his favorite dish and encouraged him to take seconds.

AS THEY APPROACHED the cluster of blue supergiants, Heather searched the radio band for transmissions that were not overwhelmed by static from the great black hole. She found a radio source coming from the tenth planet out from one of the blue giants nearest the black hole—though the transmission was broken and garbled, she could make out voices.

As they approached the planet, Zahara grew more impatient. She spent all her waking hours on the bridge—pacing back and forth, staring at the viewscreen, listening to the garbled transmissions in an attempt to find words in the hash of static. Sometimes, Bailey sat on the bridge with her, listening and looking.

They were coming into orbit around the planet when Zahara, while adjusting the viewscreen, panned across the face of the smaller of the planet's two moons. "What was that?" he asked.

"What?"

"A flash of silver on the face of the moon. Polished metal."

Zahara focused the viewscreen on the planet's moon. The flicker of reflected light that had caught Bailey's eye was a round metal plate, maybe three meters across by Heather's reckoning. Beside that silver plate was what looked like the blasted remains of a living dome, perhaps some sort of base camp.

"A doorway of some sort?" Lotus suggested. "The Old Ones favored circles and spirals."

Not long after Bailey spotted the doorway in the moon, Zahara first began to hear words among the static. "There—that was a voice saying something about a colony. Listen."

Bailey listened. A man's voice beneath a hash of noise. "Indigo Colony transmitting . . ." Static. ". . . do you read . . ." Static.

And so they made contact with the colony on the planet Indigo, an outpost of human civilization in the center of the galaxy.

INDIGO WAS A wet planet; more than ninety percent of its surface was covered with water. There were two land masses: a large island and a small one. Over the oceans, clouds swirled in grand typhoons. In the viewscreen, Bailey watched the swirling clouds with discomfort, imagining what it would be like to be down on the planet's surface beneath such a changing sky. What an uncivilized place to live.

The colony was on the larger of the two islands, located on a wide, green coastal plain where a large river flowed down from the mountainous interior. From orbit, Bailey could see the intricate branching of the river's tributaries, joining to make a single stream. On the plain, the river spread out into a fan, forming a wide delta with small streams threading their way among patches of vivid, jungle green. No signs of the colony were visible.

Their conversations with the colony had been intermittent, broken by static from the black hole. The radio operator had assured Zahara that there was a landing strip that could accommodate their landing craft. But in-depth conversation was impossible. Every other sentence was lost in the static.

Zahara, Jazz, Poppy, Iris, and Lotus elected to go down to the planet on the landing craft, leaving Lily and Heather on the ship. Bailey would have been happy to stay on the ship, avoiding the discomfort of a planetary visit, but Zahara asked him to join the landing party. Just as Gitana had predicted, she had come to trust the norbit's abilities.

They squeezed into the landing craft, a small ship designed to transport people to a planet's surface and bring them back. No frills. Basically, seats for six people, tightly packed, in a craft equipped to enter the atmosphere and land. Their radio contact had given them the coordinates of the landing strip. Zahara guided the craft to that location and landed without incident.

While Zahara completed the mandatory atmospheric

tests, they remained in the landing craft, staring out the ports at the jungle that pressed close to the landing strip. It was late in the day, and the planet's sun, a hot blue-white star, was setting over the jungle. Great, thick-trunked trees draped with creeping vines and moss reached upward for the sky. The leaves were a deep purple, the color of violets and royalty. In the setting sun, the vegetation looked velvety and soft.

An ancient landing craft was parked at the far end of the strip. It was painted in the Farr colors, but the paint was worn and chipped.

"All right, the atmosphere passes," Zahara said at last.

"Of course it does," Iris grumbled. "Violet's colony has been living here for the past couple of hundred years. It's got to be compatible with human life."

Zahara popped the hatch and they climbed out into the humid air. Bailey looked up at the sky. It was a brilliant, cloudless blue. He breathed a sigh of relief. He really hadn't wanted to worry about that stuff called rain.

The air was warm and moist, reeking with the exotic fragrance of alien plants and with the pungent odor of decay. High in the canopy of the trees, moths the size of small birds flew among leaves the size of dinner plates. A beetle-like creature the size of Bailey's foot was deliberately making its way across the concrete.

"Here they come," said Lotus. Iris, who was sitting cross-legged on a rug she had spread on the ground, struck up a lively, slightly martial tune on her qanun. Before the landing, Lotus had discussed the need for a certain amount of pomp and ceremony in their initial meeting with representatives of the colony. For that reason, Zahara was dressed in her finest silver and black jumpsuit, looking very much a leader. The others, all wearing Farr colors, formed a semicircle, with Lotus at her right side and Jazz at her left.

Bailey took a place behind her, feeling a little out of place. The others were all of a height; they looked good in their jumpsuits. In their company, he felt short and shabby; he did not belong.

The approaching dignitaries were dressed in what appeared, at first glance, to be jumpsuits in the Farr colors, identical to the ones that the sibs wore. But as the people came nearer, Bailey realized that their jumpsuits were made of natural fibers and dyed with natural dyes.

A woman was at the head of the group. Her blonde hair was cut in a crewcut; her face was decorated with tribal tattoos that looked strangely familiar. As Bailey studied her, he realized that the tattoos were identical to the ones on Violet's face. When the blonde woman stopped a few paces away from Zahara, Iris finished her tune, letting the qanun fall silent.

"Welcome," she called to Zahara. "My name is Levana and I am the Keeper of the Truth. We have come from the Great House to welcome you. We have been waiting for you for many years."

Levana had the high cheekbones and hazel eyes of a Farr, but her face was thin, not broad. She was not a sib of the clone, but she had Farr blood. Her face was bright with anticipation; her eyes shone with tears.

Zahara began to answer. Lotus had coached her on the appropriate language for this occasion—something high-blown and pompous. Bailey wasn't listening. Instead, he found his eyes drawn to the blue-eyed man who stood at Levana's right. Unlike Levana, he had not been moved to tears by their arrival. Rather, his eyes were wary and he studied the faces of the sibs, as cautious as any Farr.

"These are my council." Levana introduced the others. The man with the skeptical blue eyes was Piero. He was the one who had made the first contact with the sibs on the radio.

"Now you must come to the plaza," Levana said. "You must show the people you are here at last. It is a time for great rejoicing."

Bailey could see other people gathering at the far end of the landing strip, staring at the landing craft, at the sibs. Men and women dressed in robes woven of natural fibers were huddled together and staring at the sibs.

At a nod from Lotus, Zahara and the others followed Levana. At another signal from Lotus, the sibs began to sing a Farr marching song, a tune they had all learned as children.

> *All for one,*
> *And one for all.*
> *United we stand*
> *And divided we fall.*

The crowd parted before them and surged after them, following them along a trail through the jungle into the city.

It was a city of wood, built on a grand scale from the trunks of the jungle trees. The buildings seemed a part of the jungle, blending with the jungle that pressed so closely around them. Climbing vines wove their way up elaborately carved facades; low-lying creepers threatened to overwhelm flat-roofed lodges built low to the ground.

Bailey, following along at the end of the group, stared about him as they walked, not attempting to join in the song. He didn't like the open sky overhead. He felt more comfortable as soon as they stepped under the canopy of the trees. The branches and leaves overhead enclosed him like the hull of a ship, like the walls of the Restless Rest.

Piero walked beside Bailey. "You don't sing with the others," he said softly.

Bailey shook his head. He had been self-conscious

about his singing since the Trancer episode. "I don't sing at all."

"You're not a Farr. Who are you? Where are you from?"

"I'm Bailey Beldon. I'm a norbit from the Earth system. I came along to help Zahara."

"You came to help open the door into the moon and learn the secrets of the Old Ones."

"That's right."

"I only hope you will also take the time to teach us the secrets you already know." Bailey looked up at Piero, startled. The man smiled. "I would trade all the secrets of the Old Ones for a working star ship."

There was no more time for talk. As they walked through the city, the crowd grew. Some of the people who followed the sibs joined in their singing. A group of drummers added a percussion beat to the music—the hollow thumping of wooden drums. People were shouting and dancing and climbing trees and roofs to get a better look at the sibs.

At last they reached a spacious brick plaza. Here, the trees had been cut back, revealing the sky overhead. The sun had set and the sky was bright with stars: the brilliant blue giants so near to Indigo, the distant red giant with its flaming comet tail, and the great glowing disk that filled the sky, surrounding the blackness that was the Heart of the Galaxy. In the east, a full moon—the larger of the planet's two moons—hung above the trees. The smaller moon, half way past full, was high overhead. Where the line of shadow crossed the face of the small moon, Bailey could see a smudge of darkness and a gleam that might have been metal.

The facade of the building that faced onto the plaza was ornately carved. Torches had been lit, and Bailey studied the carvings in the flickering torch light. The light glinted on the wooden scales of a mighty flying creature, a dragon of some sort. Wings spread, the dragon was swooping downward. At the base of the building, carved people clustered around what could have been a laser cannon.

"It's the Boojum," Piero said, his lips close to Bailey's ear so that he could be heard over the drumming. "Legend says that it lives in the moon called the Bellman's Folly." He gestured to the moon overhead

Then Levana was leading them all up a winding wooden stairway to a balcony that overlooked the plaza. Levana was declaiming to the crowd below, shouting to be heard over their cheers. The sibs had stopped singing, but the drums still played. "They have come at last!" Levana was saying. "Our sisters from far away. They have come from the stars to open the door and bring us great wealth."

There was a great deal more about the wonders they would find inside the moon, about the wealth and glory that the Farr sibs would bring their sisters. At Levana's urging (and with a nod from Lotus), Zahara spoke. She didn't say much about what they planned to do, but spoke at length on their difficult journey, their adventures on the way, their joy on finding Violet's descendants. What she said didn't seem to matter. Everything was greeted with cheers.

That night, the sibs were housed in that building, which was known as the Great House. They had dinner in a comfortable room, warmed by a crackling fire in a great brick fireplace. The walls were hung with tapestries woven of fiber from jungle vines. Dinner was splendid— an assortment of tasty dishes in spicy sauces. Generally, they found themselves taken care of in a very satisfactory fashion.

But even after eating good food and drinking good wine Bailey couldn't seem to relax. He kept thinking of the carved dragon and what Piero had said about it.

"Legend says that it lives in the moon called the Bellman's Folly."

During dinner, Levana told Bailey and the sibs more about what had happened when Violet and her crew came to this planet called Indigo. As Levana told it, the story had the tone of a myth, a legend of divine events. She spoke with reverence.

Leaving out the references to the divine, Levana's basic story was this: Violet and her crew had noted the door in the smaller moon, the one that the colonists called Bellman's Folly. Violet had established a base beside the door and had tried to enter the door without success. Eventually, low on supplies, members of her crew had established a base on the planet Indigo. At that point, Violet had sent a message pod home, but had decided (with typical Farr stubbornness, Bailey thought) to try to force her way into the door. She tried explosives. After her first blast, the door opened and something unexpected came out.

"A monster came out of the moon. A Boojum, like the one that the poem foretold," Levana told them. "There were flames in the sky."

A monster, a dragon, an alien warship—it wasn't clear what it was, but something emerged from the moon. It blasted Violet's base, destroyed Violet's star ship, and flew over the base on Indigo, spouting flames and setting the jungle afire. The crew fought back with laser cannons taken from the ship. Then the monster returned to the moon, never to emerge again.

As Levana spoke, Bailey watched Piero. The others—Levana and her other disciples—seemed like true believers. They accepted this story of the past with the fervor of religious zealots, without thought, without question. They accepted Zahara and her sibs as saviors.

Piero was the sort of person that every religion needs but no religion likes. Thoughtful, rational, scientific. He asked questions and did not accept the easy answers on faith. He was the only one of the group who did not listen to Levana with rapt attention.

All this had happened some two hundred years ago. (During that same time, Zahara had been zipping around the galaxy at near light speed, a much shorter time had passed for her.)

After the visit from the Boojum, the crew members had rebuilt their base, creating Indigo Colony. Over the years, the colony had survived with much hard work. The colonists had made use of solar power for heating and electricity. They had not lost space travel entirely— the landing craft that had brought them to this spot was still functional; it could carry a group to orbit and back.

Piero had, in fact, piloted the craft to orbit and had returned safely. A successful test run, but there was no reason to go to orbit, no reason to leave the planet's surface. They had, Levana explained, no way to go any farther. The Hoshi drive had been destroyed with Violet's ship, and they lacked the technological capabilities to build another.

Levana explained that over the passing years, some had forgotten Violet's original quest. That was no longer important, these unbelievers said. But some faithful few remembered the truth, maintained the landing strip and the radio transmitter, watched for the ones that Violet had said would come. For two hundred years, they had been watching and listening and waiting. And now, they would be rewarded.

Later, after Levana had left them, Lotus interpreted the situation for Zahara and the others. "We are dealing with a group of religious fanatics. The other members of the colony have, quite reasonably, given up on Violet's quest, relegating it to the distant and legendary past. Why bother to believe in Violet when you have crops to plant, houses to build, a new civilization to create?

Believing in Violet doesn't contribute to day-to-day survival."

"Then why do Levana and her disciples believe?" Bailey asked.

"Basically, we're dealing with a cargo cult."

"What's that?" Zahara asked.

"The original cargo cult was a religious movement in Melanesia, a set of tropical islands on ancient Earth. The islands, which were inhabited by a technologically primitive culture, were colonized by a more technologically advanced group. Envious of the goods and technology of the newcomers, the islanders came to believe that some day a special cargo would arrive for them, brought by tribal divinities, cultural heroes, revered ancestors. To prepare the way for that cargo, the islanders built wharves and landing strips and warehouses, creating the symbols required for the divine cargo. By maintaining the landing strip and the radio, Levana and her group are serving a divine purpose. Don't think of it as science; think of it as religion. We aren't just visitors from Farr Station. We're divine."

Zahara nodded.

"They aren't all religious fanatics," Bailey said. "Piero, the blue-eyed man, doesn't trust us."

"You're right there," Lotus said. "But the others accept without question."

IT WAS DARK when they went to sleep and still dark when Levana and Piero came to wake them. On Indigo, a full day—from dawn to dawn—was seventy-two hours long. Since the human body was adapted to a twenty-four hour day, the Indigans had come to divide this lengthy day into three days of twenty-four hours each: Zada, the day of light; Una, the day of light and shadow; and Lisha, the day of darkness. They put these together to make a week of seventy-two hours. They talked of the light end of the week, a good time for beginnings, and the dark end of the week, a good time for completion.

That dark morning, the morning of Lisha, Levana took them on a tour of the Great House. Stranded on an alien planet, her ancestors had adapted to local conditions, preserving some elements of the technology that had brought them there, inventing their own culture, and generally making do.

The story of the Boojum's attack was, as Bailey had already observed, carved on the facade of the Great House. Levana talked of how the colonists reenacted that battle each year at the Festival of the Boojum Battle. The laser cannon, salvaged from Violet's ship, had been kept in working order for that occasion. In addition, the colonists had fireworks, which they blasted aloft through great cannons constructed from ironwood trees.

"For many, it was just another festival," Levana told the sibs, with a hint of bitterness in her voice. "Some said the Boojum was a myth, that Violet was a legend. Now they believe again."

Zahara asked about the ship's log, but of course that had been destroyed with the ship. In place of that, Levana showed them the story of Violet's journey to Indigo, painted on an elaborate mural that ran the length of the largest hall in the building.

The colonists had kept the radio working. And they had preserved Violet's original map, the one that Violet had duplicated in the message in holographic form. The map was, for Levana, a holy relic, but she willingly let the sibs examine it.

Zahara showed Levana the fragment from the Curator. The Keeper of the Truth watched with rapt attention as Zahara matched the fragment to the broken corner of the original map. It fit perfectly.

Later, Levana took them on a tour of the city, a sprawling metropolis overgrown by jungle. Each day, the colonists cut the vines and creepers back lest the vegetation strangle the buildings and make the paths among them impassable.

Bailey found Levana's relentless enthusiasm for the expedition a bit wearing. She acted as if they had already succeeded in entering the moon, as if they had already gained the maps they had come for and made their way safely home again. Bailey knew better.

He preferred the company of Piero. Levana was a believer. Piero was a doer. He had come to the Great House as a boy because he wanted to learn how things worked. He had learned to read so that he could read the old manuals. And now, he was in charge of keeping the ancient devices in working order. He kept the radio functioning, he serviced the laser cannon that was used in the colony's annual festival.

During the week that they stayed in the city on Indigo, Bailey made several trips to the radio room, where Piero contacted Fluffy for him. Bailey found it a comfort to talk to the construct, rather than the overly optimistic Farrs and the starry-eyed disciples of Levana.

Over the course of these conversations, Piero and Fluffy hit it off. This didn't surprise Bailey, since both had a reckless streak that he feared and admired.

"So has it rained on you yet?" Fluffy asked Bailey. She knew of his concern about the water that fell from the sky and shared it.

"Not yet," Bailey said. "With any luck, it won't." He looked at Piero. "I don't like the idea of water falling from the sky."

Piero shrugged. "It's not so bad. You can get used to it."

"Sure. You can get used to just about anything," Fluffy said in a skeptical tone. Doesn't mean it's a good idea. Hey, speaking of bad ideas, tell me about taking that landing craft into orbit."

Piero told her about his flight in the ancient craft.
Fluffy was amazed.

"You got some kind of death wish?" she asked.
"That's got to be one obsolete spacecraft."

"That's true," Piero agreed. "But it's the only spacecraft we've got."

"You've got me there," Fluffy said. "Well, if you ever
get up this way, I'll take you on a spin and you'll see
what a real machine can do."

"I'd like that."

After one of these talks, Piero said, "I think that you
are an honest man, Bailey Beldon. And I enjoyed talking
with your friend Fluffy. But I must say that I question
the wisdom of your endeavor. There are those who say
that the Boojum will come from the moon and destroy
you. That would be all right, but the Boojum may destroy us as well."

Bailey nodded, unable to dispute this possibility.

"There are others who question the Farrs' willingness
to help a colony that is not made up of Farrs," Piero
went on. "Some of the stories that have come down to
us speak of the Farrs' selfishness and distrust of others."

Bailey nodded again. The Farrs were treating him
very well. They gave him full credit for the escape from
the pirates and the spiders; they all, even Lily, treated
him with respect. But he remembered their attitudes in
the past and noticed that none of them expressed any
concern for how their plans to enter the moon might
affect the jungle city that was welcoming them with such
hospitality. Zahara had mentioned the mixed nature of
the colony with a bit of surprise (and discomfort Bailey
thought). Of course, she had known that Violet's crew
was mixed, but somehow, she had expected the colony
to be dominated by Farrs. Not a logical expectation, but
an emotional one.

"It is possible that they will treat us fairly," Piero said

thoughtfully. "But it is also possible that they will not."

Though Bailey was warm and comfortable and well-fed in Indigo Colony, he was far from happy. He kept remembering the grim look of the blasted dome and the smudge of blackened rock around it. At night, he dreamed of the carved wooden Boojum on the facade of the Great House, swooping over the colony and burning the buildings. And he didn't sleep at all well.

11

Just the place for a Snark! I have said it twice:
That alone should encourage the crew.
Just the place for a Snark!—I have said it thrice!
What I tell you three times is true.

—"The Hunting of the Snark," Lewis Carroll

THEY LEFT INDIGO ON THE FIRST DAY OF THE WEEK OF THE LUN-
atics, a celebration of the lesser moon conducted by the
Society of Moon-Faced Men, one of the many Secret
Societies of Indigo Colony. Levana told Lotus that it was
an auspicious day to begin their endeavor, being Zada,
the Day of Light, in a week dedicated to the moon.

As the sibs walked from the Great House to the landing strip, drummers played intricate rhythms and people
sang. Bailey could not follow all the words—the lines
repeated in a complex pattern, tangling around one another so he couldn't make heads or tails of them. There
was something about Snarks and something about Boojums, but it made no sense to him at all.

When he asked Piero, who was walking at his side,
the Indigan said that the song provided instructions for
the hunting of Snarks.

"How's that?"

And Piero sang in a fierce baritone:

"You may seek it with thimbles—and seek it with care;
You may hunt it with forks and hope;

You may threaten its life with a railway share;
You may charm it with smiles and soap."

Bailey frowned at Piero. "I don't know if all that applies to this Snark."

"Perhaps not. Except, perhaps, for the line about seeking it with care. That seems like advice that Violet could have used."

Bailey nodded. "It seems like good advice."

As the drums played, they took off in the landing craft, leaving the people of Indigo behind. They returned to the *Odyssey*, then headed for the moon that the people of Indigo called the Bellman's Folly.

"Not very big, is it?" Zahara commented as they orbited the moon.

Bailey peered at the small satellite as they orbited. It seemed quite large to him, much bigger than the Restless Rest and other asteroids. About the size of Phobos, the smaller of the Martian moons. He had visited Phobos when he was a young norbit, and it had seemed terribly large to him.

Staring down at the moon's surface, he could see the metal door he had glimpsed on their way in. Surrounding the door, he could see the ruined remains of Violet's camp.

"All right. It's time to get to work." Zahara was enthusiastic.

With the *Odyssey* on autopilot in orbit around the Bellman's Folly and Fluffy keeping watch, they took the landing craft down to the surface of the moon. They landed beside the remains of Violet's camp. Despite the passage of years, the devastation by the Boojum was unmistakable: a great black mark sliced across the dome site, the blast mark where the Boojum had cut the dome in two.

In the center of the ruined camp, they found the doorway. A round piece of metal, about the size of a manhole cover, was set into the hard basalt of the moon's surface. The fine lunar dust that covered everything had settled on the metal and the surrounding stone. Zahara brushed it away with a gloved hand.

On one side of the circular plate, the rock had been blown away, leaving a crater. The result of Violet's impatience, Bailey thought. He shook his head, looking at the crater. He didn't approve of Violet's strategy.

And of course, it hadn't worked. The explosion had removed five feet of rock, revealing that the metal plate capped a tube constructed of the same metal. The tube extended into the moon and out of sight.

In the center of the metal plate, undisturbed by the violence of the explosion, was a panel of twelve buttons, each one marked with one of the alien numerals. Below the buttons was a handle.

While the group was gathering, Zahara pulled on the handle. "It's solid," she said. "Not a bit of give." She stared at the door for a moment, then turned away. "Let's set up camp. Then we can get to work on this."

They labored in space suits to raise a bubble camp, a set of inflated plastic domes that would serve as temporary living and working quarters in the airless environment. Norbits often used bubble camps when setting up mining stations. Bailey had been constructing these domes since he was a lad. Since the Farr sibs had little experience with bubble camps, Bailey became the default supervisor on the construction of the camp.

Bailey's experience on asteroids also made him the best among them at taking advantage of the low-gravity environment. The trick to running in low gravity is to stay low to the ground, pushing forward rather than up, and moving in long, low bounds. The sibs tended to push upward, so that they wasted a lot of time going up and coming down, rather than moving forward. Many times during the construction, Bailey sighed as he watched one of the sibs take twice as long to fetch a tool as it would have taken any norbit he knew.

Their first task was to clear away the remains of the plastic domes of Violet's camp. When Bailey and the sibs tried to roll up the great plastic sheets, they crumbled instead of rolling. Over the years, meteors the size of grains of dust had been raining down, tearing microscopic holes in the plastic. Intense ultraviolet radiation from the brilliant blue star had weakened the chemical bonds that held the material intact. The sibs had to gather fragments of plastic into awkward bundles and carry them outside the site.

It was during this process that Poppy found the remains of Violet's expedition. "I've found them." Her voice on the radio had an hysterical edge. "I found Violet and the others."

In an area that had once been covered by the dome were the remains of five sleeping cots and five bodies. Two of the bodies were still on their beds; the others had fallen nearby. By the look of it, there had been just enough warning to wake them, but not enough to save them.

On the airless moon, the bodies had not decomposed. Rather, they had mummified: flesh drying tight to bones; skin contracting to hard leather. Moon dust had covered them, a fine powder that colored them a uniform gray. The tumbled bodies did not look human now; they were display mannequins, artist's props. Bailey looked away from their grimacing faces, telling himself that their expressions were the product of drying skin pulling taut, not indicative of the agony in which they died.

"Violet," Zahara said softly, kneeling by one of the fallen bodies. She reached out and took Violet's withered hand. As she did so, something fell into the dust.

Zahara picked up the object that had been in her

daughter's hand and held it out on the palm of her glove, for everyone to see. It was a piece of burnished metal in the shape of an arrow, about the length of Zahara's palm. The head of the arrow was etched with the spiral that signified zero in the numbering system of the Old Ones.

"An artifact of the Old Ones," Lotus murmured.

Zahara slipped the arrow into a pouch at the belt of her suit. Bailey could not see her face; the starlight reflected off her face plate. But her voice was soft as it crackled over Bailey's suit radio. "We'll take the bodies with us when we go, and release them in deep space. No Farr wants to remain bound by gravity in death." The others were silent. "Now let's get back to work."

When the remains of Violet's domes finally had been cleared away, Bailey and the sibs laid out the domes for the new camp on the same site. They worked steadily: sealing the edges of the domes to the lunar rock, installing the anti-meteor screen, inflating the domes. Finally, weary and subdued, they entered through the air lock and removed their helmets.

"And now we'll open that alien door, move into the alien base, and all our work will have been wasted," Lily said, running her hand through her crest of red hair. Damp with sweat, it stood on end. From the start, Lily had argued against setting up a camp, confident that they would quickly open the alien door.

Zahara shrugged. "Even if we open the door, we'll need a base while we analyze our find. Let it go." She looked around at the group. "I'm going to the door now. If you want to join me, keep your suit on. We have no idea what atmosphere might be inside."

Though everyone was tired, they all put their helmets back on and joined Zahara around the metal plate. The dome over the alien door was separated from the others by airlocks and tunnels, so that any atmosphere in the alien base would not contaminate their living quarters.

"It's a beautiful piece of work," Jazz said. "It's a shame Violet tried to blow it loose."

"Violet was not a patient woman," Zahara said. She knelt by the door. While the others watched, Zahara carefully punched in the sequence of glyphs from the Curator's crystal fragment into the control panel. Each time she pushed a button, the panel emitted a pure musical tone, barely audible through Bailey's helmet. She punched the last glyph, the pair of arrows, and stopped, staring at the metal plate intently. No one spoke. Bailey listened for a sound that might indicate some response to the numbers. He could hear only the hiss of his suit's air conditioning system.

Zahara grasped the handle and pulled hard. The door remained stubbornly in place.

That was the beginning of a long and frustrating time. Zahara tried punching in the numbers again, with the same result. The others made suggestions. Try reversing the order of the numbers. Try punching each one twice. Try this and try that. No success.

Finally, Zahara gave up and Lily gave it a try, then Lotus. Gradually, one by one, each sib tried and gave up. Jazz wandered off to set up sleeping quarters in another dome; Poppy, to set up a galley and make dinner.

"Let's sleep on it," Zahara said at last, pulling off her helmet. The sun had set and the lunar night had begun. Everyone had switched on their head lamps, illuminating the door in their golden beams. When he pulled off his helmet, Bailey could see the stars shining steadily through the clear plastic of the dome. "In the morning, maybe we'll think of something new."

Weary and discouraged, they went and ate dinner. After dinner, when the others were going to bed, Bailey was still restless. Unwilling to get involved in the sibs' quarrels, he had not yet punched a single number on the door. "I'll stay up a bit," he said.

Iris, Lily, Poppy, Heather, and Zahara went to bed. Jazz and Lotus stayed up with Bailey. When he said he wanted to take another look at the door, they went with him. They sat on the cold rocky surface together, staring at the panel. They had their helmets with them, but had not put them on.

"Remember the pattern you found in the numbers," Lotus said quietly to Bailey. "I wonder if that could help somehow."

"What did you find?" Jazz asked.

Bailey shrugged. "Well, I noticed one thing. If you put those six numbers into base ten, you get this series." Using his finger, he wrote these numbers in the dust that had settled on the metal door. "1, 1, 2, 3, 5, 8, 13. Add two numbers in the sequence together, and you get the next number in the series. One and one makes two; one and two makes three, and so on up to thirteen."

Jazz leaned forward, studying the numbers in the dust. "So the next number in the series would be eight and thirteen, which is twenty one."

"That's right."

Lotus nodded, looking at the series of numbers in the dust, then looking back at the alien hieroglyphs, which Zahara had copied from the crystal fragment and left by the door. The last glyph was two arrows, pointing onward. "You know, that last symbol looks like it's telling us to keep going."

"Sure," Jazz said. "We could do that. Add thirteen to twenty-one and you get 34. . . ." She mumbled to herself as she wrote more numbers in the dust. "21, 34, 55, 89, 144 . . ."

"Wait a second," Lotus said. "Stop there."

Jazz stopped, looking at the numbers she had written.

"We had seven numbers. Now we have twelve," Lotus

said. "The Old Ones operated in base twelve."

"Maybe we need to punch in all twelve numbers," Bailey said, excited now. "Let's translate them into the alien glyphs."

Jazz leaned over the series of numbers she had written. "Twenty-one is one twelve with nine left over, so in base twelve that would be nineteen." She consulted the list of alien glyphs. "In alien glyphs, that would be:

Thirty-four would be:

She kept going until she got to the last number in the sequence: 144. "That's twelve times twelve. So in base twelve, that would be one hundred. In the Old Ones' glyphs, that would be this." In the dust, she wrote:

"Let's try it," Bailey said. They put on their helmets and Bailey punched in the series of numbers. He tugged on the door, but nothing happened.

Taking her helmet off, Lotus shook her head wearily. "Good try," she said. "But no luck. I'm done for the night. Maybe we can think of something else to try in the morning."

She and Jazz clambered to their feet, but Bailey remained where he was. "I just want to sit here and think for a while," he said.

"Don't stay up too late," Jazz said, briefly resting a hand on his shoulder.

"I won't."

When he heard the air lock close behind them, he lay back on the ground and looked out through the clear plastic at the cold blue stars that surrounded them. Such alien stars. He wished, not for the first time, that he could sit in his solarium, just for a moment, and admire the view of the constellations that he knew and loved. He shook his head, thinking about his conversations with Heather and Poppy about the passage of time. Back home, one hundred fifty years had passed during the time he'd been traveling. So much could have happened to the Restless Rest in that time. Rationally, he knew that some other norbit was probably living there now. He knew that all his friends and relations would be dead by the time he returned. He knew that.

But he didn't believe it. In his mind, the Restless Rest was just as he had left it, with fresh fig bread in the cupboard and his best parlor still cluttered with the dishes and wine glasses from that last party with Gitana and the Farr sibs. Try as he might, he could not imagine it any other way.

He had reached a turning point and the Restless Rest was behind him. Every point is a turning point, he thought, wondering where Gyro Renacus was right now. Weary from the long day, he drowsed and stared at the stars. Gyro was out there somewhere, drawing spirals and translating bits of text from obscure Earth languages. *"Eadem mutata resurgo.* Though changed, I arise again the same."

Bailey shook his head, thinking about what that meant. Changed, yet the same. You go around the spiral and end up back where you started.

His eyes were closing. He knew he had to get up and go to bed, but he was so tired that he could sleep right where he was. Fall asleep by the alien gateway, thinking of pataphysical spirals that somehow returned to the point from which they had started, thinking of the alien numbers that seemed, at that moment, so expressive. Of course, the two arrows meant keep on going.

He thought about the last number in the series they had calculated: an arrow pointing forward followed by two spirals. In his drowsy state, as he imagined the spiral started to uncoil and the uncoiling end slithered like a snake to attach itself to the beginning of the arrow. The spiral, he thought, takes you back to where you began.

He blinked, still half asleep, and propped himself up on his elbow to stare at the figures that Jazz had made in the dust, especially at the last glyph, the one that meant 144. The spiral lead you back to the beginning, he thought sleepily.

Sitting up suddenly, he stared at the sequence. Could that be it? Go back to the beginning? Quickly, he pulled on his helmet and began punching the alien numbers, completing the sequence once, then returning to the start and completing it again. As he was punching in the second spiral of the final glyph, he realized that one repetition was not enough. There were, after all, two spirals. He punched in the entire sequence again.

Finally, he placed both hands on the handle. When he pushed it down, it slid easily. When he tugged on the handle, the door opened and Bailey gazed down a long tube that led into an alien world.

12

→ ◉

I engage with the Snark—every night after dark—
In a dreamy delerious fight:
I serve it with greens in those shadowy scenes,
And I use it for striking a light. . . .

—"The Hunting of the Snark,"
Lewis Carroll

SUDDENLY, HE WASN'T AT ALL SLEEPY. HE TAPPED THE WRIST
control that commanded his suit to analyze the air coming from the moon's interior, and as chemical sensors
processed the air, he stared down into the tube.

It led straight down, its smooth sides studded with bars
that looked like ladder rungs. The walls of the tube
glowed with a pale golden light that reminded Bailey of
the light of Sol. Such a warm and inviting radiance.

His suit chimed the all-clear signal, indicating that the
air in the tube was safe for him to breathe. He took off
his helmet. After a moment's hesitation, he took off his
suit. Dressed only in his jumpsuit, he could feel the
golden light on his hands and face, warming him. He
felt so much happier.

He knew that he should wake the others. But he
didn't. For most of the day, he had been listening to the
sibs squabble amongst themselves—about how to put up
the domes, about what numbers to punch into the panel,
about what to make for dinner. At times, he had felt
almost invisible. Now here he was, with an alien world
open to him. He wanted to savor this for a moment,

before waking the others and starting a new set of discussions about what to do and how to do it.

He slid the Moebius band onto his wrist—just in case he had to make a quick exit. Then he swung his legs over the lip of the hole and got his feet onto one of the rungs. It was a narrow tube, but not too narrow for a norbit who was used to small spaces. He'd only go a little way, he told himself. He just wanted to explore a little before the place was filled with the sibs and their noise. The golden light invited him in, and he accepted the invitation.

He had, for the moment, forgotten Gitana's advice: "Some things that look innocent are really quite dangerous." The golden light looked quite innocent, but the Curator, had she been there, might have reminded him of the sphere that had caught Lotus. She might have advised him that some artifacts of the Old Ones could mesmerize a person, lulling him into a very suggestible state.

Bailey climbed downward, smiling as he went. The rungs were warm in his hands and they seemed perfectly suited to his grip. In the light gravity, it felt as if he could climb forever.

His feet touched down on a smooth surface. High above him, the gateway was a circle of pale blue star light in the center of a field of golden light. It looked cold, uninviting. The tunnel that led away from the ladder was hewn from the lunar rock, but the floor was the same smooth, glowing material as the walls of the tube. He could feel the floor humming faintly beneath his feet, and he thought that it would be pleasant to stroll on that floor for a time.

Without thinking, he placed his right hand on the wall—a habit he had acquired as a child when exploring mining tunnels. "When you go off exploring tunnels that wind and twist, put your hand on one wall and never lift it off," his old uncle Cuffy had told him. "To retrace your steps, just turn around to face the other direction and put the other hand on the wall."

A very old habit, and Bailey did it without thinking—which was just as well, because he wasn't thinking much anymore. He was mesmerized by the light, and it seemed a pleasant thing to go strolling in a labyrinth of alien construction, his right hand running over smooth rock, polished by some alien drilling machine. He didn't have a destination in mind. He just kept his hand on the wall and kept walking, his footsteps sounding a steady rhythm that got into his head, along with the humming of the floor. The two blended to make a tune in his head, a familiar tune, and he found himself humming as he walked. The tune that he hummed was the Trancer's song and that was, in the end, what saved him.

The alien light sent him into a deep reverie. He was strolling along, admiring the light, when he found himself walking through a cavernous room, illuminated only by glowing golden lines that floated in the air around him.

"I've been here before," he thought. "When was that?"

He heard a familiar voice, whispering something he couldn't quite understand. And that seemed familiar, too.

"Who are you?" he said to the voice.

He felt the tickle of curiosity, not his own, but a feeling coming from outside him. "?" The symbol of a question mark came through clearly. Who? Then a series of sensations. He caught of whiff of musty air, like the smell of a room that has been closed off for many years. Closed off, stored away, left alone. His tongue tingled with the taste of an ancient wine that he remembered having at his great uncle's home. His uncle was ancient; the wine was old, very, very old. Under his fingers, the texture of the wall seemed to change to a slick metal surface: cold and smooth beneath his hand, and he imagined that he felt something ticking away inside it, a clicking like the turning of gears. Not a living entity, he thought. A machine. A very old machine that has been locked away for many years. An intelligent machine made by the Old Ones.

"Yes." The affirmation was so clear that he heard it as a word, spoken in his ear. An artificial intelligence that had been trying to communicate with him for some time. He remembered now why the room seemed familiar. He had visited it in his dreams each time the ship had traveled through a wormhole.

He could be dreaming now. He could be wandering the corridors of an alien base and dreaming alien dreams, caught, just as Lotus had been caught by the sphere at the Curator's.

He thought about this for a moment, then focused on the steady rhythm of his feet, taking step after step. The rhythm of his footsteps seemed to tap into a deeper rhythm. He followed that deeper rhythm and found the rhythm of the Trancer tune that he was still humming under his breath.

He blinked and found that he was not in a room with golden lights. He was strolling down the alien corridor, going deeper into the alien base. He stopped right where he was, blinking and shaking his head like a sleepwalker who has just woken up.

The corridor stretched away from him, gradually curving. He could not see the end. Both walls of the corridor were lined with shelves and the shelves were packed with crystal cubes, like Violet's map.

His right hand was still on the wall and his fingertips felt a little chapped and sore from rubbing against the stone. He had no idea how far he had walked. Through the soles of his feet, he felt the steady humming in the floor. He felt an echo of that steady humming in the Moebius band on his wrist.

For a moment, he stood motionless, staring at the map nearest him. A transparent cube, like Violet's map, it rested on a shelf carved into the rock. Like the floor at his feet, it glowed with an internal light. He reached out and touched the crystal surface.

He lifted the cube from its rocky shelf and held it for a moment, staring into its crystalline depths at the bright points of light inside. Those stars could be part of the Milky Way galaxy or the Andromeda galaxy or some galaxy so far from him that no human had ever seen it. He was holding a piece of the universe in his hand. Gazing into the depths of the crystal, he understood Zahara's passion for this quest. So many unknown worlds to explore; so much to learn. A universe of possibilities.

He cradled the map in his right hand. Carefully, deliberately, he turned 180 degrees and put his left hand on the wall.

Then he felt something change. The corridor looked the same, but he felt chilled, as if a cold wind had just blown past him. A new voice spoke in his mind. It didn't speak in words. Rather, he sensed a communication coming from outside himself. He had a very strong impression that someone or something was asking him something like: "Where do you think you're going?" Or perhaps it was more forceful, more like: "Where the hell are you going? Stop right where you are."

The emotional overtone reminded Bailey of his great grandmother Brita. He knew somehow that this was someone who was accustomed to being obeyed without question.

He remained where he was, one hand on the wall, the other one holding the alien map. He had stopped humming the Trancer tune, but now he started again, humming in time with his footsteps.

"I'm going out," he said aloud. In his mind, he imagined himself climbing the ladder to the lunar surface, meeting the sibs on the outside. As he pictured this, he did his best to project a feeling of complete confidence. Of course he was leaving. Nothing could stop him.

Another communication came through, this one with a different emotional texture. The first voice, he thought. The voice from the room of golden lines. It felt a bit like his mother, when he had misbehaved. A sense of disappointment, the feeling that she had expected better of him. The disappointment seemed to be connected to his eagerness to leave. Translated into words, the gist of it might have been something like: "Do you really have to go so soon? You've just gotten here."

He managed to take another step. "I've had a lovely time," he said, just as if he were speaking to his mother. "But my friends will miss me soon. I really must be going."

This time the communication was quick and hot, with an edge of anger. Not a reproach, but a warning from the authoritarian voice. There will be trouble if you pursue this course.

He kept walking, still humming the Trancer tune. A question mark, this one from the first voice, the friendly voice. Who are you?

Bailey hesitated before answering. Who was he? Bailey Beldon was his name, but what sensations should accompany that name? Was he the norbit who saved the sibs from spiders and pirates or the norbit who would rather stay home and have a nice dinner? Was he the norbit who flew in space battles or the norbit who played games with his nephew? And what would an ancient alien artificial intelligence make of any of that?

He thought about the Restless Rest, and that was where his mind settled. He was the norbit who belonged at home. He imagined himself in the solarium, looking through the glass of the greenhouse into a riot of greenery, and sent out a feeling of peace and warmth and belonging. He felt the strength of that connection to his home, to his friends, to that place. That was who he was; that was where he belonged.

The strength of his image of home helped him take a step forward. That step led to another, and then another. As he walked steadily toward the ladder, his left hand always on the wall, he felt an echo of emotion from the first entity that had communicated with him. Homesick and sorrowful, wishing and yearning for the familiar, the commonplace, the everyday. He thought about talking to a friend on the radio, checking a mining station, tending the aquaculture farm in the Restless Rest. Such simple things, so ordinary, so commonplace.

His footsteps slowed, faltered. Some of that terrible sorrow was his and some came from outside, but he could not tell which was which. No matter where the feeling came from, it was overpowering. He almost stopped then, overcome with the burden of his homesickness, but he fought the feeling.

It was a very, very long walk to the ladder, and the yearning kept on tugging at him, drawing him back. As he walked, the feelings that pressed on him changed subtly: still sorrowful, he also felt the edge of hostility and bitterness. An angry sorrow followed him. But he didn't let it stop him.

He paused at the bottom of the ladder to figure out how he could keep the map yet have both hands free to climb. He unbuttoned the top of his jumpsuit and slipped the cube inside, where it rested against his belly, prevented from falling by the waistband. Without hesitation, still humming the Trancer tune, he began to climb.

Even in the low gravity, the climb seemed endless. His arms and legs were weary, heavy, and his head felt leaden. It took all his energy to keep on humming the Trancer's tune and continue climbing.

As he climbed, the emotions coming from outside him began to fade. Humming the tune became easier; climbing became easier. He still felt homesick, but the feelings were his own—bearable, familiar. He felt lighter, and he climbed faster.

"There he is!" Lotus' voice echoed down the tube. "He's coming up."

He heard the clamor of other voices, but he paid no attention to what they were saying, thinking only of his hands and feet on the ladder rungs. His heart was pounding and his legs were trembling. He wasn't humming the Trancer's tune anymore, but he kept repeating it in his mind, moving his hands and feet in time.

The sibs were standing around the gateway when he came popping from the tube like a jack-in-the-box, red-faced and panting. Lotus grabbed one shoulder and Jazz grabbed the other and they lifted him from the hole and laid him on the ground.

"Where have you been?" "How did you open . . . ?" "What have you got there?" "What's down there?" Bailey lay on his back, catching his breath and letting the questions wash over him without even trying to answer. He fumbled in his jumpsuit and pulled out the cube, then rested as the sibs passed it from hand to hand, exclaiming over it.

"I'll use my computer data base to determine whether this is a region of known space," Heather was saying to Zahara.

"Are you all right?" Jazz asked Bailey gently.

He nodded.

"Lotus and I were just about to go in after you," she said. He noticed a pack on the ground beside her. "We shouldn't have left you alone."

"How long was I gone?" His voice was hoarse. He realized that his throat was dry.

Jazz dug in her pack for a water bottle and gave it to him. He propped himself up on one elbow to drink, realizing at that moment how hungry he was, how dreadfully his legs ached.

"I don't know when you went down. But we left you here about twenty-four hours ago. We didn't realize you were gone until we woke up and came in here." She shook her head. "Why did you go down alone? Why didn't you wait for us?"

"Good question." Zahara had turned her attention from the cube to Bailey. "And what did you find there?"

Bailey took another sip of water, appreciating how cool and sweet it tasted. "Many maps," he said. "Too many to count. And a guardian . . ." He hesitated, considering how to describe the entity that had contacted him. "Two guardians. One friendly; one dangerous."

"What kind of guardians?" Zahara asked.

"One was curious," Bailey murmured. "The other was just waking up. It was angry."

"How do you know? Did it talk to you?"

"Not exactly." He struggled to a sitting position, and Jazz reached out and helped him. He took another sip of water, thinking hard about the guardians and how they had communicated with him. "I don't trust them. I think . . ."

He didn't finish his thought. Beneath them, the rock trembled and a low rumble echoed through Bailey's bones.

"Moonquake," Lotus said.

The trembling intensified, rattling the flexible plastic of the domes. Jazz helped Bailey scramble into the suit he had abandoned by the gateway. The others snapped their helmets into place. Bailey could not help thinking of the mummified bodies they had found, the agonized expressions on their dried leather faces.

"Can you feel it?" he asked, his voice trembling.

"The quake?" Jazz asked.

"No. The guardian." Still sensitive from his time in the tunnels, Bailey could feel the thoughts of an alien entity, a distant bellow of anger and confusion. Fully awake now, that entity, the hostile voice, was searching for the thief who had crept into its home and stolen a map.

The sibs looked around them, feeling some of the emotional blast. "What is it?" Poppy asked on the suit radio.

"The guardian. The Boojum." An image filled Bailey's mind: flickering flames and the sensation of heat, like a fire at his feet. The image grew clearer: a gout of fire raking across the bubble camp, the plastic bursting and blackening. Then another image: Indigo, seen from space, with the flames licked at the edge of the continent where the colony was.

"It's coming." His voice echoed inside his helmet. "It will destroy the camp. It will destroy Indigo. We have to warn them and get to safety. The only safe place is the tunnel."

Zahara hesitated, but only for a moment. She had seen the devastated camp; she, like Bailey, remembered the bodies of Violet's expedition. She gave orders: "Everyone suit up. Bailey, Jazz—warn the colonists. Poppy, Iris—bring as much food and water as you can carry. Lotus, Lily get the weapons. Let's move."

"What about Fluffy?" Bailey asked. There was no way they could take XF25 into the tunnel.

"Warn her to get clear," Zahara said. "Nothing else we can do."

As they moved, hurrying to accomplish as much as they could before fleeing to the safety of the tunnels, the moon shook beneath them. Jazz raised Fluffy on the radio and Bailey spoke to her. "You'd better clear out of here for now," he said. "The Boojum is awake."

"That's great," Fluffy said. "It's been kind of dull out here waiting for you guys. This should stir up some excitement."

"You need to put some distance between yourself and the Boojum," Bailey said. "It won't be safe around here for a while."

"I think safety is an overrated concept," Fluffy said. "Boring, if you ask me."

"Look, Fluffy . . ." Bailey started.

"We don't have time to argue," Jazz interrupted. "You have your orders, Fluffy."

Jazz raised Indigo colony on the radio and spoke to Piero. No time for a lengthy conversation. "We opened the door," Jazz said. "But the Boojum has awakened. Protect yourself however you can. Hurry."

And then they were all rushing back to the door, carrying the radio equipment with them. The moon shook beneath them. The thoughts of the alien entity grew stronger, a constant clamor in Bailey's mind, a roar of fury that made his hands tremble as he led the way down the tube into the heart of the moon.

"I'll leave the door open," said Lily, the last one into the tube. "We want to make sure we can get out."

"Please close it." Bailey could feel the alien entity coming closer, its wrath a heat that seared his consciousness. "We want to live long enough to get out."

"But if I close it . . ." Lily began.

"Close it." Zahara's tone brooked no disagreement.

Lily pulled the great metal door closed behind them. It snapped into place with a bang that echoed through the tube with a repetition that sounded ominously like "Doom. Doom. Doom." Bailey took a deep breath and kept climbing.

Just a moment later, the moon shook again and the air in the tube resonated with an explosion from above. Bailey's teeth rattled and he clung to a rung of the ladder, imagining the devastation above as the Boojum's flames raked the bubble camp. Though his arms and legs trembled with fatigue, he kept climbing downward.

It seemed to him that he had been doing nothing but climb for days and days. The tube still glowed with golden light, but its warmth did not comfort him as it had before. He was exhausted.

"How much farther do we have to go?" Lily called from above him. "I don't much like this tube."

"We have to go until we reach the bottom," Zahara called, answering for Bailey. "Save your breath for climbing."

Bailey continued descending for what seemed like forever. At last, his feet touched bottom. He tottered a few steps away from the ladder and sank to the floor, leaning against the tunnel wall. As the sibs reached the bottom, they gathered around the norbit.

"I think we could all use a bite to eat," Poppy said, sitting beside the norbit on the warm floor.

No one disagreed. Poppy opened her pack and brought out a ready-heat pack filled with tea and a handful of food sticks.

The hot tea and food revived Bailey enough to answer Zahara's questions about where they were and where they were going. He described how he had found his way to the chamber of the maps, described how he had felt the presence of the Boojum.

"You know," he said thoughtfully, "the Boojum is gone, but I think the other guardian is still here. Can you feel it?"

The presence he felt was not heavy and overpowering like that of the Boojum. Meeting the Boojum was like having a conversation with a large man who stood too close and had onions on his breath. This presence flitted about, never coming too near.

"Feel what?" Zahara said.

"Something nudging at your mind." Bailey struggled to describe the sensation. "Something coming from outside, but pushing on your mind."

The sibs fell silent as they tried to sense the feeling Bailey described. "I might be feeling something," Zahara said at last. "Something a little bit shy. Uncertain."

"That's it." Bailey nodded, glad to have his sense of the presence confirmed.

"So what do we do now?" Zahara looked to Bailey for suggestions.

Despite his fatigue, the norbit was cheerier than the Farrs. Norbits were used to tunnels and burrows and life in the heart of asteroids and moons. The Farrs were not: they liked to be on the move, exploring, looking out at the stars. To them, the tunnels were oppressive. To Bailey, they were alien but homey.

"We go on," he said. "You wanted maps—let's go get them."

He lead them through the winding tunnels, following the right hand wall as he had before. Lotus insisted on stopping at each intersection of tunnels to record the glyphs on the tunnel walls. The sibs talked as they walked, filling the tunnels with chatter.

As he walked, he tried to sense the presence he had detected earlier. Tuning out the sibs' chatter, he listened with his mind, extending his consciousness, reaching out as best he could. He could not feel the Boojum's presence at all, but he sensed something else, an entity that felt careful, contained, well-ordered.

He turned a corner and entered a corridor filled with maps. The sibs stopped, struck by the wealth of knowledge that the maps represented. "So many places to explore," Zahara said, her voice touched with awe. "So much to learn."

Zahara and the sibs wandered down the corridor, inspecting map after map. The corridor stretched on for miles, it seemed. Heather stopped counting when she reached a thousand maps, but with each turn of the corridor, she exclaimed again about how wonderful it was to have the universe open to them.

After walking for what felt like a mile, they came to a great circular room from which other corridors radiated. More corridors, each one filled with maps. The sibs continued to explore.

Bailey followed them, feeling overwhelmed. On his earlier visit, the Boojum's mental presence had oppressed him. Now that the Boojum was gone, he felt suffocated by the enormity of the place. So many crystal cubes, so many tunnels. He no longer felt lost—as they wandered, he was constructing a mental map of the place: a sort of spiral of corridors, reaching out from that central room. It was an amazing construction, but he had had enough of it. He kept thinking about the Boojum, wondering when the monster would return.

13

But oh, beamish nephew, beware of the day,
If your Snark be a Boojum! For then,
You will softly and suddenly vanish away,
And never be met with again!

—"The Hunting of the Snark,"
Lewis Carroll

WHEN BAILEY WAS CLIMBING THE LADDER TO RETURN TO THE moon's surface, something was stirring in the heart of the moon. A guardian, Bailey had called the entity that had touched his thoughts. The Boojum. An artificial intelligence with one job: protecting this storehouse of knowledge until its masters returned. An intelligent fighting machine that could make decisions, devise battle plans, observe a situation and modify its strategy in response.

When Bailey had opened the door, the Boojum had begun to wake up. Its sensors had detected Bailey as he climbed down the ladder and walked the corridors, minor tickling, barely enough to awaken the creature. Then Bailey had taken the cube from the shelf.

A thief was in the house. Still half-awake, the intelligence that was the Boojum had tried to stop him with a warning—but that was not enough. The thief had escaped with the precious map.

And now the Boojum was awake. On the far side of the moon, the side away from the planet Indigo, an enormous hatch creaked open. The rumblings of the ancient machinery sent tremors through the moon, the quakes that had sent Bailey and the others hurrying down the tube. For a moment, the moon had a gaping mouth, a dark and sinister smile from which anything might come. Then the Boojum emerged into the light.

Magnificent and terrifying, awesome in its chilly splendor—this was no stiff human-designed battle craft. The Boojum resembled an alien beast, a flying reptile with scaled wings and fearsome jaws. Its eyes glowed with pale blue fire. The scales on its body were iridescent in the light of the blue star, glittering in a rainbow of colors.

Before Violet had come, it had slept peacefully for thousands of years. Violet had roused it, but only for a little while. After destroying Violet's camp and ship, the Boojum had settled back down to sleep, conserving its energy and waiting patiently. Now, awake once again, the Boojum's sensors were active, reaching out into the world to detect signals that might indicate the source of the latest threat. It detected radio signals coming from the lunar surface and from the planet Indigo.

The Boojum took flight, launching itself from the moon and sending a tremor through that satellite. Flying low over the lunar surface, the Boojum blasted the bubble camp with a great burst of flames. As the domes collapsed, the monster turned toward Indigo.

In Indigo colony, a group of revelers were on their way home from the Feast of the Lunatics, the final event in the week-long celebration. It was the end of Indigo's three day week, late in the evening of Lisha, the dark day at the end of the week. One of the revelers, a Moon-Faced Man who had been drinking steadily since Zada, glanced up to see a red-gold flare in the dark portion of the crescent moon. "Fire on the moon," he called drunkenly. "Is that lucky, do you think?"

There was no time to discuss whether the flash of flame on the moon was a fortunate omen or not. At that moment, the fire siren shrieked. Its shrill note ripped through the sleepy chirping of insects in the night-time jungle, interrupted the merriment of the revelers, and cut short the dreams of solid citizens who had gone to bed at a reasonable hour. Set atop the fire house and operated by an enormous bellows, the fire siren was an gigantic wooden whistle used to call the people to help fight fires, a constant danger in the wooden city.

"Where's the fire?" An old woman in a nightshirt leaned out her window and shouted to the young man who was pumping the bellows. "I don't see a fire."

"The Boojum is coming!" he bellowed over the screech of the siren. "There's no fire yet, but there will be. The Boojum is coming! Members of the Battle Crew to your posts!"

"Witten! Wake up! They need the Battle Crew!" The old woman rapped her knuckles on the window next to hers. A sleepy, gray-haired man pushed aside the curtain and looked out. "The Boojum is coming, Witten! Get to your post!"

The old man was the Captain of the River Gun, the fireworks cannon at the northern edge of the city. Like all the members of the Battle Crew, he had been chosen by his Secret Society to operate the laser and fireworks cannons on the Festival of the Boojum Battle. Being a member of the Battle Crew was a position of great ceremonial honor.

He opened his window just long enough to take in the pandemonium in the street below. "The Boojum is coming!" the Moon-Faced Man shouted drunkenly. "Battle Crew! To your posts!"

"To your posts!" Witten shouted, and hurried to get dressed and get to his post.

Drunken people in the street and sleepy-eyed people peering from balconies took up the cry. "Battle Crew to your posts! The Boojum is coming!"

Several of the Moon-Faced Men who had been carousing in the street took off running, heading for the places that they had served in the last Battle.

A great roar of rockets joined the wailing of the siren. The crowd fell silent, watching as the ancient landing craft took off, leaving a trail of fire that sliced across the eastern sky.

Piero was at the controls. Following the radio call from Jazz, he had lost no time. He had immediately awakened Levana, who sounded the alarm to rouse the house.

She sent a group of disciples to move the sacred artifacts away from the Great House into the jungle where they would be safe if the Boojum burned the city. She sent others into the city to blow the fire siren, to organize fire crews, to prepare for battle.

While Levana prepared the ground defense, Piero headed for the landing strip with a team of friends to arrange for air defense in the only aircraft the colony had: the ancient landing craft. He had been preparing the landing craft for launch since the sibs' first communication, not knowing when or why it might be needed, but anticipating that he might go to the moon to join them. He had not anticipated a need as great as this.

Piero strapped himself into the cockpit, lowered the cockpit canopy, and watched his friends rush down the runway, setting flaming torches into the ground at five-meter intervals. To them, he looked heroic—a brave man prepared to do battle with an ancient enemy. But he didn't feel heroic. He felt a bit like a fool. He had no experience with aerial combat. He didn't know what he could do to prevent the Boojum from destroying his city. He only knew that he had to try.

As he accelerated down the runway, the flickering flames of the torches blurred together to become a line of red-gold light. Then he lifted off, heading upward into the darkness of the long night.

As a child, Piero had heard tales of the Boojum while sitting by the fire in the Great House. Over the centuries, the creature (for that is what it had become in legend— not a machine, but a living thing) had taken on mythic proportions, the ultimate bogeyman, the monster that lived in the moon.

Bailey had shaken his head when Piero had mentioned that some said the Boojum took the souls of the dead. "Zahara thinks it's a machine of some kind," Bailey had said.

Thinking of that now gave him heart. He understood machines. Unlike the mysterious forces that Levana dealt in, machines were predictable. You could break them; you could fix them. If it was a machine, he had a chance.

That's what he thought, until the moment he saw the Boojum itself. Emerging from its lair, the Boojum had been awesome. In flight, wings spread and eyes glowing, it was overwhelming. It dove past Piero's landing craft without hesitation, ignoring him, dismissing him as unimportant, no threat at all. The landing craft, which had always seemed so swift and maneuverable, felt slow and clumsy. The Boojum's glowing eyes were fixed on the lights of Indigo colony below.

Piero lost sight of the monster for a moment, then rolled the craft, forcing the clumsy lander into a maneuver it was never intended to execute. He initiated a downward loop to build airspeed, bringing him lower and closer to the speed of the Boojum. As he was leveling out, he caught a glimpse of the Boojum, still below, speeding upward toward him.

The Boojum had completed its first sweep over the city and was circling back. Beneath it, the jungle was ablaze. Flames leaping from the tallest trees illuminated the deep purple foliage with red-gold light. Below the canopy of leaves and flames, Piero knew the city was burning. The wooden buildings were crackling as the flames licked at the wooden carvings; people were shouting as they tried to douse the fire, choking on the smoke that billowed along the jungle paths.

As the Boojum swooped low again, the sky below Piero blazed with fireworks, futile bursts of glorious light. At the River Gun, Witten was overseeing a team of sweating Moon-Faced Men. "Fire!" he shouted. A brilliant blossom of golden fire exploded at the Boojum's head, causing the monster to change course. "Fire!" A starburst of blue and green and violet exploded to the Boojum's left. They were beautiful fireworks, intended to dazzle and delight, not destroy.

As Piero dove, trying to catch up with the monster, a laser beam sliced through the fireworks, a crimson sword running straight and true. It touched the Boojum, flickering over the monster's scales. But the touch was ever so brief: the monster dodged, evading the beam before it could do any harm.

Piero saw all this as he dove down to meet the Boojum. The words of the song of the Snark echoed through his head:

> *"But oh, beamish nephew, beware of the day,*
> *If your Snark be a Boojum! For then,*
> *You will softly and suddenly vanish away,*
> *And never be met with again!"*

For that was the threat of the Boojum. Not merely death, but elimination. You met the Boojum and you were erased, gone, disappeared. The colony would be erased from the surface of Indigo, just as the sibs had been eliminated from the surface of the moon.

He dove toward the monster. Though his ship had no weapons, he thought he might bring the Boojum down by crashing into it, a kamikaze maneuver that would destroy his ship but save the city.

As the landing craft sped downward, he caught a glimmer of light on metal out of the corner of his eye. Another ship—small and fast—flashed past him. "Hey, Piero! That you?" Fluffy's voice crackled on her radio. "What the hell are you doing up here? I think this calls for someone with a little more gunpower. Stay on my tail if you can."

Piero dove after the XF25, gaining air speed as he lost altitude. As they dove, Fluffy was talking fast, though Piero didn't understand half of what she was saying.

"Got a tally on that bandit at angels 16. Going to the merge with a high alpha. Target locked on. Firing."

Piero watched a missile leave the XF25 and dive toward the Boojum, as Fluffy rolled and turned. Piero managed to execute a slower, clumsier version of the maneuver in the landing craft. He ignored Fluffy's jabbering.

"Damn that bastard. He jinked out of plane. Clean miss. But I'm on him this time. Here we go!" Fluffy sounded cheerful, happy to be in the fight. "Stay out of the way, if you can!"

Piero leveled out and saw Fluffy completing another turn. Fireworks were exploding around the landing craft, rocking the air with their blasts. Below, a new fire—this one from Fluffy's missile—was blazing. Piero forced the landing craft into a climb, gaining altitude and putting some space between himself and the fireworks, gaining altitude that he could convert to air speed when he needed it.

The monster flashed past below him, with the XF25 in hot pursuit. Another missile shot away from the XF25, trailing smoke and fire. The Boojum dropped and turned.

Just then, a burst of crimson fire exploded right in

front of Piero, momentarily blinding him. The concussion rocked the landing craft. For a moment, he was aware only of his own craft, fighting for control in the smoky, turbulent air. Confused, disoriented, trying only to keep his craft aloft.

As the smoke cleared, Piero looked for the Boojum, the XF25. On the radio, Fluffy was talking steadily, using jargon Piero didn't understand, about angels and aspect angles. Below, he could see the flames of the burning city, the XF25, coming up fast, but no sign of the Boojum.

"Piero!" Fluffy's voice on the radio. "It's behind you. Shake him if you can."

The monster was behind him now, and closing. Shake him how? There was no escape. The Boojum had come from nowhere to pursue him, just as it had in the old tales. It had emerged from the dark smoke of the burning city, the instrument of chaos and confusion. It would return to the void from which it came, taking him with it.

As the Boojum closed the distance between them, Piero dove toward the city. If he was going to die, he would die while leading the monster into the guns of the city. He dove toward the River Gun, skimming just above the tops of the jungle trees, luring the monster down.

A blast of laser fire just missed him. The landing craft bucked and rocked in the turbulent air.

"I'm behind you, Piero." Fluffy's voice was jubilant. "I've got him in my sights."

IN THE CITY below, Levana clutched a hose, holding it high to spray the facade of the Great House with river water. Somewhere, beyond the smoke, the sun was rising. She had been working on the fire crew all night. Her arms ached but she would not relinquish the heavy hose. Behind her, the jungle burned with a fierce heat, singeing her hair, her exposed skin. The air was thick with smoke and her lungs labored for air. Her throat ached from breathing smoke, from shouting encouragement to the fire crews.

At that moment, a puff of wind momentarily cleared the air of smoke and steam. Levana looked up and saw the landing craft, high above the city, with the Boojum in pursuit.

Levana watched, frozen in place. The landing craft seemed so slow, and the Boojum was so swift, so relentless. But then, flying out of the smoke came a small fighter, tiny and fast.

Now the little fighter was behind the Boojum, closing in on it, so close that she thought for a moment that the two would collide. A fireworks rocket went up from the River Gun, exploding into a violet and silver starburst in the Boojum's path. At that same moment, there was a flash of flame, and a missile darted from the tiny fighter to hit the Boojum. The Boojum exploded in a burst of flame and smoke, and a moment later, the city rocked with the sound of the blast.

As burning wreckage of the Boojum tumbled down into the jungle, the landing craft rocked and plunged, struck by the concussion from the explosion. As Levana watched, the landing craft soared away from the debris and the smoke, circling back toward the landing strip.

WHEN THE SUN was high in the sky, the people of Indigo were still struggling to put out all the burning buildings—the ones set ablaze by the Boojum's fire and the ones struck by Fluffy's missiles. They fought the fires all through the Day of Light and half the Day of Light and Shadow. By sunset, they had quenched the last of the fires.

Piero had landed safely, first swinging out over the

jungle to find the place where the Boojum had fallen, then returning to the landing strip. He landed in time to help in the fire fighting effort. Though he was tired, he had rushed to the pumps and the buckets, throwing himself into the task with a frenzy. He carried water; he shouted encouragement until his voice was hoarse.

At last, as the sun was setting, he returned to the Great House, walking along the main path, through a blackened landscape that stank of ashes and river water. The fire had burned the jungle on either side of the path, sweeping through the underbrush and leaving the tallest trees scorched but intact. All along the way, families searched the smoldering ruins, weeping for those who had died, salvaging the few possessions that had survived the blaze.

Entire blocks had been destroyed by the flames. The Great House had survived the conflagration. Now it was crowded with refugees whose homes had not. So many homeless people, their faces weary and smudged with soot, came to the Great House where all were welcomed.

As Piero approached the Great House, he saw Levana sitting on the steps to the verandah, gazing out to the east, where the Bellman's Folly was rising over the burned trees. Levana looked weary, as well she should. Since the fire had been driven back from the Great House, she had been busy tending to the needs of the refugees, making beds in rooms that had once housed sacred artifacts.

Piero sat down beside her on the steps. Their past disagreements were unimportant now, insignificant beside the devastation that surrounded them.

"It looks so calm and peaceful," Piero said, staring at the moon. "It looks as if nothing has changed, as if nothing has happened."

"Yet so much has changed," Levana murmured. Her voice was hoarse from breathing smoke. "Now we live

without fear of the Boojum. We can build again, knowing we are safe from that threat. Thanks to you."

Piero studied his hands, blackened by soot. It had
done him good to fight the fires. That, he could do. He
had felt so helpless in the aerial battle, so inexperienced
and powerless. He could not accept Levana's praise.
"Thanks to Fluffy. Thanks to good fortune."

Thinking of Fluffy reminded him of Bailey. "I wonder," he said. "has anyone been listening to the radio?
Has there been a signal from Bailey and the others?"

"There's been no time for that," Levana said. "But I
think there's no doubt that the Boojum dealt with them
first. They disturbed the monster's rest and they were
the first to pay the price."

"They said they opened the door," Piero said. "That
means they got inside." Though he gazed at the burned
jungle and the rising moon, his thoughts were filled with
the wonders that might be inside the moon. His heart
burned with yearning for the secret knowledge of the
Old Ones, now unprotected. "I'm going to check the
radio."

Levana followed Piero into the Great House, through
corridors that stank of smoke, to the radio room, one of
the few rooms that remained free of refugees. As Levana
watched, Piero switched on the set. "Indigo Colony
transmitting," he said. "Do you read? Zahara? Bailey?
Indigo Colony transmitting."

A burst of static, then an unfamiliar voice answered
Piero's hail. "We read you, Indigo Colony. This is Gyro
Renacus, Vice Curator of the College of 'Pataphyics and
captain of the pataphysical research vessel, the *Ethernity*."

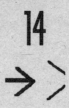

14

If it once becomes dark, there's no chance of a Snark—
We have hardly a minute to waste.

—"The Hunting of the Snark,"
Lewis Carroll

WHILE PIERO AND FLUFFY DID BATTLE WITH THE BOOJUM, ZAHARA
and the sibs explored the heart of the moon known as
Bellman's Folly. Bailey did not explore with the others.
Exhausted, he found a warm place in the circular room
in the center of the corridors of maps. There, he helped
himself to a ready-heat pack of cocoa from Poppy's pack,
grateful that he could remain still for a time. It seemed
to him that the adventure was, by all rights, over. They
had reached their destination. They had found the treasure that they sought. True, they still had the Boojum
to attend to. But fighting monsters surely wasn't his business (though, after all their adventures, it wasn't precisely
clear to him what his business was).

In any case, monster or no, he was done in. He lay
down on the warm floor of the circular room and pil-
lowed his head on Poppy's pack.

"Wake me at breakfast time," he murmured to Poppy,
before she and the others set off to explore the corridors
that radiated from the central room, leaving their helmets and packs with him.

As he drifted off to sleep, he felt something tickling at
the edges of his awareness. Not the Boojum, but that

other presence, the one that felt friendly. Then he sank into a deep sleep.

ZAHARA LED THE way at first, but after a time the sibs scattered, some falling behind, others rushing ahead. Their excited voices faded from Zahara's consciousness as she wandered like a sleepwalker, mesmerized by the cubes, by the golden light. She picked cubes off the shelves at random and stared in wonder at the patterns of stars and golden arrows.

So many maps, Zahara thought. So many worlds to explore. All her life she had lived in such a tiny space, extending just three hundred light years in all directions from Farr Station. She and all the Farrs had been constrained by the limits of the known wormholes.

But now the Universe was open to her. Map after map showed routes to the farthest reaches of the Galaxy, to places to which no human had ever traveled. She felt as if she had stepped from a tiny closet into the great wide world. If only Violet had lived to see this.

In this moment of triumph, she mourned for Violet. She sat on the floor of the corridor, staring at the shelves and shelves of maps. Thinking of Violet, she reached into the pouch at her belt and took out the alien device she had taken from her daughter's withered hand. A metal arrow, marked with a spiral on either side, about as long as her palm, a finger-width wide, and the thickness of her hand. It was a comfortable weight in her hand.

Artifacts of the Old Ones always made Zahara feel foolish, impatient, a little bit incompetent. They followed an alien logic, suited an alien purpose. Until she had seen Violet's map, none of them had made much sense to her. But Violet had died, clutching this arrow in her hand. It must be important. What did it do, Zahara wondered?

The spirals were slightly indented. When she pinched the arrow between her fingers, the ball of her thumb and the tip of her index finger fit neatly into the indentations. She squeezed gently—that seemed like the right thing to do—and the arrow came apart in her hand into two arrows, each half as thick as the original. She felt it vibrating, ever so slightly.

She lifted her head, listening. Was that a voice? Not a voice, exactly, but a sense of warmth, a feeling of collegial friendship, and a hint of a question. She felt as if someone had taken her hand and asked "How can I help you?"

"Who are you?" she said aloud, speaking to the presence in her mind.

Then she had the strangest sensation that something was rummaging among the images in her mind in search of the one it needed. She remembered an encounter that she hadn't thought of for a long, long time.

When Zahara was a child on Farr Station, she had won a writing competition. The goal was to write an adventure story, and Zahara had written about diving down an uncharted wormhole and bringing glory to her family.

As part of the prize, Zahara's story was placed in the Great Library, the repository of all the Farrs' knowledge. Zahara's teacher had taken her to the library and had introduced to the Librarian, a soft-spoken sib with a tendency to slouch.

At the mental touch of the alien entity, Zahara remembered that moment in the Library. The air was warm and it carried the Librarian's perfume, a light floral scent. The Librarian wore a comfortable sort of robe in a fabric patterned with flowers. "Hello, youngster," the Librarian had said. "I'm very pleased to meet you. We will be honored to include your story in the data banks."

At that moment, the Librarian's praise had warmed Zahara. She was proud of her work. She was certain it was good.

Now, in the alien corridors, she felt that glow of pride again. Throughout their journey, she had struggled to lead her sibs, wondering sometimes if she made the right choices. Now all doubts fell away. She was certain of herself.

The mental image of the Librarian grew clearer and brighter. That was her answer. She was speaking to the Librarian.

Zahara smiled. The Librarian was a reassuring presence. The Boojum was dangerous, but it seemed to her that the Librarian was there to help those who sought knowledge. How can I help you? No words, but the Librarian's message was clear. I want to help you. You deserve my help.

The pair of arrows hummed gently in Zahara's hand. She closed her fist around them and reached out to the Librarian. "What is this?" she asked. "What can it do?"

No words, but a mental image: she saw the dark sphere that marked the wormhole that had brought them to Indigo; she recognized the stars in the background. She was apparently in a ship, approaching the wormhole. That won't work, she thought, knowing that she could not approach the wormhole from this side. Wormholes go one way, and this was the wrong way.

Then the view shifted to her hand: she saw her hands holding the arrows and fitting them back together—not with arrowhead to arrowhead, as they had been arranged, but with the head of one arrow lining up with the tail of the other.

She looked up from her hands. Ahead of her, the dark sphere flickered and then she dove into the wormhole.

Violet's device could reverse a worm hole, making a two-way street where once there was a one-way street.

An incredibly valuable device, it would make her fortune at Farr Station.

A sense of pride swept over her. In that moment, she clearly imagined the glory that would be hers. Farr Station would shower honors on Zahara and her kin. There would be songs about Violet's quest, about Zahara's triumph; tales would be told of their adventures. Perhaps the wormhole that Heather had dubbed Zahara's Hope would be called Zahara's Triumph. Myra would give Zahara the respect she deserved. In Zahara's mind, the glory, the praise, the respect were already hers. They were hers by right, and no one could take them away.

WHILE ZAHARA WANDERED, Bailey slept and dreamed. He dreamed, as he had so often before, of the Restless Rest. In the dream, he was curled up in his own bed, thinking back on his adventures. How fortunate he was, he thought in the dream, that he had found his way back to his own place and time.

In the dream, he opened his eyes and got out of bed—and found himself in a cavernous room, surrounded by glowing golden lines. The Moebius band was on his wrist; he could feel it humming gently.

Here I am again, he thought. I'd rather be home.

He felt a wave of sympathy from outside himself. The alien entity, the one he thought of as friendly, was communicating again.

"Can't you just let me sleep?" he muttered, irritably. "If the only way I can go home is in my dreams, then leave me be and let me dream."

Again, the wave of sympathy and he felt the Moebius band growing warm. He had the sense that the entity was trying to call attention to the Moebius band. Carefully, he slipped it off his wrist. As he held it in his hand, he caught a glimpse of a flash of light through the loop of the band. Frowning, he held the band up and looked through the hole in the center of the band.

He saw the Restless Rest, floating against a backdrop of familiar constellations. He could see in through the solarium windows and it was just as he had left it. He could see his comfortable chair and the plants in the greenhouse.

"Home," the alien entity said, as clearly as it had ever said anything. "This will take you home."

BAILEY WOKE TO the excited voices of the sibs, all talking at once as usual. For a moment, he lay still, listening to the sibs talk of the treasure they had found. For a moment, he savored the feeling that he could go home. He did not know how, but he knew that he could. The Moebius band would make it possible.

He struggled to a sitting position, blinking and rubbing his eyes.

". . . found a route that leads to a Farr colony near Achernar. And another one that leads back here. We can send for help right away," Zahara was saying.

". . . found a route that connects the Fomalhaut system to Epsilon Indi via Groombridge," Lily was saying. "We could make a fortune by cutting our transportation costs."

". . . so much to learn about the culture that built this," Lotus was saying. "The glyphs are a beginning, but there is so much more. . . ."

Bailey shook his head. They talked as if the Boojum were already dead and the treasure won. "What about the Boojum?" he said loudly. "Haven't you forgotten about the Boojum? Maybe that's a minor matter for you, but it seems important to me. We've found the treasure, but we're not home free yet."

"That's true," Zahara said, nodding. "We are now the masters of the galaxy, but we still need to figure out what our next step should be."

Masters of the galaxy? Bailey wondered at that. Yes, the maps were important, but she seemed to be over-stating the case. She was smiling broadly, a rare expression for her.

"These maps are all very well, but you can't eat them," he said. "We need to find a way out, so we won't be caught napping when the Boojum returns. We need to get into radio contact with Fluffy."

"I found a passage that leads toward the surface," Jazz said. "Followed it for a little way, and it looks promising."

Zahara nodded, still smiling. She seemed distracted. "Let's check that out," she said. "We'll find a way to the surface and contact Fluffy."

JAZZ'S PASSAGE LED away from the corridors filled with maps. A long upward trudge, but that seemed a good sign. They were climbing toward the surface, and Bailey liked that. Sometimes, the passageway opened into rooms filled with strange instruments and softly glowing panels, but the group did not linger in those places. Caught by Bailey's urgency and concern about the Boojum, the sibs kept moving. Among them, only Zahara still seemed completely confident and cheerful: she talked merrily of all the wonders they would see when they used the maps to explore.

As she chattered, Bailey kept thinking of the Boojum. What would the monster do when it returned to find its home occupied? Bailey had no idea, but he really didn't want to find out.

At last, the winding passageway opened into a large room. Bailey looked up and saw a pale blue light shining dimly through a dusty gray filter. Squinting upward, Bailey realized that the ceiling of the room was thick glass, covered with a thin layer of lunar dust. He could see scratches and dings where tiny meteors had struck the window, could make out a few bright stars, shining dimly through the dust. Just a few stars, just a glimmer of reflected starlight from the planet called Indigo, but it cheered Bailey immensely.

Bailey and the sibs cautiously explored the cavernous room. At the far end of the room, a chamber that appeared to be an air lock seemed to exit to the moon's surface.

"Let's see whether we can raise Fluffy," Jazz said. She set up the radio and scanned the communications frequencies, searching for radio traffic.

"XF25 to *Odyssey* expedition. Do you read?" Fluffy's recorded voice, obviously on a continuous loop. "Please respond. XF25 to *Odyssey* expedition . . ."

"We read you, Fluffy. Jazz here."

A crackle of static, and Fluffy's voice again, live this time. "Finally! Where have you been?"

"Exploring the alien base inside the Bellman's Folly. Out of radio contact."

"Well, it's about time you showed up. You missed all the excitement. We shot down the Boojum."

"You shot it down? You destroyed it?"

"I certainly did. Piero helped, of course, but in that antiquated ship of his, he couldn't do much."

"You destroyed the Boojum!" Jazz was jubilant. "We're safe here. The maps are ours!"

All the sibs cheered and shouted Fluffy's praises. "Good flying, old girl!" "Amazing work! Excellent job!"

When they let Fluffy speak again, she described the battle in detail. Bailey listened, but he couldn't keep his mind on the intricacies of the aerial dogfight. With the destruction of the Boojum, it seemed to him that the adventure was really over. He was thinking about going home, and wondering how he might learn how the Moebius band would help him get there.

"Glad you finally got in touch," Fluffy said, after she

finished her description of her own heroics. "Things have been pretty lively. You see, Indigo Colony is certain the Boojum got you. That's what they told the pataphysicians, anyway."

"Pataphysicians?" Zahara's smile faded and her expression became grim. "What are they doing here?"

"Gyro and the Curator are here with the Pataphysical Research Expedition," Fluffy said. "I listened in when they were contacting Indigo Colony. Right now, they're assisting the colonists. But then they're planning to visit the alien base. I get the feeling they think it'll be easy pickings, being unprotected and all."

"Not so," Zahara said softly, her voice suddenly savage. "We are protecting it. It is ours." She spoke to herself and the words sent a chill down Bailey's spine.

"Yeah, well, they don't know that."

"The jackals are gathering." Zahara's her voice was sharp. "This is our treasure. We opened the gateway. It belongs to us and we will defend it."

"Against the pataphysicians?" Bailey said. "But surely they are not our enemies."

"Anyone who wishes to take our knowledge is an enemy," Zahara said. "That is clear. It is ours, and we are taking it back to Farr Station."

Bailey frowned. It wasn't clear to him. "Where's Gitana?" he asked. "If she's with the pataphysicians . . ."

"This is not Gitana's expedition," Zahara said. "She made that clear when she abandoned us at Ophir. The treasure belongs to the Farrs."

"I thought that I had an interest in it," Bailey said, hesitantly.

"Same here," Fluffy said over the radio.

"We will discuss that later. Now we must marshal all our resources to protect what is ours." Zahara's eyes were fierce. "There is no time to waste."

Bailey studied the faces of Zahara and the sibs. For

months he had been learning to notice the differences among them: the laugh lines around Poppy's eyes, the broken line of Jazz's nose, the thoughtfulness of Lotus's eyes. But now, the differences faded. He was struck once again by how much alike they were. All of them burned with a desire to possess the station and the knowledge it contained. They would not share it willingly.

In that moment, he felt very much alone. Among the friends with whom he had shared the adventures of many months, he was an outsider. The treasure belonged to the Farrs and he did not belong.

"Yes," Zahara said. "All this is ours by conquest and ours by right." Her gaze focused on Bailey. "The Moebius band," she said. "I think that may be an important weapon in protecting our treasure. Let me take that now."

Startled by her words and by the intensity of her stare, Bailey took a step back. "The band?" he stammered. "But that's mine."

Starlight reflected in Zahara's eyes. "We need all our resources to defend ourselves," she said. "That band belongs to the expedition."

Bailey shook his head. His hand was in his pocket, gripping the band. The band was his path home. He could not let go of it. "Why are you doing this?" he asked.

"As expedition leader, I require that all our resources be under my control," she said. "It's for the good of the company."

"I have already done a lot for the company," he said. "And I don't think you have the right to demand this."

"I don't have the right?" She glared at him and he remembered the ferocity of Myra's gaze; he remembered how small and alone he had felt, back in Farr Station. There, the other sibs had helped him.

He looked at the others. Identical eyes, watching him.

He was the outsider here. The sibs were family; he did not belong. Zahara's demand that he give up the band was unjust, but no one here would defend him. "No," Bailey said. As Zahara reached out to take his arm, he pushed the tab. Her movement slowed to a crawl and he stepped away.

The other sibs were frozen. Lily and Lotus and Iris were watching Zahara, their expressions neutral. No, he would get no help there. Poppy looked concerned; Jazz looked miserable. They were his friends, but their first loyalty was to their clone.

He was still wearing his suit and his tanks were still full of oxygen. At times, during the long trek underground, he had been sorry to have to carry them, but he was glad of them now.

He went to the airlock and stepped inside. He let the tab slip back to normal time as the airlock cycled, releasing him on the airless surface of the moon. Above him, he could see Fluffy.

"Fluffy," he called on the suit radio. "Can you hear me?"

"Loud and clear, little partner. What's going on?"

"Where are you, Bailey?" Zahara's voice cracked over his headphones. "What are you doing?"

"I'm leaving," Bailey said to both Zahara and Fluffy. "I'll jump into orbit. Will you pick me up?"

"You'll do what?" Fluffy asked. "Is this another idiotic norbit scheme?"

"When I was a kid, we used to jump off asteroids. This is about the size of Phobos, and I jumped off Phobos once. I'll go into orbit around Indigo. Just be ready to pick me up."

"Can do." Fluffy was cheerful as always.

"You can't leave." Zahara's voice was harsh.

"I think I can," Bailey said. "I have a piece of paper that says I take a share of the proceeds. I found this along the way, so I don't know if it counts as part of the proceeds, but I'll take it as my share."

"You are a thief. You are a disgrace to your family. You are betraying the company."

"I don't think so," Bailey repeated. As he spoke, he started running with long, low bounds toward the point on the moon's surface right below Indigo.

"I have to get to the sub-planetary point," Bailey said to Fluffy. "That's where the pull of Indigo is the strongest. That's where I can jump off."

He kept moving, traveling across the surface with great long leaps. Even if the sibs reached the surface, they could not overtake him. Running under low gravity, they would be clumsy, lacking the rhythm and ability that Bailey had built up over years of wandering on asteroids in the Belt.

"Why are you betraying us?" Zahara asked.

"I'm not betraying anyone."

"Small wonder Myra trusts so few," Zahara said, her voice bitter. "This is a hard lesson to learn."

Zahara continued to talk to him, raging over the radio, telling him that he was a traitor and a fool. He did his best not to listen, keeping the radio channel open so that he could contact Fluffy. He ignored Zahara's ravings as he leapt across the satellite's surface, covering twenty meters with each low, flat bound. He wished he could speak with Jazz or Poppy, wondering if they thought he was a traitor, too.

But there was no time for that. He was approaching the subplanetary point. "I'm on my way, Fluffy," he said.

The technique for jumping into orbit had been perfected by generations of norbit children, playing in the Asteroid Belt. Bailey hadn't tried it for decades, but the reflexes were still there. He remembered the last time he had done this—a drunken teenager romping across the surface of Phobos—and he knew exactly what to do.

Without hesitation, Bailey took a long, low leap that would carry him to the sub-planetary point. While in the air, he brought his back leg forward. When he struck the surface, both boots hit simultaneously, with his legs bent and ready to spring. He pushed off with all his might, hurling himself out away from the Bellman's Folly.

He was soaring toward the great orb of the planet Indigo. He remembered this too—the disconcerting sensation of vertigo as he spun free in the great void with a planet above him and a moon far below. In that moment, he was disconnected from everything, he had no attachments.

"Fluffy!" he called.

"May we never meet again, Bailey Beldon," Zahara snarled over the radio.

"Fluffy!" he called again. Already, he was leaving the Bellman's Folly behind. He was spinning slowly, a motion that had started with a slight unevenness in the push from his two boots. Now, he was looking down at the Bellman's Folly where he could see the tiny figures of the sibs bounding across the surface, their leaps carrying them too high to make good speed. Now, he was looking out into the blackness of the Heart of the Galaxy. Now, he was staring down at Indigo, where scraps of clouds drifted across a wine-dark sea.

If Fluffy did not find him, he would drift into orbit around Indigo, a tiny satellite endlessly circling the globe. The air in his suit would run out after a few hours. His suit's temperature regulation systems would fail and he would freeze.

"Fluffy! Where are you?"

"Coming right up, little partner." Fluffy's voice was comfortingly loud. "Matching your orbit."

He saw the XF25 now, as Fluffy blasted the jets once, giving the craft a gentle push toward him. As the ship drifted past, Bailey caught a hold of a tether hitch near the cockpit canopy and pulled himself in.

It was the work of a few minutes to find the canopy release, to strap himself into the pilot's seat, to close the canopy and fill the cockpit with air once again. He pulled off his helmet and leaned back, exhausted and despondent.

"Where to, little partner?" Fluffy said cheerfully.

"To the pataphysicians," Bailey said.

15

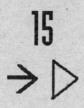

For the Snark's a peculiar creature, that won't
Be caught in a commonplace way.
Do all that you know, and try all that you don't:
Not a chance must be wasted today!

> —"The Hunting of the Snark,"
> Lewis Carroll

BLACKBEARD SMILED AND TOOK A SIP OF TEA FROM A WOODEN cup. Levana, Piero, and Hamilton, the mayor of Indigo Colony, were meeting with the pirate captain in the mayor's temporary office, a warehouse building that had survived the fires. They sat on a salvaged pillows that reeked of wood smoke and on rugs, thrown over the wooden floor.

Blackbeard sat cross-legged on a rug, his big hands resting on his knees. Even seated on the floor, Blackbeard loomed over the others. He knew very well that he cut an impressive figure.

He was wearing the full dress uniform of the Director General and Captain of Rogue's Harbor, a garment of his own design. A talented tailor on Rogue's Harbor had created the flamboyant garment, working from the Captain's description. A silver shirt with billowing sleeves; jet-black pants with crimson lightning bolts running down the sides; a crimson coat with polished platinum buttons, each one bearing the insignia of Rogue's Harbor: a grinning skull above crossed lightning bolts.

Blackbeard's presence filled the room; his voice echoed from the bare walls. "I hope that the little we have been able to provide will aid you in your reconstruction efforts."

When the pirates had arrived in the Indigo system, having tracked the *Odyssey* to its destination, Blackbeard contacted both Indigo Colony and the pataphysicians by radio and learned of the colony's destruction. The Captain was a pragmatic man, as well as a romantic. It seemed to him that it would be wise to befriend the people of Indigo Colony. He planned to exploit whatever it was the Farrs had found no matter what happened. But down the road, if his actions were questioned, it might be useful to have established a legitimate connection with the local planetary government. Besides, coming to the rescue of a primitive colony was such a glorious gesture.

So Blackbeard and several members of his crew came down from the battle cruiser, bringing food and medical supplies, supplementing the supplies that the pataphysicians had been able to spare. When the Captain landed, a work crew was building temporary quarters to accommodate the refugees. Blackbeard had shed his finery, pulled on a jumpsuit, and labored with the people of Indigo colony, assisting them in felling trees and constructing simple huts of forest logs. Though Blackbeard was not skilled in woodworking, he was a large and powerful man. He lifted logs it would have taken two men to carry. He laughed and sang as he worked, rallying the spirits of the people.

Now, after a hard day of work, he had washed in the river and gone to meet with Levana, Piero, and the mayor.

"Your assistance has been invaluable," Hamilton told the pirate. The mayor perched on a pillow, looking ill-at-ease. Blackbeard claimed he was a businessman, but he did not look or act like any businessman Hamilton had ever dealt with.

The mayor was a businessman himself. He ran a lumber mill and had been elected mayor because of his practical plans for city improvements. He was a member of Old Growth, one of the most respectable of Indigo's Secret Societies. Until the arrival of the Farr sibs, he had never believed that anyone from Farr Station would come to the colony's rescue. When the Farrs arrived, he had done his best to adapt to the changing circumstances. But events of the past few days had left him baffled and overwhelmed.

"So tell me what happened to Zahara and her sibs," Blackbeard rumbled. "As I understand it, they accepted your hospitality and then woke the guardian that came to destroy you."

"Well, yes. I'd say that was an accurate assessment," Hamilton agreed.

"It was not their intention to injure us." Levana stared up at the big man. She still felt a certain loyalty to the Farrs. "No doubt, they were the Boojum's first victims."

"Of course not." Blackbeard nodded genially and poured more tea in Levana's cup. "But their actions did bring devastation to your colony. I think it is reasonable for you to expect some compensation for that. What share were you promised in the wealth of the alien base?"

He watched the three colonists over the rim of his cup, confident that no promises had been made. The Farrs were not noted for their generosity.

"They made no specific promises," Levana said hesitantly.

"They promised nothing," Piero spoke quickly. "And even if they had, we would be in no position to hold them to their promises." The blue-eyed man met Blackbeard's gaze. "Just as we are in no position to hold you to any promises you might make."

Blackbeard nodded, regarding Piero with respect. A realist, this one. "There are ways that you could be helpful," Blackbeard said. "I could be quite generous if you told me, for example, what the Farrs expected to find in the alien base."

"Maps," Levana said. "Maps of the wormholes. Maps that would have put us in touch with the rest of the galaxy. That was all we wanted. That would have been enough."

Maps. The Captain's smile grew broader. Of course. The Farrs were searching for knowledge that would increase their hold on intragalactic navigation.

Blackbeard turned his gaze to the mayor. "If that base is filled with maps of the wormholes, it could be very very valuable. As a salvage expert, I'm just the person to exploit that value—and of course I would generously contribute to the rebuilding of your planet. I could, of course, begin salvage work without your permission, but I would much prefer working in cooperation with your colony."

"We could certainly use assistance in rebuilding," the mayor muttered.

"Of course you could. And it is only fair that you be compensated for your losses." Blackbeard's voice was soothing. "Well, with your permission, I'll go take a look and then we'll know what's there. What do you say?"

Levana looked vaguely troubled, but Piero leaned forward. "I think perhaps you need a representative of Indigo Colony along on this investigatory expedition. I would be more than happy to come along."

Blackbeard smiled at Piero, recognizing a fellow adventurer. "I would be delighted to have you aboard."

"That's a fine idea," the mayor said. Piero, like Blackbeard, made him nervous. "You take a look and let us know what's there. You certainly have my permission."

"Excellent," said Blackbeard. He clapped Piero on the shoulders. "Let's go!"

AT ABOUT THE same time that Blackbeard was making a deal with the mayor of Indigo Colony, Bailey was stepping out of the airlock onto the pataphysical research ship, the *Ethernity*. (The name, incidentally, is a blend of the words "ether" and "eternity," a symbolic blending of space and time.)

Gyro greeted the norbit with great enthusiasm, wrapping him in a warm embrace. "How wonderful you survived the Boojum's attack. The colonists on Indigo were certain you had all perished. Curator Murphy and I are delighted with your successful entry into the alien base."

Bailey shook his head wearily. "It's all gone so badly."

"Badly? I don't agree. Of course, the business with the Boojum was unfortunate, but other than that . . ."

"Zahara believes that you are here to steal the knowledge they have gained. She says I am a traitor for defending you. And she wants to take the Moebius band, and I can't let her have that." Bailey shook his head, downhearted and confused and frankly at the end of his rope. He did not know how to describe what had happened. "I don't know what to do."

Gyro put his arm around the norbit's shoulders. "Did I tell you when we talked on Farr Station that 'Pataphysics is the science of imaginary solutions?'"

"No."

"We must talk about that. But first, perhaps you would care for a shower, clean clothes, and a nice dinner."

Gyro provided Bailey with a clean jump suit with a silver pataphysical spiral over the breast pocket and showed him to a bath room where he indulged in the luxury of a long, hot bath for the first time since he had arrived at Indigo. It was wonderful to wash away the dust of the alien base, to be warm and clean and among friends. Then he thought of the sibs, huddled in the halls of the alien base, and felt bad that he was enjoying this without them.

Then Gyro took him to the Curator's quarters. The old woman took his hand and smiled. "First, we will eat," she told him. "And then you can tell us what has happened."

They dined on fresh-baked bread and a hearty stew, made with vegetables from the vessel's greenhouse. Over dessert, a sweet custard flavored with cinnamon and nutmeg, Bailey told them of the events of the past few days—from Zahara's discovery of the artifact in Violet's hand and Bailey's entry into the alien base to the unfortunate moment when Zahara demanded the Moebius band and Bailey had fled. He felt rather uncomfortable admitting that he had a Moebius band, since he had not revealed it to the Curator earlier, but she seemed unsurprised.

"And why didn't you give her the band?" Gyro inquired with a raised eyebrow.

"I found it myself when they had left me behind. And I think . . . I believe . . . that it can help me get home. Besides, I had an agreement with Zahara that I would get a share of the profits, and this is the only profit I really want." He hesitated, feeling embarrassed and uncomfortable.

"And you have kept it. So why aren't you happy?" the Curator asked gently.

"Perhaps I should have given it to her." Bailey looked down at his hands, wishing he were wiser, wishing he had been certain of the best course. "I don't know what's right."

"Ah," Gyro sighed. "There's the problem. You want to know what's right."

"What's wrong with that?" Bailey frowned at the pataphysician.

"Nothing is wrong with it, exactly," Gyro said slowly. "It's just that being 'right' is as difficult as seeking the 'truth.' And the idea of 'truth' is the most imaginary of solution of all."

"But you said that 'Pataphysics is the science of imaginary solutions."

"Of course. It certainly is." Gyro smiled at the norbit. "And imaginary solutions work quite well, as long as you realize that problems are also imaginary."

Bailey shook his head, frustrated. The problems felt quite real to him.

The Curator leaned forward in her chair. "Leaving all that aside, I have a question. Why do you think that the Moebius band will help you get home?"

Bailey shrugged uneasily, feeling rather foolish. A respectable norbit, he didn't usually pay much attention to dreams. "Just some dreams," he muttered. "When I was traveling down the wormholes, I kept dreaming of a room filled with golden lines. And there was this voice that I couldn't quite understand."

The Curator nodded sagely. "And when you reached the Bellman's Folly?" she asked.

"Inside the alien base, the dreams were more vivid. And I started to understand the voice. Not the words, but I could understand what it said." He described his communications with the guardians. "Even after the Boojum left, there was a presence in the station."

"Of course." The Curator nodded slowly. She clasped her hands beneath her chin and studied Bailey thoughtfully. "And this entity told you how to use the Moebius band to achieve your heart's desire."

Bailey nodded. "I can use it to get home."

"A helpful entity," the Curator said. She exchanged a look with Gyro. "The worst kind."

"Why is that bad?"

"What you want is not always what you should have," the Curator said. "Sometimes, it is better that your heart's desire remain out of reach. I think perhaps that Zahara would be better off without this entity's help."

Gyro nodded. "The seed of this misfortune was in her. The Farrs tend to be suspicious and a bit greedy. But it took the alien presence to make that tendency grow. There was nothing you could have done to forestall it." Now Gyro turned to the Curator. "She certainly won't be happy when she realizes that Blackbeard is here, too."

"The pirates?" Bailey was taken by surprise. "They're here?"

Gyro nodded. "Apparently Blackbeard followed the *Odyssey*, tracking the ship by means of Hoshi drive emissions in the space between wormholes. He's here and he is talking with Indigo colony about salvage rights."

Bailey nodded. "He held us captive for a while."

"I see. He told us that you were his guests for a time." Gyro nodded. "A slightly different perspective."

"So tell us," the Curator said. "How did you come to send that message pod to summon us here?"

Bailey shook his head. "I didn't send a message pod."

The Curator frowned. "I received a message pod telling me to come quickly. Zahara needed my help." She hesitated, studying Bailey's face. "I thought it came from you."

Bailey shook his head. "Not from me."

That night, Bailey slept aboard the pataphysicians' ship. For the first time in many days, he slept in a comfortable bed on clean sheets with no alien presence nearby, but even so, he did not sleep well. He kept dreaming he was back on Bellman's Folly, wandering the map-filled corridors and arguing with Zahara about his right to the Moebius band. When he woke up, he still felt tired and miserable.

*　　*　　*

BACK ON BELLMAN'S Folly, Zahara and the sibs were busy. Though Jazz and Poppy were unhappy about Zahara's demands of Bailey, feeling as he did that the Moebius band was his, they remained loyal to their leader. Under Zahara's command, the sibs prepared for attack as best they could.

Heather and Iris made their way out the airlock and across the lunar surface to the ruined camp. Remarkably, the landing craft had escaped destruction. The two sibs returned to the *Odyssey* and, at Zahara's command, dispatched a message pod through a nearby wormhole to the Farr colony near Achernar. The colony, which was located near a sector controlled by Resurrectionist forces, was well armed. In her message, Zahara described their situation, requested reinforcements, and provided a wormhole route that would bring ships from Achernar swiftly to Indigo.

Then Heather and Iris brought the *Odyssey* into the alien base, entering the base through the hatch that the Boojum had left open. There, a landing dock accommodated the ship. From the *Odyssey*, the sibs brought food and supplies, so that they were ready for a siege.

It was then that Blackbeard's ship came to orbit Bellman's Folly. Through the glass ceiling of the room that had become the sibs' headquarters, Zahara saw the battle cruiser.

"A Lupino battle cruiser?" She shook her head in amazement. "What are they doing here?"

She hailed the battle cruiser on the radio. "Attention," she said. "You have entered space that is under the control of the Farrs. What business have you here?"

When Blackbeard's voice responded, Zahara was startled and dismayed. "Hello, Zahara," the pirate boomed genially. "So you've survived after all. What a pleasant surprise! I come on behalf of the colonists on Indigo, who have suffered from the attack of the Boojum. I had thought to begin a salvage operation on their behalf."

"Indeed," Zahara replied. "Well, you are wasting your time here. We have claimed this base for Farr Station."

"What? You claim the base for yourselves, with no thought to the troubles of those who helped you on your way?"

"What concern is that of yours?" Zahara snapped. "We claim this base. When we have determined what we will do with the artifacts here, we may decide to assist Indigo Colony. That's our business, not yours."

"We are here in a humanitarian capacity," Blackbeard said smoothly. "Surely we can discuss a fair settlement for Indigo Colony. And perhaps a share to pay for your room and board on Rogue's Harbor."

"We will not help anyone who sends a battle cruiser to demand our assistance," Zahara snarled over the radio.

"I see." Blackbeard's voice remained jovial. " "Well, we will wait for a while and see if that situation changes."

Zahara switched off the channel and glared up through the glass ceiling at the battle cruiser, so angry and grim that the other sibs did not dare speak with her.

On the bridge of the battle cruiser, Blackbeard leaned back in his command chair and grinned at Red.

"So," she said, "shall we send the crew to roust them out?"

The Captain shook his head, still smiling. "That could be messy. They've had time to learn the ways of the alien base and set up an ambush or two. Why walk into that? We're in no rush. Let's wait a bit and give Zahara a chance to change her mind."

16

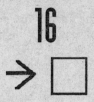

But if ever I meet with a Boojum, that day,
In a moment (of this I am sure),
I shall softly and suddenly vanish away—
And the notion I cannot endure.

—"The Hunting of the Snark,"
Lewis Carroll

FOR A TIME, THE BATTLE CRUISER REMAINED IN ORBIT OF BELL-
man's Folly. Bailey remained on the pataphysician's
ship.

Gyro and the Curator spoke with Zahara by radio, a
conversation that was unpleasant and unproductive. Bailey listened in without participating.

"Zahara! The Curator and I were delighted to learn
you had survived the Boojum's attack."

"We survived and we have occupied the alien base."
Zahara's voice was flat.

"I understand that," Gyro said. "But you have sealed
yourselves off there, as if you expect us to attack. Come
out. We are here in peace, in the spirit of investigation."

"Then why is there a battle cruiser lying in wait? We
have no friendship with Blackbeard and his crew of
scoundrels."

"Blackbeard has come to this place independently,"
Gyro said.

"He says he represents the colonists of Indigo. Is that
true?"

Gyro raised an eyebrow. "True? I can't say for certain. I know that he has offered aid to the people of Indigo Colony in their time of need."

"That is no business of mine." Zahara's voice was harsh. "If they wish to accept his assistance, that is their business. My business is here."

"And what business is that, Zahara?" the Curator said softly.

"Learning the ways of the Old Ones," Zahara replied. "Bringing our discovery home to Farr Station."

"But that's not something for a few people to accomplish alone." The Curator's voice was gentle. "That's something that we can help with, something we can all share in."

"No. This place is ours. Why would I trust you to share in it?"

"You don't trust me?" The Curator sounded surprised. "What causes your mistrust. Remember how I helped you along the way?"

"You helped us, and then you followed us here to demand that we share what my daughter Violet gave her life to discover."

"I have demanded nothing," the Curator said. Her voice was growing less gentle. "I followed because I received a message pod indicating that you needed assistance. Bailey says . . ."

"So the traitor has found his way to you," Zahara spoke bitterly. "I should have known that he would go running to you for comfort. So much for *jen chi*. Far from balancing our group, he has left us in disarray."

"The disarray is not his doing," the Curator said. "I suggest that you look in your heart for wisdom."

"I suggest that you leave this place and take your friends the pirates with you."

Gyro cut off contact and traded glances with the Curator. "She was arrogant and headstrong before," the Curator said. "Under the influence of the alien presence, she has lost sight of what wisdom she had."

Not long after that conversation, the pataphysicians spoke with Blackbeard by radio. Blackbeard invited them to come aboard the battle cruiser for dinner. "I prefer to meet in person when I can," he told Gyro. "You learn so much more about a person that way."

So Gyro, the Curator, and Bailey went aboard the battle cruiser and had a lovely dinner of Lupino cuisine. (It was prepared by a chef who had once served the Lupino Admiral, but had defected to the pirates. That, however, is another story.) Fortunately, they were in synch, all eating left-handed food.

Piero joined them. Bailey was very glad to see the colonist again.

"Tell me about the fight with the Boojum," Bailey asked him.

Piero grinned, looking happier than he ever had on Indigo, and shook his head. "Fluffy makes a better story of it. I barely knew what was going on."

Blackbeard clapped the young man on the shoulder. "Just taking off in that landing craft is a feat worth a story," the pirate said. "Actually trying to fight in it is the stuff of legend."

Throughout dinner, the pirate captain was jovial. "I've never met a pataphysician," he told Gyro. "None have passed through Rogue's Harbor. Do you folks have something against piracy?"

"Not at all." Gyro smiled amiably. "I believe piracy, like other criminal activities, is necessary to the social fabric. Crime interrupts the monotony of everyday life, protecting us all from stagnation and creating a restless tension that is an essential stimulus to productivity."

Blackbeard stared at the pataphysician. "You're joking."

Gyro shook his head, still smiling. "I would never joke. I think it's rude. I was actually paraphrasing an ancient philosopher of Earth, a man named Karl Marx."

"Protection from stagnation," the pirate repeated. "Creating a restless tension. I like that."

"Glad to be of service."

Blackbeard poured more wine for Gyro, then glanced at Bailey. Several times over the course of the meal, the pirate's gaze had lingered on the norbit. "Mr. Beldon, I'm just not sure how you fit into all this."

Bailey hadn't been saying much, content to eat and listen to the conversation around him. Though Blackbeard didn't know him at all, Bailey felt he knew the pirate captain rather well, having listened in on many of his conversations.

Bailey shrugged, taking another sip of wine. "I have an interest in the profits," he said, in a businesslike manner.

"I see." Blackbeard glanced at Piero. "My friend Piero says that you traveled with the Farrs, but you and I have never met. Where were you when the Farrs were enjoying my hospitality?"

"Around and about," Bailey said cryptically. Then he helped himself to another serving of dessert, some sort of fruit cake made with fruits he had never seen before. He rather enjoyed being mysterious.

Blackbeard studied him for a moment more, then shrugged. "Well, my interest in the matter is quite simple. I'd like a share of the spoils. That doesn't seem too much to ask. I would guess there is plenty to share. But that Zahara is one stiff-necked Farr to be sure."

Bailey had to agree with that.

After dinner, they wagered on Scrabble. Gyro won, of course, but the Captain was jovial about his losses. "Ah, never wager with a pataphysician," he said as they left. " 'Pataphysics is, after all, the ultimate weapon."

*　　*　　*

AFTER THAT, TIME weighed heavy on Bailey's hands. He was well-fed and he had a warm soft berth to sleep in. But despite his physical comforts, he was miserable. He kept thinking of the sibs in the alien base and wishing that he could think of a way out of this mess. Armed conflict seemed likely, and he had no heart for that.

Sometimes, he went flying with Fluffy, who was growing impatient with the lack of action.

"Maybe I should just start a fight," she said to Bailey. "Fire a missile across the pirate's bow. Just to see what they'd do."

"No," Bailey said. "Not a good idea."

"At least it would wake them up," she grumbled. "We could grow old and gray waiting for someone to do something."

"Maybe Zahara will come to her senses," Bailey suggested in a hopeless tone. "I suppose it's possible."

"Not likely," Fluffy said. "She's the most stubborn individual I've ever done business with."

Bailey refrained from pointing out that Fluffy was rather stubborn herself. He leaned back and stared morosely at the view in the viewscreen. The great battle cruiser lay in wait by Bellman's Folly. Beyond it was the blackness of the galactic center. He wished more than ever that he could just go home and leave all this confusion behind.

WHILE BAILEY WAS out with Fluffy, Gyro hailed the Curator, calling her to the bridge. "You'd best come here," Gyro said. "Looks like trouble on the way."

Gyro's chief radar officer had detected three ships coming from the direction of a previously unmapped wormhole. When the Curator reached the bridge, Gyro had initiated contact with the lead ship.

"Greetings and welcome," he said amiably to the grim-faced Farr sib who answered his hail. "Gyro Renacus here. Vice Curator of the College of 'Pataphyics, and head of the Pataphysical Research Expedition. With me is Curator Murphy, Satrap in charge of the College's Subcommission of Lost Missions and False Prophecies."

"Azami Farr, Commander of the Achernarian Fleet." She looked like an older version of Zahara. Her cheeks were marked with dueling scars; her eyes were fierce. "We have come from Achernar at the request of our sibs. What business have you here?"

Having received Zahara's request for assistance, the Achenar colony had sent reinforcements. To Zahara's aid, Azami led a fleet of three well-armed ships with battle-ready crews and fighter pilots seasoned by many a skirmish with Resurrectionist fighters.

Gyro shrugged. "There seems to be some confusion about that." He smiled at Azami. "Of course, as a pataphysician, I welcome confusion. You see . . ."

"What are you doing here?" Azami repeated, cutting Gyro off before he could launch into a discourse on the value of confusion. She had obviously dealt with pataphysicians before.

The Curator spoke up. "We are friends of your sibs, come to assist in deciphering their discovery. Zahara, the leader of the Farr expedition, has been influenced by an alien device and no longer recognizes us as friends. She is not herself. So we are waiting in the hope that she will change her mind."

"Friends?" Azami sounded amused. "And the battle cruiser? Is that manned by would-be friends as well?" Azami smiled grimly.

"Blackbeard, the Captain of the cruiser, declares himself to be a businessman and salvage expert. He claims to be representing the interests of Indigo Colony."

"Pirates," Azami said. "Well, we will soon see the end of them. I suggest you move on without delay. We respect our treaty with the College of 'Pataphysics, but I warn you that we will tolerate no interference with our business."

She turned her ships toward the waiting battle cruiser.

Meanwhile, Blackbeard had not been idle. As soon as his navigator had detected the approaching fleet, he had sounded the call to battle stations. Already, he had deployed a dozen fighters and had begun preparations for defending the battle cruiser. He had, of course, listened in on radio communication between Azami and Gyro and he was ready for Azami's call when it came.

"This is the *Achernar Dragon*, on course to Bellman's Folly. Yield way immediately."

Blackbeard studied the Farr commander on his viewscreen. "What's your hurry?"

Azami glared at him from the screen. "We are on a rescue mission at the request of our sibs. Any interference on your part will be considered an act of aggression, a threat to the safety of our mission, and therefore an act of war. Yield way and pull back or we will be forced to take offensive action against you."

On the bridge of the battle cruiser, Blackbeard grinned. If he let the Achernarians through, they would have the firepower to hold the station against all attack. So he wouldn't let them through.

He loved a good fight, especially when he was confident that he had the firepower to win. The Lupino fighters, piloted by battle-seasoned pirates, were circling wide to attack the Farr fleet from its flanks. The Farr ships had deployed fighters. Battle would soon be joined. Then Red spoke up from the chief radar officer's seat.

"Reinforcements from an unexpected quarter," she said. The viewscreen showed another fleet in the distance. Three ships, moving fast, and a tiny scout ship, far ahead of them. Blackbeard frowned at the screen, wondering where these ships had come from and what business brought them here.

At that moment, a radio signal hailed the pirate's ship, the pataphysician's ship, the XF25, and every other communicator in range. Gitana's image appeared on the viewscreen of the XF25, the battle cruiser, the Achernarian ships, the pataphysician's ship. The scout ship was hers, of course. Her blue eye shone with cold intensity; her capped eye glowed crimson.

"Stop your squabbling," she said, in a cold, clear voice. "The treasure you all desire may soon fall into the hands of the ones you all hate. The Resurrectionists are here. If they capture the alien base, they will spread throughout the galaxy. We must put aside our differences and fight the common enemy, or we will all perish. They are still at a distance; there is still time to join forces."

OF COURSE, THE pataphysicians were not actively involved in the battle that followed. 'Pataphysics is the ultimate weapon, but that is (as Gyro later explained to Bailey) because pataphysicians know that there is nothing to fight against. A pataphysician remains imperturbable in the face of conflict, intrigued by any possibility that comes his way. The Resurrectionists might turn the entire crew into cyborgs, and the pataphysicians would consider it an interesting aspect to the adventure of life.

But the others—the pirates and the Achernarian Farrs and Farrs from Farr Station and the Indigo colonists and Bailey and Fluffy, of course—were far more easily perturbed, being unwilling to take such a placid view.

Conferring by radio, Gitana, Azami, Zahara, and Blackbeard came to a swift consensus—they would cooperate to overcome the Resurrectionists. Following that, they would discuss their disagreements.

Bailey had heard all the radio communications, including Gitana's warning about the Resurrectionists, and he wanted nothing better than to return to relative safety of the pataphysicians' ship. But he and the other fighters were needed. Bailey and Fluffy joined the Lupino fighters, operating under Red's command.

Legends have been told about the battle that took place that day. The Achernarian Farr fighters were the first to attack. Their attack craft were swift and maneuverable, piloted by fierce fighters. Every fighter among the Achernarians had lost a close friend or family member to the Resurrectionists. The Resurrectionist fighters pursued the Alchenarians, returning fire.

As the Resurrectionist fighters gave chase, the pirate forces (with Bailey among them) circled wide and swept in from behind the Resurrectionist ships, firing missiles as they came. Bailey was bearing down on the ship, ready to fire a missile, when a Resurrectionist ship released a swarm of attack pods. "Evasive maneuvers!" Fluffy shouted, and the XF25 swerved violently, dodging the pods. In the viewscreen, explosions of red and gold fire marked the places that other pilots had failed to dodge.

The battle was terrible and fierce—and, for Bailey, confusing. A military strategist might have noted Blackbeard's expert infighting tactics and Azami's clever evasion of Resurrectionist fighters, but it was all Bailey could do to hang on and keep shooting. Bailey slid the tab on the Moebius band to slow the world down, but even then he could not make sense of it all. It was a jumble of shooting and fleeing and fighting; the radio channels were a hash of commands and confusion.

From a distance, Bailey saw fighters from the Lupino battle cruiser cut one Resurrectionist ship away from the others. He saw missiles streaking toward the black Resurrectionist ship, but he could not watch them. Fluffy was following a Resurrectionist fighter. Right when Bailey got the fighter in his sights and nailed it, a missile got through to the Resurrectionist ship, striking the engine bay. The explosion of the fighter was echoed by a larger explosion, and the Resurrectionist ship's power plant exploded, lighting the darkness with crimson fire.

No time to celebrate that triumph. No time for anything but continuing the fight. Bailey shot down fighters and attack pods. Fluffy dodged fighters and pods and shrapnel and evaded the attacks of other fighters. It was nasty and messy and Bailey kept seeing fighters explode around him. However many enemies he killed, it seemed that there were always more.

The Resurrectionists pushed forward until one ship was in orbit around the Bellman's Folly, firing on the battle cruiser. The other Resurrectionist ship, along with a swarm of Resurrectionist fighters, had engaged the Achernarian ships, driving them off for the moment. Resurrectionist attack pods swarmed around the great battle cruiser.

Bailey, watching from a distance, remembered how the pods had rasped and scraped at the hull, scrabbling their way in. In that moment, it looked like the battle cruiser was lost. The attack pods would breach the ship's defenses; Resurrectionist boarding parties would follow.

"Once they have the battle cruiser, we've had it," Fluffy said. "Might as well give up and prepare to be decommissioned. Let's go down fighting."

"Yes," Bailey said. For once he felt as bloodthirsty as Fluffy. "Let's get them."

Fluffy turned the XF25 toward the battle cruiser, heading in for a final attack.

At that moment, Bailey saw movement on the surface of the Bellman's Folly. A great hatch opened and the *Odyssey* emerged, its lasers firing at the Resurrectionist ship as it passed by. The blast was well-targeted, striking at the ship's navigational center, shearing away antennae and sensory equipment to leave the ship blind. Then the *Odyssey* rose from the Bellman's Folly, passing the battle cruiser and heading away, running away, fleeing the battle.

"She's running away?" Bailey gasped in disbelief.

"She's drawing them off," Fluffy said.

The remaining Resurrectionist ship gave chase, circling back toward the Bellman's Folly and pursuing the *Odyssey* as it fled. As the Resurrectionist ship turned in pursuit, it had to dodge the pataphysical research vessel, the *Ethernity,* which had, somehow, bumbled into the battlefield. A momentary delay, but enough to give the *Odyssey* a headstart.

"I'm going after them," Fluffy said. "All I want is one good opening," she muttered. "If I could get just one missile in. . . ."

The *Odyssey* was headed toward the wormhole called Zahara's Hope, through which the ship had entered this sector. "Where are they going?" Fluffy asked. "They can't get away in that direction." But she continued to give chase, following the Resurrectionist ship that followed the *Odyssey*.

That was why Bailey was not far behind the Resurrectionist ship when the black sphere that marked the exit to the wormhole called Zahara's Hope began to shimmer. Bands of deep red and violet spread across the face of the sphere like ripples spreading from a rock thrown in a pool of still water. The colored bands swirled, a whirlpool circling into darkness.

As Bailey watched, the *Odyssey* dove into that patch of swirling colors and the Resurrectionist ship followed. In the instant that the *Odyssey* entered the wormhole, Bailey saw an identical ship rising from the darkness, like a reflection in a pool. The *Odyssey* slipped into the darkness, merging with its reflection. When the Resurrectionist ship followed, it too was met by a ship that was identical to it in every way. And it too vanished.

"Looks like trouble," Fluffy muttered. "I'm outta here."

As the XF25 veered away from the opening, the acceleration slammed Bailey against the seat. "Hang on, Bailey," Fluffy said. "This is going to be rough."

And it was. As Bailey slipped into unconsciousness, he felt the Moebius band humming in his pocket and he felt the pressure of alien thoughts in his mind. And then he was gone, slipping into darkness.

17

In the midst of the word he was trying to say,
In the midst of his laughter and glee,
He had softly and suddenly vanished away—
For the Snark was a Boojum, you see.

—"The Hunting of the Snark," Lewis Carroll

"...WAKING UP," SOMEONE WAS SAYING. "HE'S MOVING."
Poppy's face loomed above him. "Bailey? Are you all right?"

He blinked at her, unable to speak, glad beyond measure that the generous Poppy had not been on the *Odyssey*.

"Don't rush him." Jazz's voice. Her face came into view beside Poppy's. "Fluffy said she had to pull 6 g's to avoid following Zahara down the hole. He's probably got one hell of a headache."

"How's Fluffy?" he whispered, his voice weak and hoarse.

"She's fine. Came through the battle unscathed."

"Tell me." Another hoarse whisper.

"Tell you what?" Poppy asked, leaning close.

"What happened?"

The short version of what happened was this: the battle was over and the good guys had won. Zahara had taken the *Odyssey* on its final flight alone. She had told her sibs of her plan to lead the Resurrectionist ship away and destroy it.

"I didn't really understand what she was planning," Jazz said. "None of us did."

"She had been fooling with that alien artifact of Violet's," Poppy said. "She didn't say exactly how, but she said she could destroy the Resurrectionists."

"After it was all over, the Curator explained what had happened. She said . . ." Then Jazz stopped talking. The Curator stood in the doorway.

"I thought Mr. Beldon might be coming around," she said quietly. "How is the patient doing?"

Bailey struggled to sit up in bed. "What happened to Zahara?"

Jazz gave the Curator her chair, and the old woman sat by the head of Bailey's bed. "Well, one way of looking at it is—she found her heart's desire. She'll be remembered. Her family will be honored. She destroyed the Resurrectionist ship, and that meant we won the battle."

Bailey looked at Jazz and Poppy. They were nodding, though Poppy's eyes were bright with tears.

"What's another way of looking at it?" Bailey asked.

"The device she took from Violet's hand could be set to reverse the polarity of a wormhole, changing its direction. Zahara used it to switch the polarity of Zahara's Hope, so that it led away from this sector."

"When I saw Zahara dive into the wormhole, I saw a ship just like the *Odyssey* come out to meet her," Bailey said slowly.

The Curator nodded. "When Zahara dove into the wormhole, she met herself coming the other way. The same for the Resurrectionist ship. Time is very flexible, you know."

Bailey shook his head. He didn't know.

"Meeting yourself is a dangerous thing," the Curator said softly. "If you go in the opposite direction down a wormhole you have already traveled, and you meet your earlier reversed self, the two cancel out. You disappear."

"Disappear." Bailey stared at the Curator. "You softly and suddenly vanish away, and never are met with again."

"That's one way to put it," the Curator agreed.

"The machine that attacked Indigo colony wasn't the Boojum," Bailey said softly, working it out as he said it. "We thought it was, because it was frightening. But the Boojum is the version of yourself that you meet in a wormhole. You are your own Boojum."

"That's the conclusion I've reached."

"And the Resurrectionist ship? The same thing happened to them, didn't it?"

The Curator nodded.

"Did Zahara know what would happen?" Bailey said.

"I believe she did. The Librarian, the entity that you met in the station, told her."

Bailey pulled the blankets up under his chin, wishing more than ever that he was back home in the Restless Rest, sitting in his own parlor. He shook his head, thinking of all the perils he had shared with the sibs along the way. "Adventure," he muttered. "What a terrible adventure it is that ends like this."

"Like what?" the Curator asked.

"With anger and greed and friends dying," he said. "So far away from home, with no way back." He wrapped his arms around himself.

Poppy was beside him, tucking the blanket around him and patting his shoulder sympathetically. Jazz patted his hand.

"I want to go home," he said sadly, more to himself than to the others. "It seems to me that this adventure is just about over, and I'd like to go back to where I belong."

"That's what I came to tell you," the Curator said. "I've been talking to the Librarian, you see. We have a great deal in common. And one thing that we've talked about is this." She reached out and touched the Moebius band that encircled Bailey's wrist. The band was humming softly; Bailey could feel its vibration against his wrist. "There's a chance that you can get back home."

Bailey frowned. "I can dive down the wormhole and get back to the solar system. But so much time has passed. . . ."

"Time is flexible," the Curator repeated.

"What are you saying?"

"In normal space, one can move in any of three dimensions—up and down, forward and back, and side to side. In the fourth dimension, time, one can only move in one direction—forward. However, in a wormhole, one can only move in one direction in space: forward. Therefore one can, with the proper tools, move about in any direction in time. If I understood the Librarian correctly, this device can help you shift time during your wormhole transit." The Curator gently touched the tab on the Moebius band. "As I understand it, pushing the tab this way will take you back in time." The Curator shrugged, smiling enigmatically. "It could work."

FOR THE OTHERS, the adventure was over, except for the mopping up afterward. With Zahara gone, Heather, as second in command, took charge of the sibs. She arranged for the Curator to assist in the analysis of the maps and artifacts to be found in Bellman's Folly. The maps would remain the possessions of Farr Station, but the Farrs would share their knowledge more generously than before.

Heather had a long talk with Bailey, telling him of Zahara's last thoughts. "She hoped that you could remember her with friendship," Heather told the norbit. "She wanted to take back the things that she said. She hoped you could forgive her."

Bailey nodded, tears welling up in his eyes. "I never

stopped thinking of her with friendship," he told Heather. "But this will make it easier to do so."

"Why don't you stay here?" Heather asked him. "We're just getting started. There will be many more adventures, so much more to learn."

Bailey shook his head. "I'm really not an adventurer," he told her.

"But you don't know whether this will work. You could end up stranded in some unknown sector, with no way back. The chances of things going wrong are much greater than the likelihood that everything will go right."

Bailey shrugged, smiling faintly, amused that Heather was suddenly so cautious on his behalf. "Then it will be an adventure," he said softly. "And maybe I'll get home."

Heather nodded.

"Remember when you told me that I should get used to leaving people and places behind?" Bailey asked. "You told me not to form attachments, except to things that last."

"I remember."

"It was good advice, but I can't follow it. I'll miss all of you."

Heather nodded. "You have a good heart, Bailey, and your heart doesn't follow good advice."

IN THE LOUNGE on the *Ethernity* Bailey met with Gitana and Gyro to make plans for his departure.

"Of course you'll make it back safely," Gitana said briskly, when he told her of Heather's concern. "In fact, you'll arrive before you left. That's what you did, after all."

"What I did?" Bailey asked.

"What you did, what you will do, whatever." Gitana waved a hand, dismissing the distinction. "It's what has to happen."

When Bailey shook his head in confusion, Gyro smiled. "Remember the note you found on the morning Gitana arrived?" Gyro said.

"Sure." Bailey pulled the note from his pocket. It had grown worn and tattered, but it was still legible. *"Eadem mutata resurgo,"* it said. Beneath that, a spiral. And under the spiral, three more words: "Harvest the figs."

Gyro tapped his finger on the Latin words. "Though changed, I arise again the same. I'd say that describes your current condition."

Gitana nodded, agreeing with Gyro. "You are not the same norbit that left the Asteroid Belt, but at the same time, you are."

Bailey stared at the note, written in his own messy scrawl. It was a pataphysical spiral; it was the alien zero, the beginning and the end. With a finger, he traced the line of the spiral. "Every point on the spiral is a turning point," he said. He glanced at Gyro. "Do you suppose the Old Ones believed that?"

Gyro smiled and shrugged. "I would not be surprised."

"I really don't know why you feel it's necessary to leave yourself a note," Gitana said crossly. "But obviously you do feel that way. Because you did leave yourself a note. That is, you are going to leave yourself a note. And the message pod that the Curator received—the one that told her to come to Zahara's aid—came from the Asteroid Belt. So you sent that as well. That is, you will send it."

Bailey was still wrestling with the idea. "So I'll get back home before I left? I could meet myself and tell myself not to go on this adventure?"

He frowned, thinking about that past self. Back then, he never knew all that the galaxy had to offer. He had never tasted Ergotian whiskey; he had never met a pataphysician. He had never fought giant spiders in the

Great Rift Cloud; he had never shot down a Resurrectionist fighter.

"If you did meet yourself, you could advise yourself to stay home," Gyro said. "I wonder what would happen then?" The pataphysician smiled, obviously amused by the possibility.

Bailey thought about it. He imagined telling his younger self about what would happen if he went with the sibs. Bailey shook his head. He wouldn't believe it. Even now, he barely believed the adventures had been through. "I wouldn't believe a word of it," he said slowly.

"Of course not. You didn't talk to yourself when you came back," Gitana said impatiently. "So that means you won't." She glanced at Gyro. "No need to make it more complicated than it already is."

Gyro grinned and turned back to Bailey. "You must have been out the day before Gitana arrived at the Restless Rest," Gyro said.

Bailey nodded, remembering. "I went to check on a mining station."

"You found the note after you got back. And then Gitana arrived, knowing nothing of all this."

Gitana frowned at Gyro and Bailey identified the source of her irritation. Gitana was accustomed to being the person who knew more than anyone else. It irked her that his future self had been wandering around the Asteroid Belt way back then, without her knowledge.

"So what do we do now?" Bailey asked, addressing his question to Gitana. She studied his face and smiled slowly, always happy to be asked for advice.

"Now we plan for your trip back home," she said.

BLACKBEARD HAD A farewell feast for Bailey aboard the battle cruiser. Poppy and the Lupino chef collaborated on the meal, concocting a blend of exotic dishes. The sibs toasted Bailey's courage, his resourcefulness. They wished him luck in all his endeavors.

Bailey said good-bye to Lotus and Lily, to Iris and Heather, to Jazz and Poppy, knowing that he could never see them again because he would be in their distant past and they would be in his distant future. He said good-bye to Blackbeard and Red, to Gyro and Gitana.

After the feast had ended, he went to the loading dock, where Fluffy and the XF25 were waiting.

"Hey, Fluffy," Bailey said, sliding into the pilot's seat. "I just came to say good-bye."

"So you're going back home, eh? Think you'll be happy there?" Fluffy sounded dubious.

Bailey thought of the Restless Rest and smiled. "I know I will."

"Yeah, I suppose you will. Actually, it sounds like a nice place." Fluffy's tone was wistful.

"You could come," Bailey said, but even as he said it he knew that it would never work. Fluffy would be bored in a day and looking for a fight.

"I've already made a deal with Blackbeard," Fluffy said. "I'll be working with him for a while. He's taking a route to some unexplored areas and he needs some fighters."

"Of course," Bailey said.

Bailey wore the Moebius band, and Heather gave him the hologram of Violet's map that they had been following for so long. Then he boarded Gitana's scout ship, which she had given him for the final leg of his journey.

The pataphysicians' ship, with Gyro and Gitana and Heather aboard, accompanied him to the wormhole that Heather had named "Bailey's Return." Bailey, alone in Gitana's scout ship, kept in touch by radio.

"Good-bye," he said as he approached the wormhole. "Good-bye. May your adventures be many and always end well."

"Good luck, Bailey Beldon!" Gitana responded. "Be happy. Be well."

The wormhole was ahead of him; the pataphysicians' ship was falling behind. As he approached, the stars shifted around him, doubling, tripling, multiplying impossibly in the viewscreen. "Good-bye," he said to the radio. "Good-bye, everyone." Then he pushed the tab on the Moebius band and dove into the center of the kaleidoscopic pattern.

IT WAS THE journey of an instant. It was the journey of a century. Time, as the Curator had pointed out, is flexible. Bailey was, at that moment, outside of time, moving at right angles to the usual flow.

The Curator, having consulted with the Librarian, had told him precisely how long to hold the tab in place. Bailey had set a timer on the bridge so that he would know when to release the tab. But once he entered the wormhole, he was no longer on the bridge. He found himself in an enormous room, illuminated only by glowing golden lines. "Here again?" he asked.

He felt a wave of amusement, coming from outside himself. The presence had a familiar feel; he recognized the Librarian. Can an artificial intelligence be amused? Apparently so. A soft voice spoke in his ear. "Yes, here again."

"I can understand you."

"Yes. *Eadem mutata resurgo.*"

He was a different norbit than he had been before. "But what are you doing here?"

Again, he felt her amusement. "Surely you don't think each wormhole is independent from all the others, do you? How inefficient that would be. Everything is connected, in a different plane."

"On a different plane?"

"Through a different universe, in a different dimension. I connect the wormholes; I keep them open and talk to those travelers who will listen.

"Why didn't I know about you before?"

More amusement. "Does a fish know about the water it swims through? No, a fish takes the water for granted, noticing only if the water disappears. I am the matrix in which you live."

"Where are we now?" Bailey asked. He stared at the viewscreen, which showed only gray. Nothing to see. Nothing to take hold of.

"In between. Where do you want to go?"

"Home," Bailey said.

"Release the tab when I count three. One . . . two . . . three."

Bailey heard the chiming of the timer at the moment the voice said, "Three." He released the tab, just as he popped back into ordinary space.

Through the viewscreen, he could see familiar constellations. Antares burned with a fierce glow in the heart of Scorpio; the Hyades cluster glittered in the head of Taurus; the bright red eye of the bull, Aldebaran, shone brightly among them. He stared toward Sagittarius. Out there, unimaginably far away, the colonists on Indigo were building their city while the Bellman's Folly orbited overhead. It would be many years before Zahara came to disturb them. So far away, in space and in time.

The ship's computer, making use of data from the standard navigational pulsars, calculated Bailey's position. He was just a week's journey from the solar system. Almost home.

He set a course for the Restless Rest.

18

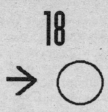

If your Snark be a Snark, that is right:
Fetch it home by all means—You may serve it with greens,
And it's handy for striking a light.

—"The Hunting of the Snark," Lewis Carroll

WHEN BAILEY REACHED THE ASTEROID BELT, HE DECELERATED and took control from the computer. He didn't need navigational help here. He knew every tumbling rock and planetoid as well as he knew his fingers and toes.

As he threaded his way through the asteroids on the way to the Restless Rest, he passed one of his mining stations and recognized the steam rocket docked beside it. His mining station; his steam rocket. Right now, his earlier self was hard at work in the station, fixing a broken valve. As he recalled, it had been an annoying and tedious task. He hadn't been able to find one of the wrenches he had needed to tighten the valve and had looked all over the station for it. He had managed without the wrench, and then, just as he was preparing to leave, he had discovered the wrench tucked away beside the air lock.

Now, older and wiser, he thought about dropping in on himself and handing himself the wrench. And while he was at it, he could tell himself about the adventures that were in store. He smiled, but kept going. He knew that his earlier self would finish the repairs, visit an orbital farm and trade figs for quail eggs, then head for the Restless Rest. He would arrive home late and wearily tumble into bed. When he woke, he would discover the note.

Bailey reached the Restless Rest, docked the scout craft, and entered through the air lock. He immediately went to the solarium, where he made himself a cup of tea and sat down in his favorite chair. He took a deep breath, luxuriating in the scent of growing plants from the greenhouse. Home at last.

But his work wasn't quite done. Not yet. He got a pen and a piece of note paper from his desk. Sitting in his favorite chair, he wrote a note, copying from the tattered note that he still carried in his pocket. The paper had been folded many times and was soft with wear, but the words were still legible.

"Eadem mutata resurgo," it said. He very carefully copied the words to make sure he got the spelling right. Beneath the Latin phrase, he carefully drew a spiral. Underneath the spiral, he wrote three more words: "Harvest the figs."

He folded the tattered version and slipped it back into his pocket. For a moment, he admired the copy. He considered adding some good advice. Or maybe just the words "Good luck!" But in the end, he left the note as it was, using a magnet to attach it to the metal file by the communicator screen.

Almost done, but not quite. His earlier self would be home soon, and he had to be gone before that happened. He went back to the scout ship and set a course for the edge of the Asteroid Belt, to the establishment of Worton Locke, who specialized in sending message pods, a service that was not much in demand among the norbits. Why send a message when everything you needed was right here?

Bailey went to send a message to the Curator. Gitana had provided him with the precise address, but it still wasn't easy to get a message pod out. Worton was a garrulous man who liked to know everyone's business.

Worton frowned at Bailey. "Interesting getup," Worton rumbled.

Bailey glanced down at the pataphysical spiral on the chest of his jumpsuit. He had forgotten what he was wearing. "Present from a friend," he mumbled.

"Where did you get that outlandish ship?" Worton asked, gazing at Gitana's scout ship in his viewscreen.

"It belongs to another friend," Bailey said.

Worton squinted at Bailey from beneath bushy gray eyebrows, waiting for him to say more. When nothing more was forthcoming, Worton said, "Your friend isn't from around here. That's an interstellar scout."

Bailey nodded. "You got that right. Now let me tell you what I need to do." Bailey told Worton about the message he wanted to send, providing the exact coordinates that Gitana had given him. He kept the message simple: "Zahara needs your help." Then the coordinates of the alien base and instructions for getting there.

Worton shook his head in disbelief. "Sending a message to the Hyades Cluster? Why would you want to do a thing like that? Who do you know there?"

"I'm sending the message for my friend," Bailey said.

"The Curator, you say? What an odd title! The name is Pat Murphy, right? Any relation to the Murphys over on Ceres?" Worton named a large clan that lived on one of the largest asteroids.

Bailey shook his head. "I don't believe so."

Worton fussed over the message pod, a sleek black one with red fins. He checked the coordinates several times to make sure he had them right. "Don't want it to go astray," he said.

"It won't."

Worton was shaking his head. "That's a very long distance," he told Bailey. "There may be postal pirates along the way." Squinting a bit, he nodded. "Things are wild and lawless out there."

Among norbits, Worton was considered well-traveled. He had been to the moons of Jupiter and had visited Earth more than once.

As Worton punched in the coordinates and double-checked the message pod, he told Bailey about his trip to the moons of Jupiter, an action-packed tale in which Worton learned about the lawlessness of the frontier when his luggage was lost by the transport company. Finally, after the last check, he slipped the message pod into the ejection tube. On the viewscreen, they watched it speed away.

"Who is this friend of yours?" Worton asked. "Anyone I know?"

"I don't think so," Bailey said. "Her name is Gitana."

Then, leaving Worton gaping and speechless, Bailey was on his way.

It was still too early to return to the Restless Rest, so he dropped by to visit his younger sister, Melita, and her family. Her family ran one of the largest honey-making concerns in the Belt—a cluster of greenhouse asteroids in which they grew flowers and kept bees.

Melita's household was noisy and chaotic. Her family was large—three sons and two daughters—and there were always hired hands and other guests for dinner. She teased him about dropping by at dinner time, but invited him to dinner, of course. It was a boisterous, noisy affair, with much food and drink.

"I think you've been working too hard," Melita said, as she offered him another helping of honeycake. "You've lost weight. And you look like you haven't been getting enough sleep."

"I've been busy," Bailey said. "But I plan to take it easy for a while now."

"Wherever did you get that ship?" Melita's husband Granger asked.

"An old friend of Great-Grandmother Brita's stopped by," he said, having decided to tell the truth, but not the whole truth. No one would believe the entire story; he hardly believed it himself. "She left it in my safe-keeping."

"I wonder how far it's traveled," Bailey's nephew Ferris said wistfully. "I bet it's been everywhere."

"I think you're right there," Bailey agreed, smiling at his nephew fondly.

A few months before, Melita's cat—a black and white mouser—had given birth to six kittens. After dinner, Bailey settled into the family room with Ferris. While Bailey and Ferris played battle simulation games on the computer, the kittens romped around them.

"Have you been practicing, Uncle Bailey?" Ferris asked after Bailey beat him for the third time.

Bailey shrugged. "Just a little." He was watching the kittens. For the past ten minutes, the smallest of them, a gray-striped tabby, had been chasing one of her black-and white brothers around and around the circumference of the room. In the light gravity environment, the kittens could cover several feet in a single bound.

Melita was sitting nearby, curled up in a chair and reading a book, oblivious to the chaos around her. To escape its pursuer, the fleeing kitten had leapt into Melita's lap, and the gray-striped one followed, landing square in the middle of Melita's book and causing a minor explosion in which kittens went flying.

"Hey, Melita," Bailey called to his sister. "Are you looking for homes for these kittens yet?"

"Absolutely. Why don't you take that little terror there?" She waved her book at the gray-striped tabby, who was now chasing another of her siblings.

"That's actually the one I had in mind."

Melita frowned at her brother. "She might be a bit lively for you," she said. "She's the troublemaker of the litter."

"That's fine," Bailey said, smiling. "I'll take her."

He left with three jars of honey and a yowling kitten in a box.

AS HE APPROACHED the Restless Rest, he saw four ships heading away from the asteroid. He recognized them: the three Farr ships and Gitana's scout. He did not hail them; he just watched them go.

Then he went home.

The note was gone from the metal file by the communicator screen. The trees in the greenhouse were no longer heavy with figs. The kitchen was a mess, as was his best parlor.

Happily, he set about gathering the dirty dishes and empty bottles. The kitten prowled around him, investigating every corner and pouncing on stray napkins and crumbs.

Finally, when all the dishes were in the washer, he sat down in his favorite chair to admire the view out the solarium windows. The kitten, tired at last, curled up in his lap and began to purr.

"Well, Fluffy," he said. "It's good to be home."

BAILEY NEVER TOLD the story of all his adventures to anyone, though he sometimes entertained his nieces and nephews with stories that he claimed he had made up. These adventure tales often involved pirate battles and Resurrectionists and alien artifacts and giant spiders in the Great Rift Cloud. He gained a reputation as a man with a particularly vivid imagination.

He kept Gitana's ship permanently docked at the side of the Restless Rest, as if, at any moment, he might decide to go adventuring again. But he never did.

Fluffy grew fat and happy. Bailey kept the Moebius band, using it only when he had to get a great deal done in a very short time. And he lived very happily in the Restless Rest until the end of his days.

AN AFTERWORD BY MAX MERRIWELL

As the astute reader has no doubt noticed, Bailey's adventures bear a striking resemblance to the adventures of Bilbo Baggins, the heroic hobbit of J. R. R. Tolkien's well-known prelude to *The Lord of the Rings*. Like so many others, I read *The Hobbit* when I was a youngster. As a child, Bilbo's adventures thrilled and terrified me.

As an adult, I admire Tolkien's accomplishment—and recognize the roots of his story. Bailey, like Bilbo before him, follows the hero's journey, described so eloquently in Joseph Campbell's *The Hero with a Thousand Faces*. The mythological hero leaves the everyday world behind and enters (willingly or reluctantly) a region of fantastic wonders. The call to adventure may seem to come about by chance—a random twist of fate that draws the hero into a relationship with forces he does not understand. But as Campbell points out, the workings of chance in an adventure tale are the result of suppressed desires and conflicts in the hero.

One way or another, the hero crosses a threshold and enters the realm of adventure. Here, he must defeat enemies and overcome obstacles that block his way. He may be aided and advised by powerful and mysterious entities: Gandalf, Gitana, Elrond, Gyro, the Curator, and others. At the center of it all, he undergoes a supreme ordeal and is involved in winning a decisive victory to gain his reward.

From this mysterious adventure, the hero returns with transcendental powers, that he may use to benefit his community. He comes out of the land of darkness and settles back into the familiar world, whether it is the

Shire or the Asteroid Belt. Bailey, like Bilbo, is quite a little fellow who becomes caught up in momentous events.

The hero's journey has deep roots in the human psyche, forming the basis for myths, fairy tales, and dreams. In writing this book, I have attempted to combine elements of that classic tale with the adventures of space opera, constrained ever so slightly by reality.

According to my physicist friends, the wormholes featured in this adventure are defensible, though unconventional, in terms of physics. For those who would like to know more about black holes, wormholes, and the enormous black hole at the center of the Milky Way galaxy, I recommend the following references:

Cosmic Wormholes: The Search for Interstellar Shortcuts by Paul Halpern

Gravity's Fatal Attraction: Black Holes in the Universe by Mitchell Begelman and Martin Rees

Black Holes and Time Warps: Einstein's Outrageous Legacy by Kip Thorne

The Alchemy of the Heavens by Ken Croswell

For those who would like to know more about Snark hunting, I recommend:

The Annotated Snark by Martin Gardner, which includes the full text of Lewis Caroll's nonsense epic, "The Hunting of the Snark."

AFTERWORD—ABOUT MAX MERRIWELL
BY PAT MURPHY

People have been asking me a simple question: Who is Max Merriwell? Though the question is simple, the answer is not.

Here's one answer. Max Merriwell is a pseudonym, a pen name under which I have chosen to write a space opera.

Here's another: Max Merriwell is a well-known science fiction writer who published his first novel at age eighteen. A prolific writer, currently in his mid-fifties, he publishes a science fiction novel each year under his own name. He also writes fantasy novels, which he publishes under the pseudonym Mary Maxwell and mysteries, which he publishes under the pseudonym Weldon Merrimax. Max is a delightful man with a wild imagination and a somewhat cavalier attitude toward reality and its restrictions on his fiction.

The second answer seems like the more accurate one to me. But that answer leads people to go to their bookstore and search for some of Max's other titles, and that's frustrating. You see, Max doesn't happen to inhabit the world in which you and I live. You could think of him, I suppose, as inhabiting some alternate time line. That's kind of how I think of him. I figure he's out there writing and every now and then a book of his leaks through into this reality.

Whatever answer you prefer, you should be warned that Max's books have just begun to leak through into this reality. *There and Back Again* is the first in a series of books involving Max Merriwell.

It will be followed by *The Wild Angel*, written by Max Merriwell under the pen name Mary Maxwell. *The Wild Angel* (by Mary Maxwell by Max Merriwell by Pat Murphy) is scheduled for publication by Tor Books in Spring 2000.

Finally, I plan to write a book about Max Merriwell, in which Max deals with the shifting nature of reality and identity. That book, *Adventures in Time and Space with Max Merriwell*, by Pat Murphy, is scheduled for publication by Tor Books in Fall 2000.

If all of this leaves you intrigued and baffled, you can find more information on my web site at www.exo.net/jaxxx

PAT MURPHY

ACKNOWLEDGMENTS

Many people offered their assistance during the writing of this book. I'd like to thank a few of them here. Dave Wright (aka Officer Dave) provided much moral support and listened to me whine and complain about exotic planets and alien artifacts. He and his brother, Gary Wright, provided information on military terms and dogfights. Ellen Klages helped me come up with the name "norbit" and loaned me the name of her cat. Physicists Paul Doherty and Linda Shore recommended books, answered odd questions, and warned me when I strayed too far from reality. Gary Crounse, Rupert Peene, and Kamishiwa advised me on the doings of the College of 'Pataphysics. Patrick Weekes, Daniel Berdichevsky, Sarah Brandel, Phil King, Miriam Rocke, Karin Willison, and Lisa Anfield, students in my 1998 Stanford class on science fiction writing, were extremely helpful in critiquing early chapters of the book. Writers Karen Fowler, Angus MacDonald, Daniel Marcus, Carter Scholz, Michael Berry, Richard Russo, Michael Blumlein, Chris Barzak, and Richard Kadrey generously read and commented on all or part of the manuscript. And finally, I would like to thank my editor Beth Meacham for her ongoing support of this project. Without her, Max Merriwell would still be in hiding.

THANK YOU ALL.

PAT MURPHY